THE ASSIGNED

THE ASSIGNED

A. D. SMITH, III

33RD PRODUCTIONS
WWW.ADSMITH.ORG

Published by 33rd Productions
www.adsmith.org

ISBN-13: 978-0-9888184-0-8

Edited By Jeremy Anderberg
www.jeremyedits.com

Additional Editing By Karolyn Miller
kjmiller_iiw@yahoo.com

To learn more about "The Assigned" or to contact A. D. Smith, please visit www.ADSmith.org

Typesetting services by BOOKOW.COM

CHAPTER 1 – ZEEK

A DELICATE LINE OF BLOOD TRICKLES FROM THE CORNER OF GLORIA'S MOUTH. "Why didn't she wait for me?" Tre asks. He looks to me for answers, but I have none. He looks to Gloria, but she can't respond. She's gone. I imagine thoughts of his brother, Martin, flood his head. Comparisons are inevitable. So much can be said, but that's not my story to tell…

"It can't end like this!" Tre sobs.

"Come on man, do your thing!" I shout to get his attention. He's the only one who can save her now. Tre places his hands around her face. Nothing. Now her chest. No response. His powers wane as Gloria's lifeless body rests in his arms. Even with his newfound abilities, Tre still finds himself in the same situation. And to think, we fight for life yet see so much death.

"Again!" I yell. Tre closes his eyes as he touches her face once more. Anxiously I watch, but still…nothing.

"NO!!!"

Cracks ripple through the ground as Tre slams his fist into the concrete floor. His eyes, now blood red, look up at me. "I'll stay here with Glo," he mumbles. "Zeek, you go after Bale."

I struggle for a response.

"Now!" Tre shouts, his voice steady as ever. "Do YOUR thing!"

"I'm going!" I yell back, attempting to regain my composure. As I focus on a point on the wall before me, I feel my gift manifest. An image of Jason Bale flashes before my eyes. Now a car—no wait—a limousine. I jump on my bike, barreling out of the parking garage. The structure itself has suffered extensive damage at the hands of the dueling factions; one good, one evil. Although the outcome has already been decided, the war continues. This has been the way for millennia.

At least this is what I've been told. So much has happened, I'm not sure what I believe. I fly down the highway like a bat out of Hell, or rather…Heaven. My gift of seeing leads me to the interstate bridge. As I ride, my mind traces back to before any of this started.

——THE ASSIGNED——

"…and do you, Angelina Moreno, take this man to be your lawfully wedded husband?" the minister asked. Angelina coyly hesitated before answering. Finally smiling, she said, "Yeah, I'll take him."

"I'm sorry?" The elderly minister replied while cupping his ear. "You'll have to speak up a bit!"

"I DO!"

I smiled as the few people who showed tried to contain their laughter. The old preacher cleared his throat. "Very good. By the power vested in me, I now pronounce you man and wife. You may kiss your bride."

I had kissed Angelina plenty of times before, but she'd given me explicit instructions for this particular public display. Funny.

At the moment, I couldn't think of the specifics. I leaned in and kissed her as only I knew how. Uncomfortable, the seventy year-old preacher man turned his head as I—how do they say—saluted my bride.

Angelina and I were finally married. Although we'd only been together for a little under two years, it seemed like an eternity. Sure, we were only 18, but I knew she was the one for me. People said that's only a few short-lived years, but if they *lived* as I had, they wouldn't consider them *short* by any means.

The sun began to set behind the old two-story farmhouse as our special day came to a close. The activities had been modest to say the least. Just six or so of Angelina's closest friends, Mr. Stanley, Angelina's forty-something year-old neighbor—who tried to act way too young—and the minister's wife, all in the backyard of her grandmother's longtime home. Of course, the strict woman said she was too tired to come outside, although I caught her peeking from a second story bedroom window.

Still wearing her wedding gown, a simple cream-colored sundress, I helped Angelina atop my pride and joy, a 1987 Harley Custom Motorbike. Actually, the motor was from an old salvage Harley. The body was a run-down Kawasaki, but it was mine. A string of *'Just Got Married'* beer cans adorned the aged chopper. Wearing a suit coat, t-shirt, bowtie, and oil stained jeans, I jumped on the bike with ease.

"So, are you ready to start your new life, Mrs. Myers?" I asked my bride.

"You bet," Angelina replied as she kissed me.

"Ok, you two. Get a room!" Angelina's teenaged younger sister, Alicia, approached from the house. *"Isn't that right?"* she continued in an unusually high- pitched voice mimicking the tone of the one year-old child she was carrying. Our child, Christina.

"There's my baby!" shouted Angelina. "Bring her here."

Drool rolled down the chubby toddler's chin. Baby Christina giggled as she drew closer to her mother.

"Hey there, Daddy's little girl," I smiled. Angelina and our daughter Christina were about the only two things that could melt this biker's heart. "Now Alicia, if you don't want us to go, we'll stay."

"And have my sister miss her honeymoon? No way. Besides, I can take care of my niece for three days."

Just eighteen months apart, Angelina and Alicia had practically raised themselves. Their mother was dead and their father…he might as well have been. He wanted nothing to do with the two after moving to the far side of the country with his new girlfriend. The sisters' elderly grandmother took them in eight years ago, but now growing in age, the woman began to slow. Angelina and Alicia pretty much handled most of the house business now. The two were inseparable, which made it hard for me to initially break through. Once I did, the three of us were more like siblings than anything else. I had no close relatives—been in and out of foster care for as long as I could remember. In fact, I'd pretty much raised myself from the age of thirteen. Being around Angel and Alicia gave me more than just a girlfriend and her obnoxious little sister. It gave me family.

"Now it's getting late," said Alicia. "You guys need to go. It's enough my sister let you talk her into riding a motorcycle on her wedding day. Now get! Scoot!"

"Thanks, Alicia," Angelina said as she pulled her sister tight. "I love you, sis." The younger sibling shrugged off the emotional display. Angelina scooped baby Christina from Alicia's arms once more using her *goo goo gah gah* voice. "I love you, Chrissy. Mommy will be back in a few days, okay?"

Angel was so good with Christina even though our little girl was too young to understand as she stared back blankly. "You wanna say bye to your daddy?"

This was the first baby I'd ever been around. I always felt as if I was too dirty to hold her or too stiff or that I may accidentally break her like one of the tools I worked with. Instead of picking her up, I opted for a soft forehead kiss. "I love you, Chrissy-pooh."

"Okay, you two. Get going!" said Alicia as she fanned us off. Smoke filled the immediate air as I started the old chopper. Alicia rushed Chrissy back inside as Angelina waved, watching her sister and daughter grow rapidly smaller.

* * *

There was nothing quite like riding on a beautiful spring day. The air ripping through your hair along with the rhythmic sound and vibration of the bike doubled as physical therapy. I considered myself an avid rider and knew the route we were traveling by heart. As we made our way to Mississippi's gulf coast, I made sure to stop at one of Angelina's favorite viewing spots.

"It's so beautiful, Zeek," Angel spoke as she admired the striking blue water. "Not as beautiful as you," I whispered back.

Angel, as I liked to call her, had brown eyes that seemed almost hypnotic and a wide gaping smile, but gorgeous nonetheless. Seemingly infinite locks of brown hair flowed through the air like dandelion seeds. To a stranger, her features resembled someone of Brazilian heritage. Being her boyfriend, now husband, I knew she took after her Argentinean father. Angelina's beauty was undeniable. Sometimes I felt as if her refined, striking countenance clashed with this scruffy biker with Irish roots. So much so, I almost never approached her. My life was filled with problems before I met Angel, but she helped change my outlook on the world, and for that I loved her. We didn't plan to have a child at seventeen, but Christina was loved nevertheless. Having these new responsibilities had changed so much in me; how I handled money, the places I went, my temper. Two years ago, I was a guy that would fight anyone who gave me a wrong look, or even race my bike within inches of my life. Not now. For the first time ever, I had a reason to live.

"I can't believe we're married, Zeek."

I loved the way Angel said my name. She made it sound important. "I know, Angel," I replied. "It's unreal."

She continued. "There's two things I thank God for everyday …"

I turned my head slightly, just enough to see her kiss the sparkling crystal cross pendant fastened around her neck. "… you and our baby," she finished.

I could feel her eyes watching me, waiting for my response. A smile, or some variable of it, endeavored to form on my face but quickly dissolved. She must have seen it. "I know you don't believe God put us together, but you'll see," she smiled.

"I've seen everything I need to see." Subtly changing the subject, my hands brushed against her face. "Now let's get this honeymoon started."

Angel's grandmother was a church going woman. Strict in her old age, it caused the girls to act out which is probably what initially drew Angelina to me. However, they never lost the faith their grandmother instilled in them. Me, on the other hand? I wouldn't even know what the inside of a church looked like. Angel and I were from two different worlds, but that's why I loved her so much. She was strong in her convictions and wasn't a pushover for anyone, including me. I didn't believe the same things she did, but I respected Angelina and she respected me.

As our ride resumed, Angel tightened her grip around my waist. Her chin rested on my shoulder as I shouted over the growl of the chopper, "We're almost there!"

"Zeek! Slow down!" she yelled, holding on. I downplayed her anxiety as I whisked around the curved highway. I'd ridden the route hundreds of times and knew those roads like the back of my hand.

"Come on babe, live a little!"

"Zeek, please! You don't know what's around the—"

"What?!" The thundering hum of the bike drowned out Angelina's plea. She tried again. "I said, how do y—ZEEK, WATCH OUT!!!"

Coming around a curve, a deer stood in the middle of the highway. Speeding, I had no time to compensate. *I swerved.* Riding alone, I probably could have regained control, but the weight of us both was just too much, especially with Angel not knowing when and to what side to shift her weight. We were immediately thrown off. It all seemed to happen in slow motion as my body propelled twenty feet into the air. I once heard when you're near death it's not your life that flashes before your eyes, but the people you love. Still mid-flight, the only woman I've ever loved raced past mine. The airborne eternity abruptly ended as I crashed to Earth, tumbling down the highway. Blood gushed from my arm and I was pretty sure I'd broken a leg and at least a couple of ribs. But those were the least of my worries. As I dragged myself to my feet, Angelina was nowhere in sight.

"ANGEL!" I cried out over and over. But my pain-writhed calls went unanswered. By this time, other motorists had pulled over to help, but I couldn't care less about my own well-being. I pleaded with them, "Find my wife! PLEASE!"

"Oh my God...She's over here!" shouted one of the drivers. I hobbled as fast as I could to my Angel. My pace slowed as I inched toward her awkwardly positioned frame.

Instinctively, I wanted to pick her up though I knew her fragile body shouldn't be moved.

Angel laid motionless, rocks and sand imbedded in her forehead and arms. Thickened blood seeped from her mouth. My mind wanted to go elsewhere but the present circumstances wouldn't allow it. Angelina was unresponsive, but I knew she was alive. She had to be.

A speeding ambulance rushed us to the hospital. Medics kept trying to work on me, but I refused. "Mr. Myers, please remain calm!" they kept shouting but all I could think about was Angel.

My entire life, I could fix most anything I put my hands on. Put bikes together like it was nothing, but now, here I was as helpless as our one year-old child. *Will her eyes just open?* I kept hoping. Just to see her eyes one more time. EMT administered medicines and fluids, none of which seemed to work.

"Please help her!" I begged, my eyes stinging from the salted tears that drenched my face. Looking down, I noticed the once polished, now deeply scratched pendant still hanging from her neck. I never believed in any of that stuff, but it had always been a source of comfort for Angelina. In a moment of sheer desperation, I rubbed the cross with blood stained hands and cried out,

"GOD SAVE HER! PLEASE!!!"

At the hospital, no one could tell me anything about Angel's condition. They wouldn't let me go back to her, always citing the same repetitive argument. "Sir, you need to let us see about your injuries." The pain was too much. Not of my wounds but from not knowing. I just wanted to see Angel.

After what seemed like an eternity, the doctor slowly made his way out to see me. The look on his face told me everything I needed to know. I—I couldn't breathe as I felt the last ounce of fight leave my body. As the room closed in on me, the world turned to darkness.

* * *

Hours later after I awakened, I found out my Angelina was pronounced dead at 7:46pm. She had massive head trauma. My body sat coiled in the corner of the waiting room as a nurse handed me a manila envelope containing her personal effects. Rage engulfed me as I pulled out the deeply scratched cross pendant. With grieved force, I threw that thing to the other side of the room. Hitting the wall, it shattered on impact.

My girlfriend of 23 months and wife of 7 hours had just been pronounced dead. Someone had to pay. I wanted to fight the paramedics who took forever getting to my Angel. I wanted to go back to that highway and find that deer—or *any* deer—and strangle it with my bare hands. Instead, the events of the day confirmed something I always knew deep down inside. There is no... *God.*

How could there be? Even with all her faith, Angelina was gone. And here I stood, the cynical, non-believing, forever doubting Zeek, still alive. Truthfully, I hated myself more than anything for surviving the accident, for not slowing down, for not knowing what was around the corner. If it wasn't for our daughter, I would've ended my wretched existence without thought. But I had to keep going for her. For Christina. My time with Angel almost made me believe. In what, I'm not sure. At least now I knew I was responsible for my own path. As that day had proven, how could there be a god?

────T H E A S S I G N E D────

"Yeah...*two* cases of menthol's," I assure the store clerk. My affinity for nicotine has grown over time.

"One dollar and seventy-five cents is your change sir. Have a blessed day," says the smiley faced cashier.

"You know what, just keep the change," I mumble, wanting nothing to do with her after such a revolting declaration.

Lighting the last cigarette of an already opened pack, I hop on my 'o1' Honda Blackbird. It takes a little longer to mount now, seeing how my leg never properly healed. After four years, I still walk with a slight limp. My injury bothers me more than usual today, having just finished what would have been a 10-hour work day at some lousy construction site. Right before lunch, they told me not to come back because of my attitude. Go figure. It's the third temp position in the last two weeks alone. Twenty-two years-old, no job, bad leg, sick daughter. And she has the nerve to say, "...*blessed day*."

"Hmph," I smirk while revving the engine.

CHAPTER **2** –TRE

"No, no…MARTIN!!!"

I jump from my sleep as the nightmare finally ends. It's as if I am a prisoner forced to watch the same haunted vision over and over. My heart races as sweat pours down my face. Part of me knew it was a dream, even in my sleep, although my body wouldn't allow me to wake. I look over to the clock. It reads 12:32pm. Sunlight beams through half-opened blinds forcing me to squint. Still dazed, I stand. My shirtless body reveals a muscular 6-foot frame, chocolate toned skin, and bald-shaven head. I step over pizza boxes and beer cans eventually making my way to the fireplace mantle. The ultra posh apartment I live in hasn't been cleaned for quite some time now. A half empty bottle of whiskey rests on the mantle…

Only a quarter remains now.

Included on the mantle are pictures and trophies showcasing my athletic career. One reads *"Tre 'TNT' Turner – Player of the Year"*. At the young age of twenty-two, some would say I've lived a great life. Not sure if I'd wholeheartedly agree.

My cell rings. The display reads 'Dad'. *It's too early for this*, I think before finally answering. "What's going on Dad?"

"Why, he's alive!" my father shouts through the phone. "Now how's my firstborn?"

"I'm fine."

"Great, Tre. Good to hear. So, you're too much of a star now to come see ya old man?"

"I'm not a star, Dad," I sigh into the receiver. "I haven't played in four months."

"So, what did this doctor say?"

I hate when my father asks me questions he already knows the answers to. "Same as the rest," I say. "If I want any chance at a normal life, I shouldn't risk returning to the field."

"Well, pray about it son. If it's to be, it's to be. You can always say you had one of the greatest rookie seasons ever for a NFL running-back."

I say nothing, hoping he gets the point. Guess he doesn't.

"Just one more thing, Tre. If you hear from your brother, tell him to come home. We haven't seen him for weeks."

I knew there was something else he wanted. "Damn it, Dad. Why do we have to go through this every few months? You know how he is. He's probably somewhere getting high. He'll be back when the money runs out."

The tone in my father's voice changes. "First off, watch your mouth son. I'm your father, not your teammate. And second, I can ask you whatever I want. You're the child and don't you forget it."

He waits. I say nothing. It's weird hearing him like this, seeing as he hardly ever gets frustrated. Guess that's one of the qualities that make him a great father…and a good Pastor. Besides, I kind of deserved it.

"Now look Tre," his voice settles. "You made it out okay. You didn't succumb to the same demons as Martin. I remember when you two were young; you guys would put on my church robe and my shoes and recite Bible verses all around the house. Now everyone is grown. Everyone is—"

I love my father, I do. But sometimes he just doesn't know when to quit. I interrupt his ride down memory lane. "—look Dad, if I hear from him I'll let you know."

"Thanks Tre. That's all I want. Me and your mother won't be here forever. After us, you're all your brother has, you know?"

"I know Dad."

"That's my boy. You know you haven't been by the church in quite some time. When's the last time you've heard one of your old man's sermons?"

"Uhh…I'd say just a couple of seconds ago…"

My father, Pastor William Turner, Jr., laughs. "Good one, son. Well, talk to ya lat—oh and Tre, never forget y—"

Like so many times before, I finish my father's words. "I know Dad. Never forget your home."

I never understood why my father would go after Martin, time and time again. He always said I wouldn't understand until I had children of my own. Maybe he's right. We both had the same parents, the same opportunities. Sure, it was tough growing up the kids of a successful Pastor, but I chose sports as an outlet. Martin chose the way of the streets.

As I head towards the bathroom, a particular picture on the mantle catches my eye. Taken five years ago, it shows my father, my mother Elizabeth, me and Martin. Wow. Funny how we've changed in five years, especially Martin. Thirteen at the time, Martin is now eighteen and tall as me.

Rehabbing back in my hometown of Memphis, I promised my Dad I'd stop by the church from time to time and that I would look out for my brother. So far, I was 0 for 2. I try to help when I can, but I've got problems of my own. My career is on the line. As a matter of fact, it's time for another drink.

* * *

The glowing neon sign at Round One Bar doesn't have quite the same effect at five in the afternoon. Inside is a mix of sports themes and contemporary furniture. Dozens of 40-inch HD television screens hang high above the bar. People wave as I take my usual seat. Guess I'm something of a local celebrity. Wish I felt like one.

Round One is one of the trendier spots in Memphis. The young, as well as the not so young, frequent here because they *are* somebody or because they want to *be* somebody.

"Whada it be, Tre? The usual?" asks Lou, the bartender. I nod as I scope my surroundings. Mostly empty, except for a few regulars, all male. That's fine for now. Besides, I need a few drinks in me before the *TNT* show can truly begin. Only girl in here is Viv, the waitress, but I've already been down that road. We really don't get along as of late.

The mirrored wall behind the bar shows a good enough reflection. Three carat diamond earrings sparkle from my earlobes. My custom-tailored shirt fits perfectly. The jeans I wear cost more than most folk's mortgage payments. Some guy three chairs down keeps eyeing my jewelry but he'll keep his seat if he knows what's good for him.

The people in this city love Tre Turner. Although there's no place I'd rather be than back on the field in Atlanta, there's no place I'd rather call home than Memphis.

"Here ya go, Tre," says Lou as he brings over my *Mr. Hyde* poison. Taking a sip from the strong concoction placed in front of me, a news report on one of the endless number of television screens catches my eye.

"…and unemployment is up seven percent," says a detached reporter. "A record 30,000 jobs lost in May alone. Yes, the recession is in full gear now."

Others sitting at the bar shake their heads in disbelief. Many order more rounds as the reporter continues. "But one company also seems to be in full gear. Bale Media, helmed by the some-times-eccentric movie mogul, Jason Bale, is sponsoring a nation-wide employment search. That's right. Bale Media plans to create 50,000 jobs in the next five years." The reporter's inflections begin to pick up. "And Jason Bale will start his massive employment search right here in his hometown of Memphis! I can't think of a better way to give back!"

Lou looks to get my take on the news. "You hear that Tre? Looks like the only Memphian more famous than you is headed back home."

I slam my drink back before responding. After two years, it still stings the back of my throat. "It's all good, Lou!" I shout, making sure everyone hears. "But nobody holds the city down like Tre Turner! Nobody does it like Tre *'TNT'* Turner! Ain't that right?!" The happy-hour crowd raises their drinks in agreement. Looks like I still got it.

"Now that's what I'm talking about! Next round's on me!" Shouts of "*TNT!—TNT!*" ring from the pub. People around the bar throw high-fives. Here, I don't have to think about my family or my career. Here, the cries of my name drown out the whispers of my thoughts.

CHAPTER 3 – Gloria

The imposing granite columns of Saint Peter's Catholic Church are hardly noticeable to me now. I've been coming here since I was a young girl and know this place inside-out. The bird's nest situated in the upper left corner of the roof. The missing stained-glass plate the crew never got around to replacing—luckily, it's high enough not to pose a security threat. The loosened pipe railing that has caused many to trip *up* the stairs—yes, the church has become like the birth mark on my back.

Not one to be late, I rush down the aisle-way to the altar and kneel.

"Early as usual, Gloria?" says a familiar voice.

"Good to see you, Deacon," I smile.

"Now, you know you don't have to come running every time I make a suggestion. Arranging my library was just a suggestion …"

"Well as you say Deacon, procrastination is Satan's way of being on time."

He laughs. "What am I going to do with you, Gloria?"

I enjoy tending to Deacon Nichols. After all, he's like a father figure to me. Especially considering I never knew my own father. A'ma never made it easy finding the man. She'd always say, *why would you want to find someone who doesn't want you?* Maybe she was right. After a while, I gave up searching altogether. Besides, Deacon Nichols fills in the gap pretty well. Now nineteen, I've known him since I was a child. Although compassionate and fatherly to all the young members, Deacon Nichols always treated me extra special. But of course, that led to the whispers. Some said it was because I was the token Hispanic girl, though I didn't let that get to me. I knew Deacon Nichols was one of the few people that truly cared.

"I don't know what I would do without you, Gloria," he says as we arrange books in his study. Unconsciously, I smile. Okay, maybe I beam. Guess something in me still desires his approval. Or maybe being around him makes me forget what awaits me at home.

"Don't mention it," I say. "You're the closest thing to a father I've had all these years." The Deacon's face lights up. Maybe he enjoys being approved just as much I do.

Deacon Nichols is a tall man of English descent. Fairly attractive even into his late-forties, older women in the church constantly tried to pair their aging unwed daughters with him. Far as I know, he never took the bait.

"Why didn't you ever get married?" I ask. "I mean since you decided not to become a priest. You would've made a great husband."

"I don't know," he quietly responds. "Guess I moved too slow for most women."

"Ahh, c'mon," I say as we share a laugh.

"Well, there was one. But that was a long time ago."

"Well, it's her loss," I say, sounding like a proud parent. Deacon Nichols doesn't share this laugh. His face tenses as if he's thinking hard about something. I'm sure there must be a lot on his mind. He's pretty much run the church since Father Macon took ill three months back. Before I can comment, he quickly snaps out of it.

"Well enough about me, young lady," he smiles. "What about you? Who's the special young man in your life? I haven't heard of anyone since that nice young fella—wait…what was his name, *Jaaason, Jaaalen*—"

"Jeremy," I finally help. "And that was like three years ago, Deacon."

"Exactly! So, you've been holding out on me, young lady."

"Nooo, Deacon. Besides, I don't have time for guys."

"Oh, come on, pretty girl like you?"

I blush slightly although he's probably just saying it to make me feel better about the whole non-dating situation. I look down at my outfit before instinctively patting my plain brown hair which rests in its usually placed ponytail. There's nothing special about my clothes, just an oversized shirt and baggy cargo pants. My mother says my wardrobe hides any hint of *femenina*. She never taught me Spanish but I'm pretty sure I know what she means by that.

"Well, I'm waiting," says the Deacon.

"With the church, A'ma, and my internship at the news station, guys are the last of my concerns." Deacon Nichols nods. "So how is your mother doing?"

"She's her usual self," I mumble.

The Deacon looks as if he's debating whether to question my last statement. I make it easy for him. "I mean she complains when I'm at home. She complains when I'm not at home. She complains when I cook. She complains when I don't cook."

Before I know it, the frustration pours out of me. "She said I spent too much time at the church and that I needed to do something with my life. So, I took up some classes and got an internship down at WREG. Now she says I'm never home. And you see why I don't have time for guys. A'ma is a 24/7 job." I stop to catch my breath, hoping I haven't rattled on for too long.

"So, she's still sickly?" he politely asks.

Sarcasm fills my tone. "She's always sick, let her tell it." Okay, maybe I didn't get it all out. "I just think she's afraid to be alone. And I don't know why. All she does is talk about me when I'm there and most of the time she does it in Spanish! I can't understand a word she's saying. I mean, what kind of mother doesn't teach her own daughter their native language. But hey, at least A'ma isn't partial. She doesn't like anything, let alone me. I don't even know why she brought me up here all those years ago. She doesn't like you or the church either!"

We share a serious look before bursting into laughter. Boy did I need that. "I'm sorry Deacon. I didn't mean to go there. It's just —" My phone rings. "Well speak of the devil," I say, sending the call to voicemail.

"Now Gloria, that's not nice," says the Deacon, trying to hide his grin.

"You're right. Sorry. Well guess I better get out of here."

Deacon Nichols steps back as he admires his newly arranged bookshelves. He places his hands on his waist in pride. "Will you look at that? You did it again Gloria."

"We did it Deacon. You think you can handle—"

"Go my child. Tend to your wonderful mother."

CHAPTER 4 – ZEEK

The ground floor employees at St. Jude Hospital are used to the roar of my motorcycle as I make my arrival. But being used to it doesn't make them like it any better. Their faces frown as I park in my usual spot, the red No Parking Zone. I take one last drag of menthol before flicking it into the nearest receptacle. Actually, it bounces off the trash bin and hits the ground.

"I hate this place," I mumble while entering the double sliding doors of the emergency room, my left leg stiffened from the ride. It makes my limp more apparent. I head straight for the restroom, turn on the faucet and begin raking the dirt from under my nails. Barely twenty-two, it's fair to say I've aged in the last four years. Bags have formed under my eyes. My hair is longer, my face unshaven, my jeans stained. The leather jacket I wear smells of engine oil. Some men do this in a fashionable kind of way, but I wasn't smart enough to plan this out. Nervously, I try to scrape the grime from under my nails but there is just too much to remove in one cleaning.

"You've got to be strong for Chrissy," I say to myself in the mirror. "For Angel."

The moment ends as the bathroom door opens. A man wearing a lab coat enters. Dr. Amali. He pauses at the sight of me, almost startled, before continuing to the urinal. We mumble pleasantries.

"Mr. Myers…"

"Doc…"

Dr. Amali is probably in his mid-fifties and of Middle Eastern descent. As I exit the restroom, a middle-aged man wearing scrubs enters. I nearly take his shoulder off with my pass. The collision loosens a high-priced gold watch from his wrist. Somehow, I manage to catch it before it hits the floor. *Now this could pay a year's worth rent*, I think. A nervous grin flashes across his face as he waits for me to return the expensive timepiece.

"Nice watch," I say.

"Th—Thanks."

A small obscure shaped tattoo on the man's wrist catches my attention. It would've been hidden by his watch. He seems to want it that way, now placing his hand in his pocket, accepting the watch with the other. The men strike up a conversation as I leave.

"So how was the trip, Phil?" asks Dr. Amali.

"Great," says the other. "A godsend."

I make my way to room 413. It's been my pseudo home for the past three long months. Unfortunately, it's been Christina's home as well. The space is deathly cold. You can hear the hum of silence as it buzzes throughout the room. I've become accustomed to this, but even worse, so has Christina. Sometimes I'm amazed at how much fight my daughter has in her. She never complains. She always tries her best to smile, even when I can tell she's hurting. Angelina couldn't have left me a better gift.

I nudge the young woman sitting in a chair beside the bed. Although upright, she's clearly asleep. Her head rests in her hand as if a ploy to stay awake. It doesn't seem to be working.

"Hey sis," I say softly. Alicia slowly comes to.

"Hunh?" She responds, still groggy. "Oh—Zeek. Hey—Sorry —I was—"

"Shhh. It's fine," I say, placing a finger over my mouth.

Angelina's younger sister has barely aged in the last four years. Now twenty, she's cut her golden-brown hair to reflect a more, independent look. Alicia yawns as she stretches. "I need to tell you something, Zeek."

Not now, I signal, turning towards Christina.

A frail five year-old rests in the over-sized bed. They say she's my Christina although I hardly recognize her anymore. This child is excruciatingly thin, even for a five year-old. Tubes protrude from her mouth and arms. Her skin seems to have paled even more since the morning. Once beautiful long brown hair is now replaced by brittle shards, even falling out in some places. Chrissy's body rejects most foods and the majority of her nourishment comes through an IV, ever present in her left arm.

To most folks, I'm an outsider, a loner. People don't even look me in the eye walking down the street. But to Christina, I was Daddy. And now, *Daddy* can't do anything but watch as my helpless child lays here dying. And I die slowly too, knowing here, I am as helpless as she is. What kind of life is this? For anyone?

I've already lost the first love of my life and that guilt continues to destroy me daily. I can't lose the second. I just can't.

Gingerly, I take Chrissy's hand. Cracks at the sides of her dried mouth indicate an attempt at smiling.

"Daddy," she whispers.

"There's my baby girl," I whisper back.

Weakened, she closes her eyes. Her small fingers continue to grasp my hand as I swallow hard. I can't let myself break down in front of my baby girl. "I tell you what. Daddy's gonna talk to the doctors for a minute and when I get back, I'll read you a story. Deal?"

Eyes still closed, Christina answers, "Deal."

Usually I get my daily report after first sitting with Christina for a few minutes. No need to search for personnel today as Dr. Amali enters the room. "Can I speak with you for a moment, Mr. Myers?" he asks.

"I was just coming to find you, Doc." We step out into the hallway. "What's with the new equipment?"

"It's a—"

Quickly, I cut him off. Gone is any remnant of the tender tone I took with Christina. "Why can't you figure out how to make her better?! I mean you can figure out she needs more machines, but you can't figure out how to take her off of 'em? I don't get it."

The doc keeps calm. "I understand your concern, Mr. Myers. Let me reassure you we're doing everything we can to help little Christina. But honestly she's just not getting better and then today—"

"What—what do you mean today?" I mutter.

"Well, today her heart stopped beating for approximately sixty seconds."

My throat completely closes. I know exactly what I want to say but it takes seven seconds before my esophagus allows any air to expel. Finally, I speak. "Why didn't you call my job? Why am I just finding out about this?"

"We did try, Mr. Myers, but we were told you're no longer employed there."

I wanted to say something, do something. But what could I do? He was right.

"I'm sorry Mr. Myers," he continues. "Christina's body isn't responding to anything and quite frankly, we've tried it all."

Christina has been misdiagnosed too many times to count. Most doctors first thought it was a rare form of cancer. Some said Leukemia. So-called specialists said Kawasaki's Disease. Truth was…no one was certain. The only certainty was that her body was diminishing rapidly.

Desperation rings through my voice. "What about…what about those experimental drugs you talked about? Can't you give her more of those?"

"It's not that simple, Mr. Myers. Her body rejects everything we've tried so far."

"So, what exactly are you trying to say, Doc?"

Dr. Amali clears his throat as he slowly backs up. "I'm sorry, Mr. Myers. There's nothing else we can do for Christina. Unless she makes a drastic change, she's looking at one, maybe two months. We'll do everything we can to make her comfortable until then."

I turn my back to the doctor. I've heard enough.

"Once again, I'm sorry, Mr. Myers."

Still not facing the doctor, I can hear his footsteps inching closer but I have no interest in the sympathy pat that's coming. Slowly, I proceed back to my daughter's room. Water engulfs my eyes as I continue to walk, my maimed leg feeling heavier than ever. Confusion, anger and brokenness overtake me.

———THE ASSIGNED———

GLORIA

I don't notice I've left my bag at church until I reach for my keys to open the front door. Luckily, I keep an extra one in a small hole in the wall outside our apartment. Thankfully, our gracious management never had it fixed. A'ma starts as soon as I walk in.

"Gloria? You know I could've died waiting on you."

I ignore her comment heading straight for the kitchen. "A'ma, what would you like to eat?" Straining her neck, she turns towards the kitchen, apparently wanting me to see the look on her face. In her mid-forties, A'ma bears the countenance of someone much older. Matted, disheveled hair rests unevenly atop her head. The difficult woman sits on a worn-down couch, wearing an old, tattered nightgown. Our outdated television is tuned to a rerun of 'Matlock', her favorite show.

Aged furniture fills the stuffy, slightly rundown apartment. We don't have a lot, but we get by. Noticeably, there are no pictures visible with the exception of one. Sitting on a small end-table near the front door is a picture of me in my high school graduation cap and gown. So far, it's the only real accomplishment I've ever had.

"I can't believe someone would do this to their own mother," she continues. "What if I got too hungry to wait on you? I could've easily burned myself or worse."

I place a TV dinner in the oven. Over the years, I've mastered the art of ignoring A'ma's comments. *Here it comes*, I think to myself.

A'ma starts ranting in Spanish. Although she never officially taught me the language, I know a few choice words when I hear them. She switches back to English to continue her investigation of my whereabouts.

"And just where have you've been, *Mija*?"

"I was at the church helping Deacon Nichols."

"You and that god forsaken—"

"A'ma!" I quickly interrupt. "Don't talk about the Lord's house like that." I usually ignore her tirades until she speaks negatively about the church.

"I'll say what I want!" she yells back. "And that damn Nichols. They nothing but a bunch of phonies and crooks!"

"I've had about enough of that A'ma. Deacon Nichols is a fine man. You don't even know him."

"I know his kind. They're all alike," she finishes before switching back to Spanish. Eventually I sigh, "Dinner will be ready shortly, A'ma."

Living with her is nearly unbearable at times, but what else can I do? She's the only family I've got.

I move to the bathroom to find A'ma's painkillers. As I search for something to put the cranky woman to sleep, my own reflection grabs my attention. Deacon Nichols' words ring through my head. *"…pretty girl like you?"*

Staring back at my reflection, I've almost forgotten what I look like. For the most part, average features stare back at me. Probably wouldn't have ever been noticed by anyone if it wasn't for my height. They say 5'7" is pretty tall for a girl. My Mexican features are predominant, though not overwhelming. Brown hair, brown eyes, round button nose, full lips. I've always thought my father could be from almost any background. Old classmates would probably say I've done little to change my look in the two years since graduating high school. Maybe I'd be considered attractive if I fixed myself up and didn't act so much like a tomboy. That's what a guy once told me. I didn't find it too complementary at the time but who knows…maybe he's right.

"What am I doing?" I smirk, resuming my search through the various prescription bottles. My hands fumble around as my mind continues to wander. I couldn't entertain the thought of dating with A'ma the way she is. I've tried that before. It lasted a whole four weeks. It's like she grows more ill whenever I grow close to someone. Some coincidence. And besides, most guys in their early twenties want more than I'm willing to offer. So, with two strikes against me, I stopped dating all together. Things are just easier that way. A'ma is the only family I have here in the states. I'm her only child, and honestly, she's done pretty well by me. As a matter of fact, I even respect my mother, Gabriela Torres, in a lot of ways. Coming to a new country on her own as a young woman, working and providing for a child, even though the father leaves her and their daughter to fend for themselves. It's a miracle

A'ma didn't deteriorate sooner than the last seven or eight years. So what if the doctors can't find anything wrong with her? They don't know everything, and she's definitely been through a lot. These are all the things I tell myself to keep a positive outlook on my non-existent life.

"Found them!" I shout, placing my hands on the missing sedatives. When I reenter our dimly lit living room, A'ma seems to be in better spirits.

"I'm sorry Gloria," she says. "I just don't want anyone taking advantage of you. You're all I have, Mija."

"It's ok, A'ma", I smile. "Now take your medicine. I'm gonna go take a quick shower and then I'll get your dinner before I leave."

"What? You're leaving me again?"

"I have to work tonight. They're doing a big interview with that celebrity in town and I have to help."

"Will you at least be on TV this time?" A'ma winces.

"I told you A'ma, that's not what I do. I'm a cameraperson."

A'ma frowns as she turns up the television. She doesn't think my job is suitable for a girl, but I think it suits me just fine. Besides, I'm glad I'm not on the tube. One less thing for her to criticize.

"Now you have your medicine, your dinner is cooking, anything else you need?"

A'ma grins. "I don't know what I would do without you, Mija."

Sometimes I'm not sure if it's the truth or if it's part of her act. The two intertwine seamlessly. "I know A'ma. Oh, I also may have to go back by the church. I left my bag there." And just like that her grin is eaten by the frown monster.

I never understood why A'ma hates the church so much. Though she never attends, it was her who initially brought me to St. Peter's all those years ago. Only nine at the time, I distinctively remember my mother combing my hair, dressing me in a homemade flowery dress and dropping me off in front of the intimidating structure. Her only words were, *"I'll be back in two hours to pick you up."* And I definitely didn't understand her disdain for Deacon Nichols. She's hardly ever interacted with the man, much less known him. Besides the few times he walked me to the car as a kid, the two never spoke. I guess there must be a small place somewhere deep inside the complex woman that wants, or at least 'wanted' faith ingrained in me. So, in many ways I'm grateful to her for introducing me to an aspect of life I hold so dear.

CHAPTER 5 – ZEEK

"What took you so long, Daddy?" Christina whispers.

"Huh?" I mumble. Distracted by emotion, I barely make sense of her words. "Oh, you know those doctors," I regroup. "They love to talk to Daddy."

"What do you talk about?" my delicate child murmurs. "About me?"

I do my best to smile as I approach the bed. "About you, about birds, about trees, about…monsters."

She slightly turns her head. "Monsters? Uhh unnn."

Kneeling beside the bed, I softly rub my nose against Christina's. "Uh *hunn*." It takes every ounce of energy to hide the anguish that brews inside.

"Uh unnn"

"Uh hunn"

Alicia smiles as Christina and I go back and forth.

"You guys having fun?" says a voice from the door.

The smile I once entertained leaves. "Can I help you, Chap?"

Standing at the door is a man dressed in faded blue jeans, slightly worn white tennis shoes, and a speckled blue blazer. Modern bifocals protrude over his nose. He wears a black button-down shirt with a white circular collar. Slight blemishes in his coffee skin tone bear signs of a middle-aged man. His coarse hair has already begun to recede.

"And how's my little Chrissy?" he asks, seemingly ignoring my question.

"Hey *Chappy Brynint*," says Christina, her front two teeth missing as she smiles. I hate to admit it but her face lights up at the sight of this man.

"Ok, Chap," I grunt. "You said your hellos, thanks for stopping —"

Alicia cuts me off. "Zeek, stop it. I asked him to come." Her tone softens as she addresses our company. "I'm sorry, Chaplain Bryant."

"Oh no problem at all," he says before glancing my direction. "I'm glad to see you're doing as well as usual, Mr. Myers."

Like him, I ignore the comment as I move closer to the door. I don't care for the Chaplain's visits, but Alicia requests his presence and Christina seems to enjoy the man.

"*Chappy Brynint?*" She could never get his name quite right. "Say the prayer with me, please."

"Sure sweetie," he answers. "You wanna join us Alicia?"

"But of course." Alicia moves to the other side of the bed. They each clutch one of Christina's hands.

"Think we should let your dad join us?" he asks.

"Uh huh," Christina nods.

"You go ahead sweetie. I'll watch," are the words that pour from my mouth although my face says more.

"Ok, suit yourself. On a count of three. 1...2..."

The three join in a synchronized prayer. *"Now I lay me down to sleep, I pray the Lord my soul to keep. If I should die before I wake, I pray the Lord my soul to take. Amen."*

I'm sure my face has deepened in color by now. The only thing that keeps me from berating this hospital preacher is the fact I don't want to upset my daughter.

I throw the chaplain a curt glance letting him know it's time to end his visit.

"I'll try to stop by tomorrow, little Chrissy," he smiles as he winks. Christina almost seems to blush. He hugs Alicia before I ask to see him outside. I don't understand why he has this effect on them.

In the hallway, I'm ready to give the reverend an earful. I couldn't care less about his white collar. To me, anything or anyone that represents a god is just as fake as the smiles people give me around the hospital. This so-called chaplain just takes advantage of families in their time of sorrow. With the door firmly closed, I begin my rampage.

"Look, I don't care who you are. Stay away from—"

"Mr. Myers, are you a man of faith?" the chaplain interrupts.

Part of me wants to ignore his question and continue with my storm of words but something compels me to answer. This may be the perfect segue to really tell him what I think of all this *god* mumbo-jumbo. I look him straight in the eye.

"If you're asking if I believe in some jolly, white bearded dude that sits in the sky determining who lives or dies, the answer is no."

"That's unusual, Mr. Myers. Especially considering your daughter is so full of faith."

"She's a child easily influenced and as a matter of fact, I don't appreciate you filling her head with this junk."

"Mr. Myers, I don't believe in an old white-haired guy that sits in the sky picking people off at random. I believe in God. A God that is kind, loving—"

"Loving?" I counter. "What kind of *god* lets an innocent five-year-old die?"

"I don't know God's reasons for everything," says the chaplain. "And frankly who am I to question God? But I do know—"

"That's just what I thought preacher man. You don't know anything. Me and my daughter are doing just fine without you or your god."

I turn my back on Chaplain Bryant as I head towards the room. He calls for me, but I refuse. The chaplain tries again, this time almost shouting. "Mr. Myers! Please!"

I stop for a moment, my back still turned.

"Mr. Myers, your daughter lies in that room fighting for her life. I've prayed for her and with her, but sometimes God wants to see what are you going to do for yourself before he intervenes. Please, pray for your daughter. What do you have to lose? If I'm wrong, oh well, life as usual. But just imagine for one moment that I'm right. Think about it, sir. Don't let the past destroy your faith. Make the first step. God will do the rest. Do it for your daughter, Mr. Myers."

I turn towards Chaplain Bryant, making sure he hears and understands every word I'm about to say. "Your services are no longer needed…preacher man." The door slams behind me.

"Why did you do that Zeek?" Alicia frowns. She's been listening. "We need all the prayers we can get!"

"Prayers?!" I nearly growl. "Alicia, god has nothing to do with this! There is no—" I glance towards Christina. Our voices have risen quite a bit and neither of us wants to do anything to upset her, regardless of the topic. We continue, more subdued. "There is no god," I say. "What kind of god would let a five year-old suffer like this, hunh? First Angel, and now Chrissy? Where's a god in that?"

"You can't keep blaming God for what happened five years ago," she says taking my hand. "Or yourself for that matter."

Not wanting to have that conversation, I turn away, but Alicia continues. "Look, I'm a wreck too, but I've gotta have faith in something. I mean with my sister and now my niece? I'd be crazy by now."

She steps in front of me, her hand stretched towards Christina's bed. "You have a beautiful little girl lying there. At least have faith in her. We can agree on that, right?"

I try to look away, but Alicia won't let it go. "Right?"

I give in, finally smiling. "You just don't quit, do ya lil sis."

"Nope," she smiles.

———T H E A S S I G N E D———

TRE

Dusk falls over the Memphis skyline. The drinks fall fast as well, the lights now dimmed at Round One, giving the spot a more club-like atmosphere. *Now this is more like it*, I observe after returning from the bathroom. Attractive young women adorn the bar like beautiful decorations. I turn on my million-dollar smile as easily as the flick of a light switch. Most return the favor. Slightly buzzed, I select my latest acquisition. It's much easier being Tre "TNT" Turner when I've downed a few.

"Hey Lou," I say, getting the bartender's attention. "Tell the one in that low-cut yellow top…" Lou points the woman out sitting on the other side of the bar.

"…yeah her. Let her know, drinks on me."

"Gotcha, TNT." Lou walks over to relay the message. The co-ed grins as she looks my way. Freckles are barely noticeable under her artificially tanned skin. Long blonde hair hides any evidence of its original color. Just like I like 'em. After a few moments, she waves flirtingly. Nonchalantly, I turn my head as I finish my drink. Never let on too quickly. After all, it's just a game. No different than the football field.

I take one more glance in *low-cut yellow top's* direction. She's still looking. Briefly I smile back before pretending to engulf myself in my smartphone. She motions for Lou. *Perfect…*

In my peripheral, I see her whisper something to the husky bartender though I pretend not to notice. She must have given him a message for me as he walks back towards my direction. Just as Lou is about to gesture for my attention, something catches *his* attention. He pauses as he gazes over my head. Must be a woman, I smile as I turn around to see the distraction. Guess I was right …sort of.

Definitely a woman, but wearing a steel-colored pantsuit with an egg-shell ruffled collar and ruffle sleeves protruding from her coat, this one definitely sticks out at the modern pub. Her attire is a mix of the Victorian Age and "The Matrix". She has to be in her late fifties, early sixties. Long, ultra-straight, platinum gray hair drops below her shoulders. Her fair skin tinges with warm hints of brown. It's hard to tell her background under that coat of hair. Maybe Middle Eastern, Brazilian, Creole? I don't recall ever laying eyes on this woman before, but there's still something oddly familiar about her.

She peers around the bar until her eyes find…me, surprisingly. We stare for a moment before I pretend to get a text message. Not really wanting to know more about the mystery woman, I turn back around on my swivel bar chair. Out the corner of my eye, I notice she is now standing right beside me. It's as if her eyes pierce through my skin. Others notice as well.

"Uhh, yeah whada it be?" Lou asks the woman, attempting to end the eerie moment. She says nothing. I can still feel her eyes penetrating the side of my face. Finally, I've had enough. "Something I can help you with?" I say, somewhat crude. What's with this lady? She continues to stare. People around the bar wait for a response. I smirk at the crowd before addressing the obviously crazed woman.

"He-he-he-hellooooo?" I mouth, insinuating the woman is slow. People laugh as I take another sip of my *act out* juice. Lou tries to intervene once more. "Look ma'am, you're gonna have to buy something or I'ma have to ask you to leave."

Then just like that, the woman turns around and heads for the exit. After a few steps, she stops. It looks as if her eyes glaze over, but it's hard to tell in this light. Suddenly she rushes back to the bar. Lou frowns as the persistent lady beckons for him to come closer.

"Look, are you gonna buy something this time?" He asks, thoroughly annoyed now. The strange woman continues to motion for Lou with her hand. He stands arms folded, resisting. She smiles, her head slightly tilted. Lou finally lets down his guard and leans over to see what the woman wants. She waits a moment before softly saying, "May you use the rest of your time wisely."

Confused, Lou stares at the woman, his tall frame still hunched over. Then comes the sound...

ZZZIPPPPP...CRRACCKK!!!

An errant dart flies over Lou's head and crashes straight into a huge display bottle on the bar counter. It shoots through the container like a bullet. Red liquid bursts from the container, soaking those closest to it, including me. I can't believe this! Do they know how much this shirt costs? —Wait a minute...I notice something odd. The placement of Lou's head—now standing straight up—and the contact spot of the dart on the bottle are nearly identical. The tall server instinctively rubs the side of his temple. Did—did she just save his life? Hell, did she just save mine? From where I'm sitting the dart could have just as easily hit me. I turn to see the woman's reaction, but she's nowhere to be found. Nah...can't be.

"Sorry about that, TNT," says Lou while handing me a towel.

"This is a $600 dollar shirt," I grumble as I continue to wipe the strawberry flavored beverage from my clothes.

"I know," says Lou. "Those college kids always in here throwing darts all over the place, like it's funny or something." Lou reaches for the side of his head again. "They done it this time!"

Just then my phone rings. Frown lines set in as I notice the number. *Better be good…*

"Yeah," I answer.

A voice whispers on the other end, "Tre…Tre…'that you?"

"Of course it's me," I say. "You called my phone didn't cha? And why are you whispering, T-Mart?"

My younger brother, Martin, doesn't sound like himself. "I—I need your help, Tre."

"Speak up! I can't hear you!" The background music of the bar drowns out his voice. "And where have you been? Mom and Dad have been blowing up my phone worried about you."

"I—I need some help, bruh," he murmurs.

"Look, just 'cause I got money don't mean I'ma give it to you to go on one of your binges."

"It's not like that," he says. "Look man, I just need—"

I cut him off as I can hear the desperation in his voice. "Oh no, you not getting a dime from me T-Mart. You still owe me for—"

"I don't want your money!" he screams through the phone. "I need your help, please!"

This desperation is not addiction-related. I can hear it in his voice. No, this is something different. Fear. I make my way to the bathroom, away from the noise.

"Okay Martin, what's going on?"

Martin's deep breathing bellows through the phone. Standing six-feet with dreadlocks and tattoos, my brother isn't the type to scare easily. A few moments go by before he begins.

"Remember when Dad used to say in his sermons, *when you're around true evil, you'll know?*"

"Yeah?"

"Well these people, man. They're evil. I can feel it!"

"Wait a minute," I say. "Slow down—back up. What people?"

Martin continues. "Mannnn, I got myself into something, Tre. A dude by the name of Los introduced me to these real business-like cats. At first, they had us doing a couple of small jobs, setting up meetings with these computer geeks, roughing them up if they didn't do the work. Nothing major. They always paid us good, and I'm not gon' lie, they made sure we had something to smoke. I mean, just one big party. Then, they said they could make us feel like we were on a never-ending high. They got me to recruit my boys and everything. But something not right wit' them cats."

"They sound like drug dealers, Martin. What do you expect?"

"No, it's not that..." Martin hesitates. "They're—they're some kind of cult or something—look Tre, I know this must sound crazy, but I'm not high. These dudes are evil. I mean *Lucifer* type evil. I've seen stuff..."

"What kind of stuff?"

"Tre, I just need to get out of here. Please. Just come get me. I can't trust any of my crew now. I'm the only one who hasn't drank the kool-aid. Just come pick me up, PLEASE!"

"Okay, okay. Fine. Where are you?"

"I'll be somewhere near that old dry cleaners on Bering. Uhhh, 242 Bering Ave. I'll see ya when you pull up."

I program the address in my phone. "242 Bering Ave. Got it. I'm on the way."

"Thanks man."

"No doubt."

"And Tre…"

"Yeah?"

"Love ya, bruh."

His words catch me off guard. I don't know how to respond. No one in my entire family, especially Martin, has talked like that in years. "Yeah man, I'll be there shortly," is the best I manage to get out. The call ends.

I stand motionless away from the bar as I try to process the conversation. The level of difficulty is increased due to the alcohol I've consumed. Not sure what to make of all this. Martin's usually the one dishing out fear, not the other way around. Walking back, I decide to stop the analytical processing going on before my brain explodes.

"Hey Lou, I gotta make a stop. Put it on my tab."

"Sure thing, Tre."

"Going so soon?" asks a soft voice to my right—the *low-cut yellow top* girl. She pouts with pink colored lips as her right index finger gently brushes against my shoulder. Man, she looks even better up close. My eyes capture a head to toe image before responding. "Yeah, I've got to make a quick stop."

"Come on. Stay," she mouths. "Next rounds on me."

The offer is appealing. I take another head-to-toe glance. Very appealing.

"What's your name?" I ask.

"My friends call me Bree."

"Ok, Bree—you're gorgeous by the way—but listen. I have to go make this one stop and then I'll be back, and I'll buy you and your girls all the drinks you want. Don't worry about buying me a drink. I'm Tre "TNT" Turner."

The seductive twenty-something licks her lips as she answers. "ONE, I know who you are. And TWO, I didn't say I'd buy you a drink. I said…NEXT ROUND'S ON ME!"

The cute blond runs to the bar—hops on top—grabs a shot glass—lies down—raises the bottom of her shirt a few inches and places the shot glass on her bare stomach.

She then points towards me for approval. "Well…"

A small crowd gathers as everyone waits for my response. Gotta give the people what they want, right?

"Now THAT'S what I'm talking about!" I shout to the crowd. "BODY SHOTS!"

The place erupts. It's as if—wait a minute—Martin. The girl—what's her name—it doesn't come right to mind, but her actions nearly cause me to forget why I was leaving in the first place. But I can't leave now. The people are depending on TNT Turner. Besides, what's a few more minutes?

CHAPTER 6 – ZEEK

"What are you doing Zeek?" Alicia asks. I barely notice her question as I scour through tattered pieces of the lint encrusted paper that line my pockets.

"Hunh," I mumble. "Thomas from the temp agency said he'd call me back in an hour. That sorry son of a—"

"Zeek, you're gonna drive yourself crazy!" Alicia shouts.

"I need to be working!" I shout back. "We're up the creek either way!" Alicia's entire face drops. The words, now freed from my mouth, seem to echo in the confined concrete reformatory. It's not so much about the job as it is keeping busy. Alicia stares at me, gauging what I really meant.

"We'll get through it," she assures me.

Alicia and I have grown close since the tragedy four years earlier. Surprisingly, she never blamed me for the accident. She knows all too well the anguish I carry inside. I guess she figured there was no need to add to it. Not that there was any room left.

"I'm gonna go down to the cafeteria," I say. "Get a paper. See if I can find something in the help-wanteds." I don't clarify my earlier statement, but Alicia knows me well enough now. She knows how I cope. "You okay for a minute?" I ask. She nods. Christina rests, her eyes closed. Walking out the door, a news story on the television above the bed catches my eye.

"The man that promises 1,000 jobs for Memphis is due to make his arrival any minute," says a young reporter. "That's right. We're here live at the Peabody Hotel downtown, and we're told that Jason Bale and his entourage will be arriving any moment," the reporter continues, trying to hide his own excitement. "As you can see, hundreds have gathered to get a glimpse of the unconventional celebrity."

Police barricades line the streets as people anxiously gather in front of the hotel. Some raise '*We Love You Bale!*' signs as a white limousine approaches.

The reporter touches his earpiece and squints as he attempts to hear over the growing roar of the crowd. "Wait! My producers are telling me…YES! The white limo is not a ruse. Jason Bale is about to be escorted in! Let's—"

The reporter and his camera crew take off towards the stretched vehicle. Running, the news staff looks almost fanatical as the crowd. They scurry around the corner just in time. Cameras flash a near blinding light as the chauffeur opens the rear door. Several men dressed in custom-tailored white suits emerge from the vehicle. Like most bodyguards, sunglasses hide their eyes. Suspiciously, they survey their surroundings, seeming to watch the crowd's every move from behind darkened specs. Their suits are impeccable, all-white from head to toe. And although the same color, each suit is designed differently. Too grand for my own simple tastes, but I can't deny their impressiveness. Just as the suits vary, so do the men in height and ethnicity.

A sixth man steps from the limousine. He's dressed in all-white, as the others, but the roar of the crowd signifies his importance. This guy is in his early forties, stands about 6'1", and looks to be in great shape. His brownish-blonde hair is cropped low, showing signs of a slight recede. Combined with a rugged 5 o'clock shadow, however, gives him a look of mystery and prestige. Now, here's the kind of guy that tries hard for that *I don't care* look.

Untanned, his skin is neither overtly pale. His eyes could be grey, perhaps blue? They change with every light that's flashed. Mr. Perfection's smile beams as bystanders take his picture. He seems to welcome the fanfare. I'm sure women, and young girls alike would consider him handsome. The fancy celebrity continues to wave to the crowd as the five men escort him through the press towards the hotel lobby. A chant of *"Bale! Bale! Bale!"* erupts from the masses as the reporter restarts his news feed. I retake my seat at the edge of Christina's bed as the news report continues.

"…and as you can see, Jason Bale has just made his way into the Peabody Hotel. That's right. Jason Bale himself is back in our fine city. Having spent the first 16 years of his life here before catching his big break in the surprise indie hit, *Drops of Heaven*, many may not remember Bale's beginnings. But I'm old enough to remember and one thing's for sure…home will always be home."

Guess the reporter is right. I had no idea the swanky star grew up here. Go figure.

"Of course, he is accompanied by his elite detail of bodyguards he refers to as his 'Angels'. And if you know anything about Jason Bale, you know those guys are always with him."

A newscaster at the studio responds. "Wow, that's great, Ted. It seems to be pandemonium down there. I'm surprised Mr. Bale didn't try to sneak in during the middle of the night."

"You know Sharon, that's a great point, but once again, if you know anything about Jason Bale, or 'Bale', as he likes to be called, you know he does nothing of the norm. This guy really loves interacting with the fans up close and personal. But not to worry, those bodyguards don't look as if they play around so…"

The studio newscaster lets out a forced laugh. The two go back and forth until time for the segment has just about elapsed.

"…and remember Entertainment Tonight is on location as well, right here in our very city. They'll be interviewing Bale as he talks about his latest movie, his expanding business venture, Bale Media, and those 1,000 jobs he's promised Memphis. I tell you Sharon, this is a great day to be a Memphian."

"You've got that right, Ted. Remember, you can tune in right here to get caught up on all the latest Jason Bale news…"

I finally turn off the television, not wanting to disturb Chrissy Pooh. *Finally some good news,* I think. I'm actually impressed by this Jason Bale guy. A lot of people talk about change, but this guy looks like he's putting his money where his mouth is. Although I've never been a big fan of his movies, (cheesy, over-budgeted, summertime popcorn flicks) he's at least brought some hope to this dying city. Impressed, I turn to Alicia. "Wow, wish I could work for that guy," I smile. She smirks and shrugs her shoulders. I guess Bale didn't have the same effect on her. Maybe she didn't see the same thing and needs a little clarification. "I mean think about it—"

My sentence is cut short by a loud beeping sound. The kind of sound that signals emergency. I immediately turn my attention towards Christina. Her heart monitor shows one elongated line streaming across the green tinted screen…flatline.

Alicia jumps up from the chair as I rush towards the top of the bed reaching for my baby's hand. "Chrissy!"

My young daughter is unresponsive. She looks as she does any other time she's resting, but the continuous buzzing of hospital equipment indicates something more.

"Help! Nurse!"

Alicia steps in the hallway to get the staff's attention. Nurses rush the room. They speak in medical jargon before beginning CPR. Ninety seconds later, Dr. Amali arrives. He shouts orders to the nurses. "Give me one amp of Epi! Now!"

People scramble around the room. Things happen so fast, it takes a minute for me to grasp what's going on.

"Nurse Statler, start chest compressions," continues the doctor.

"What's wrong with her?!" I plead.

"Mr. Myers, ma'am, you have to leave the room now."

"No!" I cry. "I not leaving my baby!" Tears flood my face as I watch the moment unfold.

"You have to let us do our jobs!" Dr. Amali shouts back. "Now please leave! NOW!"

Hospital personnel escort me and Alicia out of the room. The door slams, this time with me on the other side.

CHAPTER 7 – Gloria

"You have fifteen minutes with Bale," says a member from the celebrity's security team. His glare signifies he means business, not to mention the mohawk and tattoos that protrude from his torn off sleeves. Arnie, the cameraman, nervously thanks the guard-in-white as he fumbles with the bulky camera perched atop his shoulder. "Come on, Gloria, keep up will ya!" he shouts. Bet he wouldn't talk like that to the Scottish version of Mr. T.

Of course, I do just as he says, pulling my cables up from behind me. Assistant Cameraperson is just another name for 'servant'. My duties deal with anything involving not actually touching a camera—mostly lugging around huge cables. At least it's a form of exercise, as I try to look at the bright side.

"Uhhh, Mr.?" Arnie's shaky voice barely gets out.

"Balak," replies Bale's mohawked security dog.

"Oh, ok. Bay'lock, Ba—Ba—" Arnie fumbles worse than the old running back from State.

"Balak—Fool!"

"Oh, I'm—I'm sorry, Mr. Barack. Yeah, *Barack*. I love that name."

Balak—we all know his name now—cracks his knuckles as he stares down my near shivering superior. Nervous, Arnie quickly turns away from the irate guard only to send his camera into the sternum of another security member, who just happens to be the largest of the group. Frozen, Arnie slowly makes his way up the tree of a man. Smoke almost appears to brew from the massive man's nostrils. With a shaven head, small beady eyes, and a white suit nearly too small for his frame, the enormous bodyguard is menacing to say the least. It's a wonder the over-hyped celebrity needs anyone other than this monstrosity by his side. I've stood next to professional basketball players before and this guy measures up with the tallest of 'em. His body is made up like a World's Strongest Man competitor, muscles so swollen I don't see how he can move around.

The giant's fierce look causes poor Arnie's knees to wobble. He never speaks but instead discharges an intimidating grunt. Despite the way Arnie treats me, I actually feel sorry for him in this moment. This guy looks like he wants to eat not just the camera, but Arnie himself.

"Now Amnon, that's no way to treat our guests, is it?" says its master—err... boss. The giant's eyes squint as he leans closer to Arnie, now fully terrified.

"Amnon..."

The giant finally relinquishes and moves on. Still frozen, sweat drips from Arnie's brow.

"My friend, are you alright?"

Arnie doesn't move, probably too afraid to turn around.

"Oh, don't mind him. He's harmless as a kitten."

Slowly, Arnie turns to acknowledge the voice. "Why Mr.— Mr. Bale," Arnie smiles, relieved.

"Just call me Bale," says a set of beautifully whitened teeth.

"Why—why thank you sir. I didn't mean to—"

"Shhh, it's no problem. Go. Do whatever your team needs to do."

"Why, yes sir." Arnie's tone firms up a bit as he barks orders at me and the other intern/servant, Sam. "Whada you two doing? You heard the man, let's get moving!"

Any feelings of empathy I felt for Arnie quickly surrender.

As I work, I try to take in my surroundings. I've never been to the Peabody Hotel before. It's one of those things where you know about it because you live here, and people come to visit it from all over, but you've never been to it because…well, you live here.

The star known as Jason Bale takes a seat on an exquisite European sofa. The luxurious hotel is known for its handsome decor. Usually a privilege only afforded to the rich and famous, it has been a staple of Memphis for decades. 'Mr. Famous' removes his white suit coat to reveal a finely tailored white button-down shirt. It wraps his torso perfectly, also revealing a finely-toned upper body. Not my type at all, even excluding the age difference, but I can definitely respect a guy who works out. His white pants are creased exceptionally. Even his socks and shoes are bone colored, matching the rest of his entourage.

"So, are we ready to do this?" smiles our lead reporter, Julie Blaylock. Jason Bale smiles as well, but more from the high hem of her skirt rather than his interest in the interview.

"I'm so excited to have this opportunity," she speaks while shaking the superstar's hand.

He grips back, eyes still focused on Julie's figure. One can hardly blame him. Her skirt is so tight I don't know how she's gonna sit down. And they have the nerve to lecture *us* on professionalism. But I get it. It's about ratings, sensationalism. I'm sure God cries out for the world we live in today. As a young woman, this is what I have to compete with. Guess I'll never make it to the other side of the camera.

"An exclusive interview with Jason Bale!" Julie giggles. "Here I am just a local reporter scoring one of the biggest opportunities of a lifetime!"

"Well, life is all about opportunities," smiles the movie star.

Julie takes a seat on the sofa. She's definitely attractive; no one can take that away from her. Although I do think she tries too hard. We're only three years apart in age, but a lifetime apart in status. Casually, Julie attempts to pull her skirt down, but the already shortened garment rides up with the contour of the furniture. Jason Bale watches her legs intensely. The look on Julie's face goes from flattery to embarrassment.

"How're we looking, Arnie?" she asks.

"Ready when you are, Ms. Blaylock,"

"Great," she smiles towards Jason Bale. "Okay, so what we're going to do today—"

"It's Julie, right?" the celebrity interrupts.

"Sure is!" she beams.

"Okay, *Julie*," says the star, never taking his eyes off her legs. "I've been to the rodeo a few times, so you just fire away and I'll be ready. And what are you? About a size six? A hundred twenty …two—no, twenty three pounds?"

"I beg your pardon?" she asks, incredulously.

"Okay, we're on in 20!" Arnie shouts before glancing over his shoulder. "Get with it, Gloria!" Engrossed in their conversation, I go back pretending to be busy.

Julie takes a moment to gather herself. She continues to tug on her tight black skirt, to no avail.

"In 5…4…3…2…," says Arnie, mouthing the one and pointing to Julie.

"…Today we have a special treat everyone. We're here with none other than Time Magazine's "Man of the Year", Jason Bale! How are you today, sir?"

"I'm great Julie!" The mysterious star's tone completely changes. He continues to watch Julie intently, now only at eye level. His smile is infectious and his manner engaging. Julie is nearly thrown off guard, in fact. I'm not a fan of his movies, but maybe he is a good actor.

"…okay, so Jason—"

"Julie, just call me Bale," grins the performer.

"Okay. So Mr. Bale—"

"No sweetie, just Bale. That's what my friends call me," he says throwing his trademark smile.

"Okay, Mr—umm, Bale. Well, since you brought that up let's start right there. You are a man known for your…let's say idiosyncrasies. You go by your last name only and everyone wants to know what's up with the all-white suits for both you and your security detail. I heard somewhere you call them, *Angels*?"

Bale answers back, proudly. "Why yes, they are my angels. They protect me."

"Okay, makes sense," Julie nods.

"And I just love the color white. It's so…pure."

Bale's voice is soothing to the ear. His words are purposefully thought out, his delivery eloquent. Almost *too* eloquent. Like a mother's lullaby, his voice produces hypnotic-like effects, mesmerizing with every syllable spoken. You try your best to stay awake as not to miss anything. Although, the point of a lullaby is to put you to sleep…

"It seems you can do just about anything. Even though losing your parents at a young age, you made it all the way from Memphis to Hollywood. You're a self-made millionaire, a businessman, an accomplished actor, and I've also heard you play five instruments, speak four languages, and can even cook. Wow, what a catch!"

"Oh, stop it Julie," Bale smiles. The two certainly know how to put on a good show.

"But seriously, I just want to be remembered as a man of the people."

"Umm hmmm…so is there a chance for public office later down the line?"

"Who knows, if the conditions are right, and the people want it—right now I'm just focused on my company, Bale Media. We have an exciting announcement coming up in the near future."

"That's right. You just recently completed a huge merger with LabTech, International. That had a lot of people talking and it sent Wall Street into a frenzy."

"Yeah, but we're all about rebuilding this economy, Julie. We plan to create 30,000 jobs in this great country within just the next couple of years. Plus, many more than that within the next five to ten years."

"Wow! That's great! You definitely have a lot of tricks up your sleeve. So how did you get an established tech giant like LabTech to merge with an up and coming media firm? I mean, it's unheard of."

"Let's just say, I presented them with an offer they couldn't refuse."

Julie laughs for the camera. "Like a line out of one of your movies, hunh?"

"Hey, what can I say?! I'm an actor!" Bale laughs on cue.

"Okay, okay. So, what about this exciting announcement? Can we get a hint?"

"Come on now, Julie. If I gave you a hint, it wouldn't be so exciting now would it?"

Julie turns toward the camera. "Well, as usual, Jason Bale keeps us in suspense. I guess just like his latest movie, we'll all just have to wait and see. Reporting live from Downtown Memphis, Julie Blaylock, signing—"

Bale leans over into the reporter's parting camera shot. "Oh, and to all my fans, I'll be at the Sin City Nightclub this weekend, so come and party with yours truly, Bale."

Julie waits a second, making sure he's finished. "Wow. Most celebs like to keep a low profile when they're in town, but I guess as we've figured out by now, there is nothing usual about Jason—well...*Bale*. Reporting live from the Peabody Hotel, Julie Blaylock, signing out."

"And we're...out!" shouts Arnie—my signal to start rolling up line. Julie stands, still tugging on her skirt to magically make it longer.

"Thanks again for the interview, uh, Bale," she says. Gone is the flirtatious tone heard during the interview.

"Don't mention it," he replies. I step in closer to take Julie's lapel mike. Really, it's so I can get a better listen. Bale briefly smiles in my direction as I approach. I smile back, keeping my eye contact to a minimum. He continues the conversation as if I'm not even there.

"So, Julie, can I persuade you to join me for...let's say...*dessert* tonight?"

Any hint of Bale's "Man of the Year" persona has disappeared as well.

"Wow," says Julie. "At least you get straight to the point. Thanks, but no thanks."

I'd imagine any curiosity or slight attraction Julie held before the interview has all but left.

"Besides, I'm engaged."

This is the moment Julie's been waiting for as she flashes her over-sized engagement ring in front of Bale.

"Even better," says the unfazed actor. He moves closer, gently brushing the side of her face before she instinctively moves back.

The playboy celebrity smiles as he turns and walks away. The giant —I believe called Amnon—joins his side.

"Now, you're sure you won't join me?" Bale calls out.

Julie looks puzzled, as if she has something important to say but can't remember.

"W—we—well, I guess I can stop by for a little while," she slowly commits.

I can't believe it! What is she doing? Why would she even give this creep the time of day?

"Great, see you at 10," he says, never looking back. "My Angels will provide you with details."

The tattooed one, known as Balak, waits for us to gather our equipment so he can escort us out. I look to Julie to express my disapproval. We're not friends in the slightest, but we are two young women who both despise creeps. At least that's what I thought. As I watch Julie, I'm not so sure she even knows what she's done. She shakes her head as if she's just been under a trance. Is that the effect stardom can have on people?

"Thank you, my friends," says Bale as we pack up our equipment. "Now leave me. *I must continue to be about my father's business.*"

Before I even realize it, words tumble out of my mouth. "Wow. Quoting bible verses? Wouldn't have pegged you as a reader."

No, Gloria! What have you done! It was supposed to be a thought, but my frustrations at today's happenings materialize audibly. Everyone stops as the focus shifts to me. My eyes widen as I freeze in my tracks. Arnie, Julie, those huge bodyguards— everyone turns and stares at me—even Jason Bale stops and turns.

How did he hear me nearly out the room? Still yards away, he takes a few steps closer.

"You know what? You're absolutely right," he smirks before turning back around. His security or *angels* or whatever, follow. Whew, glad that moment's over. The men continue to the door as I hear one more statement from the shrewd icon.

"…oh, but I was referring to someone else…"

Am I the only one who heard that? Guess so—no one else turns. Or maybe they just don't care, diligently wrapping up our gear. Arnie mugs me with his eyes. I know I'll be hearing about this later.

Nearly an hour later, still no word on Christina. A steady stream of medical personnel comes and goes, but none can give specifics on what's happening. My leg stiffens as I frantically pace up and down the recently waxed floor. Alicia begs me to sit but I won't hear of it. The creaking sound of Christina's door being opened catches my attention. Dr. Amali quietly steps out.

"Doc, what's going?" I say rushing to his side. "Tell me something. Is she—"

"Mr. Myers I'm going to get straight to the point. Right now, Christina is in a medically induced coma. We couldn't revive her heart without the aid of a life support system. If we take her off the machine…she will die. I'm sorry, but we need your permission to reverse the coma."

His words barely make sense to me. I feel light headed. The room closes in. I haven't felt like this since…

I have to focus. "You said the support system has her heart running, right? You can leave her on that until she gets better—"

"You don't understand, Mr. Myers. Your daughter is—"

"That's right. My daughter! SHE'S MY DAUGHTER!"

"I know Mr. Myers, and I'm sorry. But she is not going to get any better. She's unable to hear, talk, even breathe on her own. I'm sorry, but for all intents and purposes, it's over."

Those words incense me as I grab the doctor by his collar. This can't be happening again. I won't let it. "Don't say that. Don't you ever say that!"

He pushes away. "I'll give you some time with your daughter. I'm afraid we've done all we can do."

As Dr. Amali proceeds to the elevator, I lean over, my hands on my knees—it's too much to process. The hurt suffocates me. I don't know what to do. There's nothing I can do. My daughter is —WHY ME?!?!

Alicia sobs as she embraces me. My eyes look up to catch a glimpse of the doctor right before he enters the elevator. It looks as if—no, can't be…

What appears to be a black, smoke-like haze of some sort radiates over his entire body. As the doors shut, the swaying mist lingers outside the elevator shaft. My eyes are so glossed over with tears, there's no telling what I really saw.

——THE ASSIGNED——

TRE

More than an hour has passed since I promised my brother a ride, yet my location remains Round One. Martin will understand. Besides, this isn't your typical hunny down the way. *Low-cut yellow top* is pre-med.

My phone flashes. Six missed calls. Conviction tries its best to override temptation. It's a tough battle to say the least, especially with the latter being aided by strong drinks and a college sweetie.

I try to leave…again…for real this time.

"Look, I'll be back in 20, 30 minutes, tops."

'Low-cut yellow top' grazes the side of my neck with her face. "Don't go," she whispers. "We're just getting started."

"I know, I know," I whisper back, her ginger-themed perfume further adding to my intoxication. Reaching for her hand, I'm met with a peculiar tattoo resting under her palm. Two identical shapes inverted, with a dot placed directly in between. "What's this babe? The new sign for Gemini?" I laugh.

"Maybe if you're good, I'll tell you about it one day," she smiles back.

"Well in that case, why don't we continue this party at my place?"

"Hmmm, I'm listening?" she smiles.

"I'll go scoop my brother right quick, drop him off, and then we'll meet at my place. Just me and you…"

"But I didn't—"

"—I'll call you a taxi and text you the address. All you have to do is say, yes."

"Yes."

"Now *that's* what TNT likes to hear."

Although I can't think of her name—besides the mental nickname I've given her—we kiss. Several more minutes pass before I finally leave. Martin knows how we roll. Besides, what's a few more minutes?

ZEEK

When we reenter the room, Christina looks as if she's already gone. Her skin is cool to the touch. I collapse beside the bed. It can't end like this. It just can't. We've been through too much.

"Come on, Zeek. We have to be strong," Alicia whispers. "We have to."

I caress my daughter's tiny hand, but this time she doesn't squeeze back. Eyes bloodshot red, my body has no more tears to produce. Alicia is silent. Guess even she's run out of encouraging words.

"There's gotta be something they can do!" I wail. "There's gotta be someone!"

"There is," speaks a voice from behind.

I turn as quickly as my body allows, but my anticipation leaves just as hastily as it arrives.

"There is someone," repeats Chaplain Bryant. My initial urge is to pound in the man's cranium, but there's no fight left in me. Just about hopeless, I rest my head on the stony bed.

"Mr. Myers, are you a man of faith?" he asks me. I sit quietly. Neither are there words left in me, but this man is determined not to leave us in peace.

"I ask that question because some say it helps to talk to her. Give her a reason to live."

Something in his statement causes me to slightly lift my head. I turn, briefly facing the chaplain, now Alicia. She nods, agreeing. I face little Chrissy, her skin paling by the minute. The machine keeping her alive hums loudly in the still room. Even though my mouth hasn't any words left, my heart has a few.

"Baby...sweetie...Chrissy," I begin. "Daddy loves you more than anything in this world. I don't care what those doctors say. I believe in you. Daddy BELIEVES in you, baby. When you're ready to open your eyes, you just open them and Daddy will be right here. I promise. Okay baby?" Firmly clinching her hand, Christina still doesn't move.

"Now some would say that makes no sense," says the chaplain. His comment draws a stern glare from even Alicia. "Some would say that's crazy," he continues. "...that she can't hear you, she doesn't understand. By all appearances, she's—"

I've heard enough. "Look, they don't know! How can they prove she doesn't hear me?!"

A confident grin stretches from the chaplain's mouth. "You know Mr. Myers, that's the same thing I say when people question the existence of God. I have faith your daughter can get out of that bed—I really do. The question is...do you?"

I offer no answer, disregarding his sly tactics. He shrugs his shoulders as he smiles at Alicia. The two share a slight embrace before he exits the room. Exhausted, my head drops forward, resting between my hands.

——THE ASSIGNED——

GLORIA

Arnie gives me a good drilling on the way back to the news station. He goes on and on about my unprofessionalism, my complete disregard for protocol—blah, blah, blah. Funny, the topic of nearly being scared out of his pants never comes up when he speaks about unprofessionalism. No matter, I take it all in stride. What's he gonna do—fire me? Then who'd be his indentured servant?

Too tired to retrieve my bag from the church, I opt to head straight home for bed. Lord knows I need it. Hope A'ma is asleep. I really don't have the patience to deal with her tonight.

Coming down the hall, I reach for my key until I notice that our door seems slightly ajar. Voices now emit through the paper-thin walls. Someone is in there with A'ma. Who could it be at this time of night? It's not like she has friends, and no one comes to visit me at our apartment. Slowly, I approach the doorway.

It's a man's voice—Deacon Nichols? He must have come to drop off my bag—God, no. A'ma's probably giving him a piece of her mind. My first thought is to run straight in, but something about the way they converse persuades me to snoop instead. It almost sounds as if they're familiar with one another. But—but, they hardly know each other?

"My God, Gabriela," says the Deacon. Concern seems to fill his voice. "Gloria said you'd gotten worse but—what—what can I do?"

"What can you do? I don't need your pity!" yells A'ma. "You and ya bunch. Nothin' but phonies and crooks! I didn't need it then, I don't need it now!"

I peek through the cracked door. Using her walker, A'ma turns away. She proceeds to a bookshelf in the corner of the room and picks up a pack of cigarettes. Where she got them from, I have no idea, seeing as I threw the last pack in the trash.

"Pity?" continues the Deacon. "What are you talking about Gabriela? I never pitied you. YOU were the one—"

Deacon Nichols stops. Their voices have risen quite a bit. He looks around before speaking again. "When Gloria gets back, just tell her I came by to drop off her bag. She left it at the church. Goodbye, Gabriela."

He turns and heads for the door. Quickly, I duck out the doorway, the floor squeaking as I move into the shadows. It would always let us know when people where out front. Faintly I hear A'ma say, "Running off like you always do, hunh Nichols?"

Like a hook, the question abruptly drags him back into our tiny apartment. Did A'ma see me? I know this woman like no other and everything she does is calculated. Still not sure, I inch back towards the doorway.

"I never ran!" the Deacon shouts. "It was you! It was always you! You were the one embarrassed by your background. Not me! You thought you weren't good enough, but I loved—"

He stops as he notices the direction of A'ma's eyes. A malicious smile sets across her face. Slowly, Deacon Nichols turns to face me. I can't take being outside for another moment, literally or figuratively. I have to know what's going on.

"Gl—Gl—Gloria," he stutters. "Hi, your mother said you weren't home."

"I wasn't," I mumble.

"Right, of course. You're just getting here. Great. Well, guess I'll—"

"What were you two talking about?" I ask, my voice shaky.

"I…I…just came to drop your bag off, see?" he says, holding up my bag as some sort of evidence. "See? You left it."

"Stop it!" I shout. "I heard you two. Now tell me what's going on."

He looks at A'ma. The vindictive woman takes a seat on the worn-down front room couch, her left hand clutching a half-burned cigarette.

"Somebody's gonna tell me something. Well? Deacon? A'ma?"

The Deacon clears his throat. "Okay okay, Gloria. Me and your mother…we knew each other before you were born—we dated alright? I was a theology student at the university. Your mother worked in the cafeteria. I became very fond of her, even thought about marriage, but we just weren't on the same page. She always expressed a desire to have children, but I wasn't ready. So instead of compromising or just giving it some time, your mother went out and got pregnant by another man. I was devastated. She moved, changed her phone number, I didn't hear from her for years. Then out of the blue, you show up at the church I've been assigned to. Your mother made sure I knew who you were. But Gloria, even though you weren't mine, I took you under my wing."

I can't believe it. To think my mother has manipulated my whole religious experience, just as she has everything else in my life. My stomach tightens as disgust fills my bowels. I turn to my—my *mother*. She's done some deceitful things before, but this is the worst.

"A'ma, how could you? Why would you parade me around Deacon Nichols like that, hunh? Just because my father left doesn't give you the right to try and force another man to fill his shoes."

A'ma reaches for a pint of vodka underneath the sofa cushion. She's right. No need in hiding anything now. As I watch this pitiful excuse of a human being, a loathing spirit overwhelms me. My voice rises as the audible strike in me intensifies. "It's no wonder my father left you! Look at you!" Tears mixed with anger, I shout these words at the top of my lungs. "You make me sick!"

"Calm down, Gloria," says Deacon Nichols. "It's okay."

But it's not okay. All these years I've wasted, taking care of a woman who does nothing but lie and manipulate. A woman who has the nerve to force me in her first love's life but refuses to tell me of my own father's whereabouts!

I grab the bag that started this whole episode and head for the door. "I'm sorry Deacon, I've got to get out of—"

"I wouldn't force another man to fill your father's shoes, Gloria."

"What?"

Emotionless, A'ma stares straight at the darkened television screen. She slowly repeats the vague words. "I wouldn't force another man to fill your father's shoes, Gloria. He's quite capable of doing that himself."

"Wha—What are you talking about?"

"Good story, Nichols," says A'ma as she pulls a drag from the disintegrating stick. "Now, are you ready to tell her the truth?"

"The truth?" frowns the Deacon. "I'm sorry Gabriela, I don't follow—"

"—Nichols is right. We dated. In fact, we were in love, but he was ashamed of me. Guess I wasn't *American* enough—not a good Irish-Catholic church going woman, hunh Nichols?!"

I look towards the Deacon, but he says nothing. A'ma takes a swig from her generic bottle before carrying on. "But as those hypocritical zealots love to do, he left out one major part of the story. I didn't leave him because I got pregnant with another man's child." A'ma pauses. She looks me straight in the eye. "He left because I got pregnant with *his* child…you, Mija."

I—I—hunh? Can this be true? I look back and forth at these two people in the room I hardly know now, and I can't get a read on either. Both look away, their faces blank.

"That's right Gloria. Wonder why there's no pictures up anywhere, why I never talk about your father? You wanna know why I made sure you went to that good fa' nothin' church? Because I wanted him to see you. See what he abandoned—he abandoned us, Gloria! He found out I was pregnant and…HE…LEFT!"

I look to the Deacon for answers, but his silence speaks loudly. Guess I have my answer. "And…and so all this time, you were just being nice to me to make up for being such a horrible father?"

I stare at the very thing that drove my mom over the edge, though David Nichols dare not look me in the eye. It seems like minutes pass before I can muster up the strength to move. In reality, only seconds go by before I brush past the stranger and into the night.

——THE ASSIGNED——

TRE

"Where are you, T-Mart?"

This has to be the correct address—242 Bering Ave, right here in front of the old abandoned dry-cleaners. No sign of Martin though. Half consumed beer bottles lay scattered throughout the decaying parking lot. Pressed for time, I decide to step out and look around.

"Hello? Is anyone here?" No answer. "Hello? Martin? T-Mart, you here?"

Still, no answer. Cautiously, I search around the deserted building, but there's no one here. Back outside, I glance up at the intersecting street signs. Bering Avenue and Cross Boulevard. This is definitely it. *Man, if that blonde doesn't show, I'll kill you, T-Mart.*

Having seen enough, I step back inside my truck. This is not the type of neighborhood you want to explore in the middle of the night. I decide to give the area one more drive through before getting back to more pressing matters.

A couple suspicious characters line the dark streets. Thankfully, the car locks itself. Frowning mugs stare as I slowly drive down the mostly abandoned avenue.

When I get back, I'ma definitely need a double—something catches my eye. Sneakers lay near the edge of a high field of uncut grass. But not just any kicks. These look like shoes only two people in Memphis possess. My eyes strain to get a better view. *Can't be.*

Against better judgment, I park the SUV and hop out to get a closer look.

Before I got hurt, I was on the verge of releasing my first signature shoe. Contracts had been signed, advertising was about to begin, the works. Of course, the shoe company postponed the campaign until more clarity was given in response to my return to the field. They gave me a few pairs to tryout and share with friends. I gave a couple pairs to teammates, none of whom were from or reside in Memphis, and one pair to Martin. It hadn't been my initial intent to share them, but Martin discovered them during one of his unannounced house calls.

"T-Mart—Martin," I whisper while creeping towards an opening in the grassy field. Moving closer, I get a better view of the colorful shoes. Those are definitely the prototypes for the never released, *TNT-33's*

"What the—"

My heart nearly stops. Connected to the shoes is…nothing. I let out a deep sigh of relief before laughing at myself. I don't know if I should be relieved or mad.

"I'm outta here."

I hope Brittany—Brenda—man, what was her name? Anyway, hope she's—THUMP. I trip over a hump in the grass falling to the dampened ground. Not again! This is a $600 shirt! My head starts to spin as the alcohol coursing through my veins announces itself. Feeling particularly smashed now, I slowly make my way to my feet—MY GOD!

The cause of my fall is lying next to me—a body. My eyes widened, gazing upon the figure. Although the face is hidden, by the size and build this—this must be Martin. Wait a minute… My initial reaction of fear is now countered by assumptions.

"T-Mart?" I nudge my brother with a foot. "High as a kite! I knew it!" The nudging continues, now harder. "Get up! And you bet not get nothing in the truck!" He doesn't respond. I call again.

I listen for any sounds. Martin usually breathed heavily when he was passed out. Making my way closer, I kneel. Carefully, I turn him ov—

"AAAAHHHHOWWWWW!!!!"

A stomach-churning noise escapes from my mouth as I jump back. This is my younger brother. But not as I remember him.

Martin's face looks aged. His eyes bulge open, almost swollen. Once brown, his pupils have now turned into a faded grey. They stare into the unknown.

He's dead.

The sight of his eyes is enough to sicken anyone. Blood stains soak his shirt although I can't determine the source.

He—He's dead.

"Oh God!" I spit. Too late. A mix of alcohol and greasy food shoots from my guts up through my mouth. "Martin! What happened?!" I can barely stand to look at the body though I eventually gather the nerves to inch closer. Finally, I manage to close his eyes, caressing his head in my lap. Tears flow as I hold his hand. "Damn, Martin. What happened?" I notice an unusually shaped symbol branded on Martin's wrist. It looks fresh. He had several tattoos, but I've never seen this one before.

At least not on my brother. Two crowned shaped symbols inverted with a tiny circle in the middle. *Low-cut yellow top.* But she wouldn't know Martin. She couldn't. They're from two different worlds. What the hell is going on?

"What did you get yourself into Martin?"

A bright light shoots from my chest—my phone. I remove it from my shirt pocket. It reads '*Bree*'. *Low cut-yellow top's* name is Bree. And that's when it hits me.

"DAMN!!!"

The word scrapes against my throat as I hurl the phone into darkness. "You told me to come get you!" I scream as I pull my brother tight. "Martin! Martin, I'm so sorry!"

I can't remember the last time we embraced though only one of us will share this memory.

My brother—he's dead.

The cold air shoots through my skin like piercing needles. My nose runs in the bitter night wind. I've been walking for what seems like miles. Waking up this morning, I had no idea my life would drastically change like this.

I've wondered all this time who my father was, if he lives in the same city, if he's even alive. Now to find out he is alive and someone I've known half my life? I should've seen the signs. The way he treated me differently from the others, A'ma's disdain for the church and a man she *hardly knew*. It was all right there. At least that's the way it looks. You can never tell with A'ma. What if she's lying? But she couldn't be that cruel…could she?

So many thoughts run through my head—pick one—any one. The very least of them would immediately cause water to gush from my eyes. It's like everything I've been taught has been a lie. My family…the church…God.

"Hey, you alright sweet-cakes?"

The whiny voice startles me. I've been so busy thinking about my problems I've hardly noticed my surroundings. I'm nowhere near my neighborhood and two shifty characters now follow behind me. Quickly glancing back, I increase my pace.

"Hey, I know you hear me sweet-cakes," again says the whiny

voice. That name along with his tone disturbs me. Why does he keep calling me that?

"Now don't act funny," he continues. "Jimmy hates that. Ain't that right, Beef?"

"Yeah," answers his partner. "Jimmy hates that."

The clatter of men's boots once again increases my cadence. In the horizon is a well-lit corner grocery. *If I can just make it up the hill,* I tell myself. Preparing my body for an all-out sprint, one of the thugs grabs my arm.

"Let me go!" I yell. "Help!" I call out, but no one hears, or at the least, cares.

"Shhh," says the one named Jimmy as he pulls out a knife.

Terrified, I remain silent. Jimmy stands about my height and looks as if his name should be Snake instead. He has high cheekbones, a pointed nose, and slender frame. Alone, I could quite possibly fight him off. But he's not alone. The other brute, Beef, stands 6'3" and looks like an out of shape heavyweight fighter. There's no way I can fend off both of these guys. Think Gloria!

"Gimme all your money," scowls the snake looking Jimmy.

"I don't have any money," I cry. "I left my bag at home." And to think, my stupid bag is the object behind most of tonight's troubles. But that's beside the point now. I'm not naïve. Money isn't the only thing that concerns them. Nevertheless, I begin to barter.

"Look, you can have this ring," I plead, quickly placing the $30 coin ring in Jimmy's hand. "And you can get good money for these shoes. Just take them and leave me alone. Please!"

"An old class ring and some imitations?" he snarls. "You've got to be kidding me. But I tell ya what. I'll make a deal with ya."

The short, vile man stands eye to eye with me. He rubs my hair making his way to my face. I jerk away at the touch of his cold, brittle hands.

"Ooh, hot and spicy. My favorite!" he cackles.

"Look, just leave me—" My sentence is cut off as I am drug fifty feet into darkness through a slit in a chained-linked fence. My cries are unheard as one man drags while the other covers my mouth. My heart pounds as my worst fears rush to the forefront. I bite down on the cold, scaly hand in my mouth. The Snake screams in pain.

"I will stab you! Is that what you want? Now just give me what I want, and it'll be over!"

As if either choice is better than the other. I have given myself to no man in nineteen years and to think one, or two, will take it from me—just like that? I can't bear the thought. What have I done to deserve this?!

"Please! No! Don't do this! PLEASE!!!!"

My mind races as they pull me through clumpy patches of gravel and grass. I think about my mother, and even with all her lies, I'd give anything to be home. Even the Deacon would save me…if he could.

I'm tired and I can't fight both of them off. Maybe I should just let them get it over with. Quickly, my body instinctively denies that option as the big one lunges for my shirt. His breath smells of cheap wine and garlic. I fight back, scratching at his face, but it just makes him angrier. Viciously, he slaps me back, causing my neck to pop. The true pain sets in seconds later. I've never been so scared in my life. *Why?* I've never hurt anyone, not intentionally.

Oh God, WHY?!

"Now lie still, will ya?" says the Snake. I dare not move. "It's okay Beef. She got the message. She's cooperatin' now. Stand over there 'til it's your turn. Make sure no one's coming."

Before he starts, I make one last plea, screaming to the top of my lungs.

"Oh God! Save me! PLEASE!!!"

Suddenly, my world goes silent. I can see the men as their mouths spit out obscenities, but I can't hear a thing. For a moment, I'm not sure if I've been hit too hard or if I've just checked out mentally.

POP.

Just like that, the silence is over. I can hear again. Everything looks the same, but yet different somehow. I can't quite put it into words, but I feel a silent strength build up within me. A peace forms over me so loud, it shatters ear drums without making a sound. I feel power. *Physical power.*

The snake-looking one grabs me by the throat threatening me to be quiet. Without thought, I return the gesture, cupping his slender neck. He gags, my strength surprises him. It should surprise me too, but for some reason it doesn't. It's like my body's been waiting to feel this way.

Still on the ground, I heave the man into a collection of aluminum trash cans. "Beef, get 'er!" shouts the Snake as he writhes in pain. His dense accomplice looks back, surprised to see his boss lying on the ground.

It's obvious the big dope is trying to process what just happened. Smiling, I shrug my shoulders. This drives the Snake livid. "Get her, Beef!" he yells again. "Do it!"

Should I even be smiling at a time like this? Probably not, but it comes naturally. Even as Beef runs straight towards me.

I jump to my feet. He throws a punch with his right hand as I maneuver to the left. The momentum of the missed punch propels him forward. Jumping straight in the air, my elbow comes crashing down straight to the middle of Beef's broad back.

"AWWWW!" yells the oafish bully as he falls to the ground. "Hey, nobody does that to me!" He inches closer, cautious this time. Instead of waiting, I dart towards the coward, landing a perfect drop kick to his chest. His body is thrown backwards from the collision. Suddenly, I hear the silence again. Someway —not sure how—I just know to turn around, just in time to catch a knife being hurled at my head. Emotions swell as I sprint back for the man who nearly took my—my everything. A cry of anger fills my vocal cords as I close in, wielding the knife out in front of me. The Snake cringes. Three inches from his face, I stop.

I can hear the accelerated rhythm of his heart. It comes through so clear it sounds as if a microphone has been placed over his chest.

"I should kill you!" I sob as he begins to plead for his life. "No. Please—look, just take whatever you want!"

What am I doing?

Staring into his eyes, my assailant looks nothing more than a misplaced child. Broken. Alone. Scared. I know the feeling. I should extract justice. Instead, I leave him with mercy.

I drop the knife before running towards light. The adrenaline pumping through my body finally subsides as feelings of victimization replace the rapid chemical. I can't even begin to make sense of all that's happened. For some reason, all I can think about is running back to the home I ran away from.

CHAPTER 18 – ZEEK

I am awakened by a strange squeaking noise. Groggily, I force open one eye. Someone's kid jumps up and down on the bed— not sure—too sleepy to focus my eyes. They close as I redistribute my weight in the small hospital chair.

"Daddy, wake up. Can we get some pancakes?"

"Hmmmmpppph," I grumble. The questions persist.

"Daddy, can we go to the park?"

Sounds like Christina. "Sure baby," I mouth, eyes still closed —what is that noise?

"Daddy, look!"

Her continuous words pry open my eyes. Slowly I begin to see what looks like Christina jumping up and down in the hospital bed. "That's good sweetie." My eyes shut hoping to resume the—

"WHAT THE—!" Jumping straight up from the chair, concern sets in. "Chrissy baby, get down from there! You could—"

"Daddy, I'm hungry. Can we go?"

"I—I—I"

I can't believe what I'm seeing. Standing before me—rather *jumping* before me—is Christina. She shoots up and down the stiff bed like a baby kangaroo. Just like a father seeing his child walk for the first time, I watch in amazement. She goes for more air on every take off.

"Whoa, baby. Be careful. You could hurt your—you're not tired, sweetie?"

"No Daddy," she answers back between launches. "I'm not sleepy anymore. Nooowww can we get some pancakes?"

The moment finally hitting me, I rush to grab my Chrissy. "Baby, you can have whatever you want!" For what may be the first time ever, tears of joy glide down my cheek. I haven't held her like this in months. My baby. Little Chrissy.

Immediately I pull back, hurriedly loosening my grip. I *haven't* held her like this in months. Her body can't take this activity…at least it couldn't before.

"Wait a minute, baby. Stand still for Daddy."

Christina doesn't even *feel* the same. Her normally frail body seems to have put on weight overnight. Her skin once dry, paled, and cracked, is now soft to the touch. Christina's big brown eyes shine bright in color, her lips again pink and full of life. And her hair—her hair blooms everywhere, no signs of shedding. Each lock whimsically bounces up and down with every jump on the bed. Just like her mother.

My mind overflows with questions, but I put it all to the side …at least for now. This isn't a time to think but rather a time to rejoice. What am I doing still on this floor? I reach for my baby's hand as we jump up and down on the hardened bed.

GLORIA

"Glo-reeee-ahh!"

No one could say my name like A'ma, her Mexican accent still heavy over the years. However, I do wonder how she has the audacity to even speak it, considering last night's revelation. Guess some things never change. Staring at my bedroom ceiling, I ignore her repeated requests.

"Gloria, I need to eat! I have to take my medicine!" she shouts from the front room. My initial impulse is to go see about her. That's what I've done my whole life. But shouldn't she be attending to me now? I don't know what to feel. How could so much happen in one night? And why me? Why now? And—I could go on for days, but A'ma's periodic nags prevent my mind from keeping any kind of flow.

"Gloria! Are you gonna leave me here to die? If so, just get it ova with!"

There was no real reason to scream, other than for effect. The walls in our apartment are paper thin. I can easily hear everything she says, along with the verdict on 'Divorce Court'. Boy does A'ma hate to be ignored. *"If only you knew, you ungrateful little runt,"* she mutters under her breath.

Okay, that's it! I've had enough! Enough of the secrets, enough of the lies. Just like last night, adrenaline shoots through my body, but not the kind that produces superhuman abilities—noooo. This jolt gives me the gumption to fire back at A'ma. Jumping from the bed, I rush to the front room. I knock the vodka bottle from my mother's hand before the miserable woman has time to hide it. Shocked, her eyes widen.

"If only I knew what, A'ma?!"

"Wh—What?"

"You heard me woman! I'm sick of your lies! You said clear as day, if only you knew, you ungrateful runt. If only I knew what!?"

A'ma's eyes expand even more. She stares back, obviously amazed I had the nerve to repeat her words. "Well I'm waiting old woman!"

"Ho—How—How did you hear that?"

"Whada you mean how did I hear that? You said it loud as day!"

"Yeh. But I say it in en Espanol."

That isn't possible. I never learned Spanish. The woman only uses the language to taunt me. "All you do is lie!" I shout. "All you do is—"

POP.

My ears ring as if I'm on a jet changing altitude. Nanoseconds later, words fly from my mouth, except these words are unlike any I've ever spoken.

"*Me dejan sola mujer de edad!*"

A'ma sits straight up. Her mouth drops as she listens.

"Oh, you don't know what to say now, hunh? Well how about this. *Du riechst wie Ziegenkase!*"

My mother utters not one word.

"What's wrong A'ma? Cat got cha tongue? Why you're just a *coouuu na laaa, it nguuu, phuuu cu de heooooooooow!*"

I cover my mouth, the reality of the moment sinking in. Did I just speak...German? A'ma watches. Not knowing what to make of it, she briefly glances over at the displaced vodka bottle.

"What just happened?" I ask. A'ma opts to remain silent, merely shaking her head. "Did I just...?"

She answers with a nod, her eyes big as ever.

"Look, I'm sorry A'ma. I—I gotta get some air."

I run back to my room, slip on some tennis shoes and get my iPod. Back in the living room, A'ma hasn't moved.

"I'm going for a run. I did say that in *English*, right?"

A'ma's head quickly moves up and down.

——THE ASSIGNED——

TRE

"And how long was it from the time he called til the time you actually arrived on the scene," asks the detective.

"Dunno, maybe an hour...two."

The detectives continue their questioning in the office of my folks' home. Still wearing housecoats, my mom and dad sit close to one another, their hands clasped. Doesn't look like they've moved much since receiving my call. The sun was nearly up before I could muster enough strength to move from that...place. I called my parents, who I guess in turn called the authorities.

But this is their first time hearing any details and as police protocol dictates, the detectives ask the same questions in numerous ways in order to make sure they receive accurate answers. And telling this story over and over, especially in front of my parents is killing me.

"And you were coming from that...bar...Round One?" The detective jots down notes.

As I lean on the edge of the computer desk, my brain tries to think of any other way I can answer these questions. My body, my mind, both are wearing down. It's been nearly 24 hours since I last slept. The $600 shirt that once held my concern is now soiled with the blood of my brother and all they can ask me about is the name of that stupid bar!

"Yeah, like I said, I was—"

Come on Tre, get real. It's not the cop's fault. What's the real reason for my common practice of having drinks at the popular spot—the spot where people yell my name and treat me like royalty—what's the real reason I'm so shamed to speak about it now? I know very well why, but I can't let my mind go there. I'd go crazy if I did. With all that's brewing inside me, I'm not that far off.

My parents haven't said anything since I arrived at the house. Their silence punishes me more than words. The bleak expressions on their faces remind me of Martin's eyes—the way they looked when I turned over his body. I'll never forget that moment.

Never.

"So, he said he was scared and needed a ride and yet it takes you two hours to get to the announced location?" asks the brazen detective, never looking up from his notepad. What does he expect me to say?

My father lays eyes on me for the first time in two hours. The bold question triggers something in him. Sensing the tension, a second detective asks a more, subtle question.

"Okay, TNT. Is there anything else you can think of that may help us out?"

The unusual symbol freshly marked on Martin's right wrist comes to mind. A symbol shared by a girl I just so happen to meet hours before my brother's death. Instead, I shake my head, conceding the police will eventually find it.

"Why didn't you just go get him?!" shouts my father. The emotions swelling inside finally overwhelm him. "All you had to do was go pick him up."

Tears now flow from both my parents faces. "Why, Tre? That's all I wanted you to do. Just see about your brother."

I thought their silence was punishment enough, but my father's words produce a pain so sharp, I can barely breathe. Panic rises through my belly, now my lungs. I reach for deep breaths only to find shallow ones in their place. Before the attack can consume me, I gather enough strength to flee the room.

"Tre!" yells my mother as she calls for her only son.

What have I done…

——T H E A S S I G N E D——

ZEEK

Hours later and still none of these so-called *experts* can explain it. Less than 24 hours ago, the only thing keeping my baby alive was a cold white box attached to the side of her bed. She weighed less than 30 pounds. The tone of her skin bordered on ghostly white. She couldn't eat, barely talk, let alone jump up and down in bed. Now Christina pines for her favorite. Pancakes.

Dr. Amali suspiciously examines her vitals. He's been over them ten times already.

"I can't explain it, Mr. Myers. This child was in a vegetative state just 12 hours ago. We all saw her."

There's something not quite the same about the doctor. I can't put my finger on it. The memory of what I saw by the elevator— or at least *thought* I saw comes to mind. Oh well, who cares? And who cares about his tests? I know what I see. A healthy little girl —and man can she eat! I'd almost forgotten. She's gone through three popsicles already. I sat here and counted every bite. Heck, didn't even need to go outside for my morning smoke. Guess the excitement's got my levels where they need to be.

In the shower, Alicia missed the initial fireworks. No matter. She's taking it all in now. "She wasn't like that when I got up. My God, it's a miracle," she gets out before blowing her nose. Alicia kisses a cross medallion fastened around her neck. Wow. Never noticed how much it resembles the one Angelina wore.

Dr. Amali doesn't seem to approve of Alicia's enthusiasm. "Well, *whatever* it is, we're going to have to run some more tests," he interjects before rushing out of the room. Another visitor takes his place.

"So that's what a miracle looks like?"

"*Chappy Brynint!*" yells Christina.

"What a beautiful sight indeed," the chaplain smiles. His eyes water as he approaches the bed. Even the preacher man is thrown aback by what he sees.

"Chaplain Bryant," Alicia says nearly crying. "Can you believe it? I mean…"

"Chappy, look at me!" says my baby girl, ready to show off her newly acquired leaping skills.

"*Woooowww,*" entertains the chaplain, before turning his attention towards me. "So, Mr. Myers, I guess you are a man of faith."

I smile at Christina, ignoring the preacher man's comment. Even he can't get under my skin today.

"Well I guess God has a funny way of turning things around, hunh Mr. Myers?"

"The doctors are still running tests," I finally respond. "They don't know what happened. Those guys probably had her misdiagnosed from the jump."

Now what's he got to say? My stance on a god hasn't changed. If anything, I feel more confident in my beliefs.

"Are you serious, Mr. Myers?" he shoots back. "I saw this child less than 24 hours ago and she was—"

"Look, I don't know what happened, okay?" I make sure to look him square in the eye. "But enough of this god business— you and Alicia. All I know is, I just got my daughter back and I'm not letting her go."

"I'm sorry, Mr. Myers if I've upset you. That has never been my intention." Guess he finally realizes this is not the time to engage in useless debate. "I'm glad you've got your daughter back," he says while heading for the door. "Good day."

"Chappy," yells Christina. Never stopping, his hand briefly forms a wave.

"Zeek," says Alicia, her tone telling me everything she wants to say. What a weird day.

"Wait," I sigh while walking towards the preacher man. My hand drops from my head to the back of my neck in the time it takes me to gather my words. "Look, my daughter's taken a liking to you and you've definitely seemed to help out my sis when I couldn't be here..."

I pause. I have to. Not used to this. "...and uhh, for that... well, I appreciate it."

Preacher man's face transforms. I quickly look up and catch a glimpse of the overly-stated smile. Can't have that going on for too long. "But right now, all I wanna do is be with my daughter. Okay?"

He nods. "Understood, Mr. Myers. Understood."

"Thanks," I say, moving back to the bed.

"Mr. Myers. Could we talk for just one moment more?"

Did I miss something? Did we not just talk? "Wow. Really?" I say, now sitting.

"Please. It'll only take a minute."

I throw a wink to Christina before rising from my seat...again. My smile quickly leaves as I head back towards the chaplain. He watches. Almost intently.

"Yeah, what is it now, Bryant?"

The chaplain chuckles while shaking his head.

"What's so funny?"

"Looks like you caught a 2-for-1 sale."

"Say what?" My defenses rise on impulse.

"Your limp, Mr. Myers."

"Yeah, what about it?" I mutter, staring him down. That stupid smile never leaves his face. "That's just it. It's gone. You folks have a good day... If it can get any better."

What's he talking about? I look to Alicia but she just shrugs before twirling her index finger. With preacher man gone, I walk five paces before turning in the other direction. My walk...it's normal! I mean it's four-years-ago, normal. I'd nearly forgotten what it felt like. There's no curve in my stride, no altered motion. Not one sign exists of my former impairment. Not-a-one. My knee bends regularly as I perform a squat all the way down to the floor. Alicia snickers as I stroll around the room. She says my movements mimic a dancing flamingo, if there's such a thing. But what do I care—my leg—it's back!

"Well it truly is unbelievable," laughs Alicia. "You know what this means, right?"

"Don't start, Alicia."

I know what she's thinking and trust me, I'm nowhere near sold. Before I can declare anything else, Christina lets loose a high-pitched shriek as she laughs at my prancing around the bed.

"What?" I smile. "Not you, too?"

Almost a week has passed since the night that changed my life. Eerily enough, things are mostly the same. My hair still sits in its normal ponytail. I'm back to fixing A'ma's breakfast before heading to work. She still growls here and there, although not nearly as much as she used to. Guess she doesn't want to take a chance on me translating. I'm not sure if I could even do it again. It hasn't happened since the infamous morning after the even more infamous night before.

As a matter of fact, nothing has happened since then. No adrenaline, no super-strength, no high-jumps, nothing. I'm back to my average, run of the mill schedule. Okay, maybe that's not entirely true. Something that has changed is my presence at St. Peters. Haven't been back since 'the night', and frankly I'm not sure if I'll ever return. Some parishioners have left voicemails inquiring about the free art classes I taught, but I can't go back there as if nothing happened. For all I know, there could be dozens who already know of my mother and father's dirty little secret. It's enough I have to take care of one parent. Although she's a handful, I'll continue to fulfill that commitment. Besides, that's all I've ever known. But Nichols? I'm fine if I never see him again, let alone return his countless phone calls. What can he possibly say? After 19 years of lies? Nothing he can say can ever justify his sins.

These thoughts flood my head as the bus approaches my stop. The worthless piece of metal I own stopped running two weeks ago. Deacon Nichols was supposed to come by and take a look at it later this week...

I pull my baseball cap tight around my head as I enter the doors of WREG. No one even seems to notice as I walk through the news station. And they sure don't know any of the things I've experienced, supernatural or natural for that matter. Some may not even know I'm a girl, seeing I've been called *sir* on several occasions when my hair is stuffed in the back of a cap. But that's fine, I like it that way. Other than the occasional pick-up game out back, I'm a nobody at this station. Just an ant delivering debris back and forth.

As I near my desk, the stench of overly sprayed perfume saturates the air. It could only mean one thing...Sandy. Now, that woman can talk. She says we're friends, but oddly enough she knows nothing about me, although I somehow know everything about her. I wouldn't be able to get a word in even if I wanted to tell her about all that's happened.

Sandy is an up-and-coming producer—though some disagree as to how the 24 year-old college dropout got promoted so fast. I'm an assistant cameraperson—translation: lackey to the great and almighty Arnie. Sandy is into boys, fashion, tanning, and Electronica—literally all the things that I abhor. So why does she continue to talk to me endlessly? I guess it boils down to the simple fact that I'm the only person who listens to, rather endures her tall tales of weekend exploits. She starts as soon as I reach my station.

"Can you belieeeeeve Julie got that exclusive with Jason Bale?" she asks. No reply is really necessary. "I would loooooovvve to have an exclusive with that man—know what I mean?" she giggles. A faint smile flashes as I check today's assignments.

Sandy's hot pink business suit is in stark contrast with my University of Memphis sweater. The talkative woman's eyes never seem to blink. A byproduct of too much mascara. "You know, they said her, and her fiancé are breaking up," she whispers.

"Who's breaking up?" I ask, already forgetting the topic of our one-sided conversation.

"Why Julie, dodo bird. I bet it has something to do with Jason—well he says 'call me Bale', but that's just some Hollywood lunacy. I call 'em Jason—but did you notice how she was just throoooowing herself on him? It's a shame if you ask me—say... you alright?"

Wait. What did Supersize Sandy just say? People call her this —albeit behind her back—not because of her size, in fact she's very petite. But because she takes any small tidbit of information she hears and blows it up or supersizes it. Nevertheless, I can't believe she just asked about my well-being. That's the closest indication of concern I've witnessed in six months. Should I tell her about my life's recent events? I don't even have to start with the out-of-this-world stuff. Just the ins and outs of taking care of a sickly parent are a conversation full.

Sandy's drawn-on eyes wait for a response. *What the heck.* "Well it's interesting you asked. I had the wors—"

"Oh my god! It's Scott Richmond!" Sandy interrupts, her annoying Electronica ringtone repeating itself over and over. "That *hhhhhhot* anchorman from WPTY! I've been waiting on this call for days! You know he has a friend. He's even *hhhhhhotter*. We should double or somethin."

I smile as I pretend to listen. Yep, things are back to normal.

—————T H E A S S I G N E D —————

TRE

Six days ago, my life changed forever. That's the only thought that runs through my mind as I peer behind tinted sunglasses at the collection of guests gathered at my brother's burial. The cheap liquor I ingested before the ceremony seems to fuel my pain rather than quench it. In some strange way, maybe that's what I want.

People have reached out from all across the country, but I could give a damn about their half-hearted condolences. They don't know me, not really, past my accomplishments on the field. And they sure as hell don't know Martin, the brother who was never the better athlete, the brother not nearly as popular, the brother who acted out.

It's my fault in so many ways. My parents will never look at me the same. I don't blame them. That's why, even with the million and a half sitting in six different accounts, I choose to drink that cheap liver killer. Maybe this slow death will serve as payment to my deceased brother.

Catching the bastard who helped destroy my family will also serve as payment. A correlation between Bree, Martin, and the tattoo proved to be a dead end with her phone now mysteriously disconnected. Convenient.

The police still have no leads and as I scan some of Martin's past acquaintances standing off in the distance paying their respects, I know it's quite possible anyone of them could have set him up.

As the minister gives his remarks, I notice a woman some fifty yards away. Too far to be considered a member of the burial party, yet she seems to be taking part in the ceremony. Her long silver-gray hair swirls in the steady wind. Even a ways off, I'm pretty sure I've seen her before. My mind, scattered with grief and cheap wine, tries to piece together the memory of this woman. That's it! *The woman from the bar!*

The same weird lady now stands at my brother's burial. But why is she here? Who does she know? WHAT does she know? Briefly, I think about leaving the burial party to approach her but when I look up again, she's gone.

My attention shifts to my folks. Solemnly they sit in the first wave of a sea of people. Mom uses a handkerchief to dab a tear from her eye. Dad, or shall I say, Pastor Turner, sits for the most part like a proud, strong father until the lowering of the casket. The finality of the moment proves too much as he wails for his baby boy. Relatives and church staff rush to his side. I don't know what to do. Part of me wants to go to my father, but what if he doesn't receive me? I couldn't live.

I watch as he cries out in pain. My mind—my body can't take this. It's too much. Everything. Few hardly notice as I bolt for the car and take off.

——T H E A S S I G N E D——

ZEEK

With so much time spent at the hospital, I've nearly forgotten what my apartment looks like. Needless to say, the place is a mess when I bring Christina home for the first time in months.

"Daddy, it's stinky!" yells the blunt five-year-old.

"I'm sorry, baby. Why don't you go to your room for a minute while Daddy straightens up?" Guess I hadn't planned for this part. Over a year of on-and-off sickness, four months of complete hospitalization, and now in what seems like overnight, we're back home.

As I run around the place throwing away molding food, my mind finally takes a moment to process the last few days. It was a job in itself just getting out of that prison. Nobody wanted to sign off on Christina's discharge. They kept waiting day by day for the cancer, or whatever it was, to return. Nearly a week went by before they got tired of the now healthy Christina making requests, running up and down the halls, eating up everything in sight. Finally, the suits who run the place agreed it would be easier to just send her home. Guess children's hospitals are not meant for healthy kids.

"Daddy, it's stinky in here too!" Christina yells from her bedroom. I can't help but laugh as I remove what I think is pizza from the crease of the couch. "Okay baby. Why don't you—"

A sharp pain suddenly shoots through my head. It's like nothing I've ever felt. As quickly as it comes, it goes away.

"Daddy, why you looking like that?"

"Hunh?" I hadn't even noticed her standing there. "Oh, Daddy's okay. Just a little—AWWWGGHHH!!!"

Nerve endings spark with pain while flashes of light run across my eyes. I clinch my head—it feels like it's about to explode—and it just might if I let go. The light begins to shape itself into blurry images.

"Uggghhh, what's happening to me?"

Vaguely I hear the screams of my daughter as I stumble around the room. The images become clearer by the second. My eyes are wide open, but all I can see is this picture, like it's right there in front of me. There's a vehicle of some kind. Truck? Van? White or light gray—the images are still a little hazy. My eyes flash to a rooftop, people fighting. Next a silver haired woman with burning eyes. Now to my deceased wife, Angel. Dizziness emerges as the images consume me. It's too much.

"Stop it!" I shout. Immediately, the images disappear, as does the pain. "What in the world?" My apartment slowly comes back into focus. I call for Christina, but she doesn't answer.

"Chrissy, baby?"

I sense motion to my left. There Christina hides, balled up in the corner.

"Christina!" I yell. Her coiled body tenses up even more.

She's afraid.

Of me.

"Oh baby, I'm so sorry. Daddy's sorry."

"You're scary, Daddy," she says. The words nearly break my heart. I stretch out my hands, slowly approaching. "Daddy's fine, see? Just had a little headache, that's all. Everything's okay now. I promise."

Slowly, she lets down her guard. Kneeling, I make her a deal. "I tell you what. How 'bout we get out of this stinky house and get some ice cream?" Reluctantly, she nods her head.

"Can we ride the swings?" she asks.

"You wanna ride the swings too? Sure baby, we can ride the swings. Now can Daddy pick you up?" Christina nods again, this time a little faster. Carefully, I scoop her up just as I've done since she was a baby. I'm rough on bikes and tools and even apartments, but never her. Not Chrissy. "Daddy's right here baby. I'm right here."

——THE ASSIGNED——

TRE

Still daylight, I drink from a silver flask. I have to. The funeral, burial, and then my Dad's breakdown? Reality can't die quick enough. The music in my truck is cranked all the way up. What do I care? I speed down a narrow boulevard breaking more and more traffic laws with each turn of the burly vehicle. I can't tell how fast I'm going anyway.

A picture of my family sits on the dash. My mind can't get past the look of Martin's lifeless face. Tears flood my eyes as cars honk around my erratic driving. Part of me hopes I wreck. Maybe my self-destruction will count for something. Or maybe—just maybe, I can trade my life for my brother's. Or, maybe the 90-proofed alcohol coursing through my blood stream is getting the better of me. I grab the picture—it won't stop moving. It's like I've got three families instead of one. Funny. "Three families," I smile—oh god, look at Martin!

A beep from my phone signals a voice message. I haven't checked it in days. Maybe it's a hunny. I could use some company. Or maybe not. My temperament sways like the wind. Thoughts jump from the divine to the morbid. Tears erupt right behind fits of laughter. I decide to listen to the message before the alcohol gets the better of me. If it hasn't already done so.

The message starts off garbled. Or is it just me? No, I think someone is…running? Now noise, like something's being thrown. A commotion of some sort. The next voice I hear makes me wish I never listened.

"No, please. I'm sorry. Just leave me alone!"

I can hear Martin begging for his life. His words make me wish I could end it right now.

"PLEASE!"

That's the same word, the same tone he used in pleading with me to come pick him up. And now he uses it before his executioner. The severity of my actions truly hits home.

I am to blame for my brother's death!

Before I throw the phone out the window, I hear another voice emerge. I listen intently. The voice of his killer will be a voice I never forget.

"I…ask…question."

The husky voice talks in disjointed sentences as Martin sobs uncontrollably.

"Wrong…answer. I…take back…mine."

99

The last sound I hear is Martin's scream. Only a scream like that could make the face I last laid eyes on.

"T-Mart, I'm sorry!"

My apology goes unanswered. I laugh. He better not answer. The world spins as my weighted foot rests on the gas pedal. It's becoming increasingly harder to determine what lane to stay in. People blow their horns. Will they just…

"Leeeeaaave me alone!" I shout to the window. "Stop it! All of you!"

They're no good. All of em! Except Martin—Martin was good. He was a good brother—he was. I shouldn't have—

"LADY WATCH OUT!!!!!"

I swerve to avoid the woman crossing the street. My body jolts as the truck flips…

I'm awake. Not sure how long I was out, but…

I—I—can't move.

——THE ASSIGNED——

GLORIA

"So whada ya say, hunh? Scott Richmond? His frrrrriii-ieeeend?" Sandy nags. Naturally, she doesn't give me a chance to answer. "Well it's done! I just texted Scott that we'll double next Friday! We can get you a pedi, a mani, heck—even a wax!"

It's days like this that make me wonder why I even put up with Supersize Sandy. "We'll talk about it later, Sandy," I defer. "I think I'm leaving a little early today. I need some fresh air—"

"Hey, that sounds great! I was thinking the same thing! We could get a little shopping done—ooh I saw these grrreeeeaaat shoes at Melodies. They would go great with my tan jumper..."

My mind zones her out, a feat not hard to accomplish. It drifts to one of my favorite spots, Lincoln Memorial. The sprawling park never fails in clearing my mind. In fact, it seems like I've been by there nearly every other day lately. No A'ma. No Sandy. No Arnie. Nothing but me, my music, and the trail.

"...or maybe I'll get those red six-inch. They've been dyyyinnnggg for me to buy them."

Wow, she's still going. "Every time I walk in, they're just like, *heeeeeyyyy Sandy. Buy me. Pleaaaasssseee...*"

Yeah, definitely a Lincoln day.

——T H E A S S I G N E D——

ZEEK

Maybe it's me, but I don't remember the park ever being this crowded. People are everywhere; playing, jogging, riding bikes. It's the warmest it's been in about a month and looks like everyone's taking advantage.

Lincoln Park is huge. Six or seven basketball courts, miles and miles of trails, a track, three playgrounds to choose from. They have some of the best swings in the city and Christina loves it, so I bite the bullet and blend in with the rest of the sappy population. Actually, I stick out in my Road Hogs leather fatigues as some kid embarrasses his mom by pointing to my tattoos, saying, *"mommie why does he have those pictures on his arms?"*

She gives a nervous, anxious grin before whisking the kid away. The comment actually makes me smile. Heard a lot worse.

Christina bubbles with anticipation. It's been a long time since she's had a day like this. Seeing the look on her face has made everything worth it…already.

I hold her hand tightly as we navigate through the large crowd. Still, it doesn't take long for the white ice cream truck sitting off in the distance to catch her attention.

"Daddy, ice cream! Ice cream!" she shouts. "Can I have some please?!"

"Don't you wanna play for a while?" I ask, as if her young mind will be persuaded by the option.

"Daddy, please! Ice Cream! Ice Cream!"

Right. No chance.

Chrissy jumps up and down, full of life, like every five-year-old should be. How can I possibly refuse her after all she's been through? "Sure baby," I say. "But only one popsicle. You don't wanna mess up your tummy before we ride the swings."

With the ice cream truck sitting about 30 yards away, we cross a narrow asphalt path, cutting across the grass. Several kids hover around the truck like birds circling their prey. As we near the adolescent chaos, I clutch Christina's hand even tighter.

Some of the children make faces at Christina as they run around, free from their parent's grasp. Chrissy mimics the children as she tries to break free from my hand. "Whada you doing?" I say firmly. Christina points to the other children who scurry about as their parents order their favorite treats. *Couldn't be more than ten feet*, I think to myself. A few more visits from those eyes and I eventually let go. Christina bolts like a stallion from the barn, showing the other kids what she can do. Wearing forest green shorts, an orange pullover, and socks pulled up over her calves, Christina plays her heart out. So, what if she looks like a single father dressed her, she's happy. Standing just five or six large steps away, she waves to me. I wave back of course, just as proud as the rest of the parents that congregate on this beautiful Saturday morning.

————T H E A S S I G N E D————

TRE

What happened? Sirens howl in the distance. And everything —everything is upside down.

"Sir, don't move," says a voice to my left. "We've called 911."

Why has someone called 911? Warm liquid runs down my chin. And why am I upside down? Am I crying? I—I don't think so.

"What's going on?" I ask, hoping the voice will hear me.

"Sir, you've been in an accident. You should just lie still."

I try to focus but my eye, it won't open. And that liquid—it's blood—my blood.

Struggling with the seat belt, panic sets in. A white object in front of me makes it hard to move. Then I realize, it's the air bag. My remaining good eye begins to make sense of the funny shapes. The truck—it's upside down and now my brain is sending signals to my nerve endings as pain erupts in my body.

"Oh God! Somebody, help me!" I shout. "Please!"

"Sir, lie still, you're in shock," says the voice to the left. "Paramedics are on the way."

Blood and lacerations cover my arms. I reach for my face but I can't feel anything. It's swollen. From my contorted view, I watch as feet surround the truck. I can hear their voices, though no one tries to help me—why won't they help me?!

Breathing becomes difficult as my mangled cage closes in. Will somebody just help! Not sure how much longer I can...

Something's happening. Is someone helping on my right? Can't see but my leg feels better. My eye opens just in time for me to see blood trickle back inside a deep gash in my arm. The wound closes, like it was never there. A crackling sound discharges from my body. Is that...bone? Whatever it is makes breathing a lot easier. In fact, I feel...great. My entire body feels brand new. I can now see I'm pinned under my airbag, my truck on its roof. Looks like I really did it this time.

EMT arrive on the scene. "Sir don't move. Are you alright?"

For some strange reason...

I am.

CHAPTER 12 – ZEEK

"Whada it be, sir?" asks the ice cream attendant.

"Uhhh, let me see…" I take one more glance at Christina before ordering. She playfully engages with another young child standing beside her. "I'll take a—"

The pain I felt earlier rings through my head. Blurry images fly past my eyes as I try my best to shake it off. After what feels like a few moments, it stops.

"…sir, sir? You're holding up my line. What's with this guy?"

"Hunh?" I say as my mind scrambles. What is going on with my body? What was I doing? Oh yeah, ice cream—Christina. "Hey Chrissy baby, what was it you said—"

I turn around to ask Christina what she wants, but she's not there. My eyes pan through dozens of children playing around the ice cream truck. It takes a moment, but none of them are Christina. It's not like her to run off, but maybe this small taste of freedom has overwhelmed her. We will definitely have a long talk about this. But first I have to find her.

"Christina?" I call. So many people, it's hard to focus on anything past 20 feet. The nearest playground is about 40 yards away. That has to be where she went.

———THE ASSIGNED———

TRE

Paramedics roll me into the ER. They refuse to let me up even though I keep trying to tell them I'm fine. How that's possible is another story in itself.

"Sir, relax!" they shout, rushing my gurney around corridors.

"Look, I'm fine," I say. "Really."

"Sir, you were just in a major accident. You're in shock." The two men confer with one another. "He is in shock, right?"

"It's the alcohol talking," says the other. "You can smell it on him a mile away. We've got to call this one in."

That's not what I needed to hear. I can't afford a DUI on my record. Not now. Can't give Atlanta any reason to cut me. This injury has got me on thin ice already.

The techs place my gurney alongside a wall. They instruct me to rest as they drop off paperwork. Carts, wheelchairs, and portable beds line the hallway, all filled with sick or injured people. Most are totally oblivious to the happenings around them, their ailments drowning out their surroundings. Being that I'm completely fine makes it all the more noticeable.

With the tech's backs turned, I ease my way off the gurney. Slowly, I crouch backwards, sneaking towards the exit. Nearly there, before a misstep lands me into the cart of an injured man. *Good going, Tre.* Quickly I lighten his load by jumping to my feet.

"Sorry," I smile. He looks up with an annoyed glare. Blood stains seep through pasty colored bandaging covering his entire right forearm. I apologize again, lightly placing my hand on the dressing. Why, I don't know. That should be the last thing I touch, although I do it almost instinctively. As I refocus my attention on a way out, I see a stairwell about 50 yards away. Walking briskly to the exit, I hear a voice beckoning for someone's attention. Carefully I turn, only to get a glimpse of the man with the bloodied arm waving wildly towards me. His face jumps with delight as he moves his arm up and down. His...*right arm.* Albeit I've moved a ways down from him now—call me crazy, but I don't see any stains in his dressing. Slipping the man a wave and nod of the head, I duck into the stairwell.

That accident must've really done something to my head. That, or I'm still a little buzzed. I'm really beginning to lose it. Whatever the case, I've got to get out of here, get my story straight. "Damn! My phone!" Probably still in the wreckage. My wallet, too.

The stairwell leads me to a basement exit. I take a few cautious moments to make sure no one has followed me. Then I make a run for the hill, leading me back to the ground level. Hopefully I'll find someone at the corner, use their phone. Of course, no one's around. I look both ways, but nothing.

"No phone. No money. Great."

"Is there someone you need to contact?"

"What the—!"

The voice frightens me half out my skin. "Where did you come —it's...YOU."

Out of nowhere stands the mysterious silver haired woman. Wearing an elegant bronze-colored, caped pantsuit, she definitely was not standing there just seconds ago. Perfectly pressed platinum colored hair hangs long around her face. Piercing light brown eyes almost glow red in the sunlight. The woman, somewhat attractive for someone that age, must be in her late fifties or sixties.

"Who—who are you lady?"

"A friend," says a proper, crisp voice.

"More like a stalker to me."

"I mean you no harm, William. Do you have any injuries from your accident?"

"Hunh?" I grimace. "First off—"

"First off, stop calling you William. You go by Tre. And how do I know you were in a collision? And how did I know you would be at this very corner at this very minute?"

My frown is replaced by confusion. "Uhh…yeah."

The woman's eyes, like before, penetrate my skin. "That is what I do. That is who I am. I know things. Have you ever felt you were destined for something great, William Turner, III? Something grander than sports? Almost as if a force much greater than your own was beckoning you—calling you to greater things?"

The delivery of her words nearly draws me in before common sense gets the better of me. "Okay lady. Did my mom put you up to this? What are you a counselor or something? Look, I'll be fine. Just need—"

Stepping closer, her pristine voice rises as she cuts me off. "I know NOT of your parents, William Turner, III! I DO know of your reoccurring nightmares, your bouts of depression, your alcoholism, and your guilt over your brother's death! I also know you were just involved in an accident that should have taken your life, at the least critically injured you. Yet you sustained not one broken bone or scratch. I know at this present time, you shall shun me. But as things continue to manifest, you will seek me out."

I stare at the obviously loony woman. Her clothes, her voice, that speech. She's off her rocker.

"...oh finished?" I mouth off. "Okay, listen. I don't know who you are, and I don't want to. And what's up with the Old English? You got King James on speed dial or somethin'?!"

I look around before taking my chances going west. Eventually, I should run into someone sane. Before I can get five steps, the nut job behind me speaks up. "That way leads to the authorities you flee."

I continue, ignoring the batty woman. A police car suddenly pulls into the hospital's parking lot. Inconspicuous, I immediately turn back the other way glancing at 'Ms. Lucky' before passing.

"At the very least, take my card, please?" she requests. I pretend not to hear. "I just gave you a forewarning, did I not? All I ask is that—"

"Okay, lady!" I shout. Can't have her following me home. "Fine!" I snatch the card, stuffing it in my pocket before setting off east.

A few blocks away is the back entrance to Lincoln Memorial Park. Several of my old high school teammates play ball there. There's got to be somebody there I know.

"Shortcut."

——THE ASSIGNED——

GLORIA

Although busy, the park is peaceful on this wonderful Saturday afternoon. Birds chirp as sunlight cuts through openings in the towering trees. Taking in all of nature, I stretch on the park bench in front of me. Looks like I made a great decision in cutting out of the station early. Arnie may bark about it on Tuesday, but right now, Tuesday feels like eons away.

I plug my ears with headphones, sprinting down the five-mile trail. Lincoln is great for running this time of year. The only thing I hear while running is...whatever I want. No A'ma, no Sandy, no Deacon Nichols. Nope. Only the song that corresponds with the button I select. Here, I have complete control over the soundtrack of my life.

Musical beats rip through my ears, pushing my pace. With the volume on full blast, another sound somehow manages to cut through. I slow down to survey the trail. Not a person in sight. The sound grows stronger. A voice. Growing increasingly loud, it keeps a child-like character. Finally, I come to a dead halt.

"I want my daddy."

Okay, I know I'm not going crazy. Removing the headphones, I listen. The voice continues to grow stronger by the second.

"I want my daddy."

Immediately my body tingles with energy as the hairs on my arm rise.

"Daddy!"

I feel...power. The same power that has eluded me for nearly seven days. It reassures me that what happened last week was not a dream. Things are *not* back to normal. Not in the least. The voice I hear is not in normal hearing distance. I just know. The feeling consumes me as I burst into an all-out sprint.

————T H E A S S I G N E D————

ZEEK

I search the entire playground and still no sign of Christina. I even circle back around to the ice cream truck. No longer calm, I shout my daughter's name at the top of my lungs.

"Have you seen a little girl?! She's five, brown hair, about this tall—she's got on green shorts—" People stare, but none offer help. I can't believe this is happening. Not now. I'm sure I look intimidating standing at the family park with a leather vest and tattoos fluttered across my arms but forget all that. Why won't they just listen to me? I'm a father and I need help! My baby, Christina is missing, and these people do nothing but stare at me!

How can my little girl go from near death to full of life, only to go missing at some stupid park? The emotions of the past seven days rise up in me like flood waters. Feelings of helplessness, grief and again…guilt.

Adrenaline surges through my veins as I scour the park. I have to find her. As I run through the trails, another feeling begins to overtake me. Not sure—it's unlike anything I've ever felt. I feel …fast. Alert. More than just the heightened anxiety of searching for a lost child. There's a distinct change all over my body and it's giving me…*power*.

Images flash before my eyes. No longer accompanied by pain, the visions are clearer than before. I see a white vehicle. *The ice cream truck!* Now, a balding man with glasses—there's Christina! Finally, a wooded trail. The images are trying to lead me to her. I'm not sure how, but I now know exactly where to find my baby.

"I want my Daddy!"

The voice. That's the voice that's been ringing through my head for the last few minutes! It belongs to a young girl who looks to be around six or seven. She squirms as a balding, middle-aged man whisks her through the winding trail.

"Shut up!" he yells. Wearing a loosened green tie and khakis, his disturbed voice sounds like three people talking all at once. The man's hand, tightly clasped around the young girl's wrist, leads the child further into a wooded area. It's not her father— or any guardian for that matter. I just know. His distorted voice softens in tone. "Don't worry sweetie. I'll be your Daddy."

Several yards away, I'm not sure if I should even have the ability to hear all this. Much like the young girl, the man's voice rings through my head clear as day. I can't let him take that child into the woods. I have to do something.

"Hey! Whada you think you're doi—what are you?"

I watch as some sort of black haze hovers around the unassuming man. Swaying with his every movement, its edges swirl about before dissipating into the breeze. The vapor like substance almost seems to take on a life of its own. Like smoke from a pipe, it falls in and out of shapes, forever moving although never leaving the man's profile.

Startled, he pulls the child close. "Oh, hi. Lovely day, isn't it?" he says. His voice sounds normal now, but the haze-like aura is still there. "My niece and I are just out enjoying this lovely weather."

I stare back, amazed. Some truly strange things have been happening, but this may be the strangest of all. Grayish-black smoke continues to hover around the seemingly common man. Otherwise, he looks like a tax collector for the IRS.

"Look, I don't know who or what you are, but I know that's not your niece."

"We have to be going, really," he says before turning his back on me. After running a few paces to catch up, I grab the Tax Collector by the shoulder. "You're not going anywhere!" I yell. The haze around him intensifies as his voice changes. "You are throwing me OFF SCHEDULE!"

Without warning, something that feels like a baseball bat knocks the air right out of me. Dazed, I lay still in the forest-like terrain. My goodness, was that his fist? I've never felt such force in my life.

"Sorry but you're not my type," I can vaguely him hear snarl in the distance. My mind races back to the young girl. If I don't get to her there's no telling what he may do. Not even sure what *he* is, I spring to my feet for another go. Quickly, my energy returns. The burst in adrenaline surprises me for a moment but I adapt.

"Hey! Is that all you got!" I shout, confident as ever. The Tax Collector, somewhat surprised, turns my way. "I said, YOU are throwing me off schedule and I HATE rushing!"

"Well, I've got all day."

"AAAAHHHH!"

Instinctively, I block his first punch with my arm before landing a side-kick to his chest. The one blow throws him back. Stunned, he rises to his feet.

"What are you, little girl?" he growls.

A grin crosses my face before answering. "I've been trying to ask you the same thing."

"What am I?" he asks. Even the haze around him looks disturbed. His chest swells as his voice multiplies. "I'M LATE!"

The Tax Collector charges again, attacking ferociously. Grayish-black mist lingers after his every move. I block his first few assaults. Not so lucky this time. He catches me with a right to the abdomen. The blow sends me into a nearby oak tree.

BAMMMM!!!!

The force of the collision cracks the trunk of the old tree. It takes everything in me to remain conscious. Even in my heighted state, his strength is beyond mine. Guess I'm not the only one with...*power*.

"You like to hit girls, hunh? How 'bout trying that on a man!" says a guy out of nowhere. He rams his shoulder into the Tax Collector's stomach, spearing him to the ground. There's something familiar about him. Black guy, bald head, looks around my age, a little older. Not sure though. Having the wind knocked out of me makes focusing fairly difficult.

"Now *that's* what I'm talking about!" he screams, like he just won a video game tournament. "TNT in the house!" boasts the brash stranger, raising his arms like a champion. He changes his stride as he approaches. The pretentious show-off tries hard to sound cool. "Hey lovely, you alright?"

Maybe I'd be better off if I was all alone.

"I'll be fine," I say, still resting on the ground. "But YOU should watch out."

"What are you talking about?" he responds, cocky as ever. "Did you see how I laid him out?" *Right*, I think to myself. *Must be a jock.*

"He's lucky I didn't—" The Tax Collector picks up Mr. Cool like a loaf of bread. Thickened black vapor swirls around him. Anger burns on the distorted face of the assailant as he throws the poor guy into nearby thorn bushes. Even Mr. Cool didn't deserve that.

"Christina?!"

"Daddy?"

"Come here, baby."

The terrified child sticks her head out from behind the large tree she's been hiding behind. "It's okay, baby," says a tattooed guy in biker threads. He leans down to her level. "You can come to Daddy." Hesitating only a moment, the child makes a dash for the familiar face.

"What's going on here?" asks the biker. He doesn't necessarily look like a parent, but for some reason I sense a genuineness about him.

"You her father?" I ask.

"Yeah. Who are you? Who are they?"

"That thing over there tried to abduct your daughter," I say resting on one knee. Wait a minute. To this guy, the Tax Collector probably looks just like a...*tax collector.*

"What the hell is with your face?!" shouts the young biker-dad as blackness pulsates in and out of the Tax Collector's profile. Wow. Maybe he does see what I see.

"And what's wrong with yours," the balding fiend sneers back. With movements like a feline, the demented man runs and jumps effortlessly several feet up into a nearby tree. Still on all fours, he growls from above.

Mr. Cool finally makes his way up from the bushes. "I think you should stay back," I say, not wanting the guy to bite off anymore than he can chew. "Ooh, and your face. It's—"

Cuts and lacerations from thorn bushes mar the jock's face. I'm sure that'll be a blow to his ego. Wait a minute. *For real?*

Mr. Cool's face clears up right before my eyes...literally! The welts and bruises disappear as if nothing ever happened. I don't know why I'm so surprised as I slowly begin to realize something.

I am not alone.

──────THE ASSIGNED──────

TRE

A deep cut in my hand heals instantly. Slowly, I'm beginning to see, this is who I am. The sting from the bushes disappears after a few short seconds. But the look in this girl's eyes says it all as she watches my face heal on the spot. Looks like she's coming to after taking a pretty good lick from Hellboy up there.

"Wow, how did you do that?" she asks.

"It's magic, sweetie," I grin back. Although kind of cute, she's much too Plain Jane for my tastes, but what can I say…I'm a flirt. Not completely sure, but I think she's different—like me. What am I saying? I don't know what I am or what I'm even doing here. Just a gut feeling telling me where to go, leading me.

Looks like the small girl over there is biker boy's daughter. Wow. A child that old, and he looks about the same age as me. Couldn't imagine what's running through his head now. But hey, not sure what's running through mine either as I watch this demon-like man hiss from the tree above us. A black mist lingers around him, mimicking his every move.

"That's your friend?" asks the young girl's father. Guess he's referring to me.

"Him?" she frowns. "Just some wannabe superhero."

"Ouch," I say. Warrior Princess then points to the guy up in the tree. "He's your only concern."

"Christina," says the child's father. "Did he…"

"No," reassures the brown-haired fighter. "I got here before— she's just scared."

"Thank you," he nods. The Latin Charlie's Angel nods back.

"And what am I?" I say flailing my arms. "Chop liver?"

"Yeah, you too," he mumbles. Guess Mr. Big-Bad-Motorcycle-Rider isn't big on words.

"Christina, you say. What a lovely name," says the demented professor perched in the tree. Or should I say professors—he sounds like three people all at once. "We'll get reacquainted later," he hisses towards the child. His words spark a fury in me...in all of us.

"Hey! Don't you EVER say my daughter's name again!" yells the girl's father.

Running with minimal effort, the motorcycle vest-wearing bad boy leaps straight in the air. Now this guy—this guy is definitely different. Mid-air, the emotional father swings wildly but misses. With cat-like movements, the possessed man jumps, avoiding the scurry. Still mid-air, he kicks the poor guy square in the mouth.

Ouch. Bad-Boy loses his balance and falls to the ground below. The nearly bald professor jumps down and lands a crushing foot to the sternum—no, wait! The biker rolls out with half a second to spare. He jumps to his feet as the professor works to free his foot from the damp earth below.

This is like something from my favorite movie. I should help the guy, but I've never seen anything like this. Plus, the biker looks like he's gaining control. He jumps up delivering a bruising kick to the professor's chest. The man-thing soars backwards, black mist and all. With the exception of his right shoe still sunk in the ground under our feet.

CRRAAACK!!!!

The one-shoed villain comes to rest at the base of another unfortunate tree. Branches fall covering the unconscious man. The black mist surrounding him evaporates, almost like a source of power, dissipating.

"Yeah, I see you not talking now!" I jaw at the knocked-out punk. He doesn't look nearly as creepy as a few minutes ago.

Speaking of jaw, looks like biker boy took a pretty good one to the chin.

"You alright, man?" I ask.

"Fine. Christina?!"

"Daddy!"

The two begin their embrace all over again.

"Freakin pedophile!" he yells, spitting to the ground.

"He was more than that," I say.

"I agree," says Warrior Princess.

"So you saw the…?"

"Black, smoke-like stuff?"

"Yeah!" I nod. "Like some kind of spirits or something."

"Enough of the spirit mumbo jumbo," interrupts the tough guy. "Dude is a doped up perv—"

He takes off towards the unconscious attacker. "Why you disgusting son of a—"

I catch him just in time. "Hey, calm down! It's over! Hey lil lady," I say, flashing the TNT smile. "Why don't you call the police? I've got things under control now."

"What?" she says, her eyes big. "You know what—whatever."

"So, you didn't see his face?" I ask the biker.

"Look. I don't know what I saw," he says trying to downplay the situation. "All I know is, my daughter's okay. That's all that matters."

For some reason, the craziness of the moment brings that insane silver haired woman to mind. I retrieve her card from my pocket. In bold font it reads:

PROPHETESS – 901-501-3377

Flipping the generic card over, it reads the same. Maybe she's not so crazy.

————T H E A S S I G N E D————

ZEEK

The only thing that matters to me is Chrissy. For a moment there, I was afraid I'd never see my baby again. I don't know what the cosmos has got against me, but I couldn't take losing Christina. To think that bastard was probably watching us the whole time. If those police allow me just seconds, I swear I will destroy him. He doesn't deserve to live, going after my child like that. A Child!

I appreciate the athlete—for the life of me, can't remember his name but I've seen him on television—and the girl for helping. Really, I do. But their talk of spirits and demons, or ghosts, or witches, or whatever else they wanna chalk it up to, is really starting to annoy me. I call 'em as I see 'em and that guy is a drugged-out businessman that preys on children. So, what if he now sits in the squad car like a mild-mannered citizen, showing no sign of his previous crazed activity. I know what he is. He knows what he is. And he's not fit to live.

One policeman has been talking to him for nearly 30 minutes now. What could he possibly have to say?! Anger fills my blood. Glad Alicia's here to comfort Christina. Don't want her to see me like this.

"A lot of stuff has been going on in my life lately," says the hometown-great. He seems to be in pretty good shape and stands a couple inches taller than me, but still doesn't look nearly as big in person. "And I don't know about ya'll," he continues. "But I don't think its coincidence we're all here at this very moment. I mean, I saw black stuff, she saw black stuff, and you don't wanna admit it, but I know you did too man."

"The name's Zeek," I say.

"Okay, Zeek. Tell me you didn't see all of that."

I think about the adrenaline coursing through my veins. I'm sure most of what I did can be attributed to just that. Adrenaline. Who wouldn't fight like crazy for their child?

"I told you *bro*, all I see is a functioning junkie perv."

"What about the fighting?" he continues. "I don't know about you two, but I consumed enough alcohol in the last 24 hours to spontaneously combust! Now all of a sudden, I get this second wind and this..." Varsity man balls his fist. "...this strength."

"He's right," says the girl. Her long brown hair dangles in a ponytail. Angelina would've allowed her locks to flow straight down her back.

"Yeah, I even saw her throw a nice swing."

"And what's that's supposed to mean?" she asks.

"I mean c'mon," smirks Mr. Memphis. "You landed a punch or two but let's face it. If I hadn't came in and saved your behind —"

"Let's get one thing straight," she snaps. "My behind is none of your concern. I was doing just fine until you showed up. Why you..."

The girl walks off muttering something in Spanish.

"Ooh la laaa!" he teases. This guy is something else. "Now listen Zeek," he says turning his attention back to me. "I'm just saying. There's something going on here, with all of us. We need to figure out what we have in common."

Mr. Personality is really starting to get under my skin. "Look bro—"

"The name's Tre. Tre Turner."

"Okay, Tre. I appreciate you and J-Lo over there, sticking up for my little girl. Really, I do. But there's nothing else *we've* got to figure out. And even less we've got in common, okay bro—uh, Tre?"

"Okay, Zeek. Yeah, I see ya with your biker vest and your tattoos. And here I am, the chocolate debonair. Yeah, you're right, we probably wouldn't have anything in common on a normal day, but I'm sure you can agree that this…is not a normal day."

Turning to join my family, I've heard enough. As I walk off, Tre blurts out a question.

"Is there anything weird or abnormal that's happened in your life the past few days or weeks…even before today?"

I don't mean to show it, especially by pausing, but for some reason his words intrigue me. He continues, "Just a few hours ago, I was in a crazy wreck. My truck flipped four or five times— blood everywhere. Now you can't find a bruise on me. Not even a single scratch."

"A week ago, I didn't know how to speak Spanish, or Russian, or even German for that matter," the girl joins in. "But now they flow from my mouth with ease. I somehow even heard your daughter's voice from half a mile away."

"Look Zeek," Tre continues. "I think we all know deep down inside, there's something going on with all of us. Spiritual, supernatural, unnatural, however you wanna say it. But there's definitely something. And I think I may know someone who can help us make sense of all this."

I glance back to watch Tre hand the girl a card from his pocket. I'm too far away to tell what it says, but they seem to discuss it in detail. I can't lie, his words cause me to reflect on the visions that led me to Christina. *Oh please.* A father's intuition. *And my baby getting well overnight?* She's a fighter, just like her dad. Plus, the doctors always said my leg could get better one day. Besides, I don't have time for this hocus pocus.

"Well whada say, Zeek? Me and Gloria here are gonna go meet an acquaintance of mine. I think she may have some answers. I'd sure like to know more. What about you?"

"Once again, I thank you...Tre. Go Tigers. And gracias to you, Ms. Gloria, but I have a child to look after."

The officer interviewing Christina's abductor comes over to ask me some questions. His line of questioning becomes more and more like an interrogation. As if I did something wrong. After a few rounds, I've finally had enough. The sheer audacity of this 'officer of the law' is unbelievable.

"What else do you need to know?!" I shout. "That guy tried to abduct my daughter!"

"Sir, please calm down," he says scanning my vest and tattoos. "So, you're a member of the Road Hog's, hunh?" he asks as if that matters.

"What? What does that have to do with anything? Did you hear what I said? That—that perv just tried to kidnap my daughter!"

"Did you actually see him take her?"

"Hunh?"

"Mr. Sanderlin states he found your daughter wandering in the woods and was only trying to help her find her parents."

My eyes hunt down the now modest Mr. Sanderlin, still sitting in the patrol car. Deceivingly reserved, the man timidly adjusts his glasses, bearing no signs of the drug-charged rage he showed just minutes ago.

"He then states you and your two buddies over there proceeded to accost him."

"To what?"

"You beat him up."

"Officer, he's full of...croc!" I say grabbing Christina's hand. "Baby, tell the policeman how that man took you from your daddy —Tell 'em."

The timid Mr. Sanderlin lowers his glasses, looking straight at my daughter. The nerve of this guy! Petrified, Christina runs, seeking safety behind Alicia.

"This is not the time, Zeek." Alicia protests.

The girl—Gloria. She tries to intervene. "Sir, we saw the whole thing—"

"Did you see Mr. Sanderlin physically remove that child from her father?"

"Well no, but—"

"Thanks."

Gloria raises her voice. "There was this black—"

Tre nudges her and mumbles, "He won't believe you."

"Come again?" says the patrolman.

"Nevermind."

"Okay," I sigh. "So, what now…officer?"

"Guess I'll have to bring the both of ya down to the precinct for questioning."

"Give me a break! Oh my g—okay, fine." It takes everything in me to contain myself. "So ya wanna cuff me too?" I say, holding out my wrists.

The cop's eyes scan me head to toe. "That won't be necessary, I guess. You can sit in the front with me."

"Fine. Alicia, take Chrissy home. I'll call you shortly." I lean over to kiss my fragile daughter, her eyes just like her mom's. She puts her trust in me, but I keep leaving her frightened. It's not supposed to be like this. I speak as assertive as I can. She's got to believe this. "Daddy won't let anything happen to you. I promise."

Those eyes. All they do is look at me. No yea. No nay. Just a look. And just like that, my baby is introduced to the real world. A world in which Daddy doesn't control everything, where Daddy doesn't win every time, or even most of the time for that matter. A world I'm tired of being a part of.

I feel a tap on the back. "Hey Zeek, I wrote down my number," says Tre. "Me and Gloria are gonna try to figure this out. I know you didn't say anything, but I bet you've got a story, too. If you change your mind, give me a call."

"Like I said—"

"I know what you said man, but just take the number as a favor to me for helping you out. Please."

It's nothing but a gesture, guess it's the least I can do. I shake my head before reluctantly taking the slip of paper, placing it into my pocket. Not even sure if these two will get where they're going the way they hassle back and forth.

"So, you wanna grab a bite to eat first?" Tre asks. The frown on Gloria's face serves as a response.

"Okay. Well can you stop me by the house considering I just wrecked my truck?"

"I don't even know you like that."

"Oh, come on Mami, I just need to change, pick up a new whip."

"Don't call me Mami. My name's Gloria. Got it?"

"Okay, okay, chill. Got it. Well I'm Tre "TNT" Turner. Don't let the grass stains fool ya."

"Como un idiota presuntuoso!" moans Gloria before storming off again.

"Tom-ay-toe, tom-ah-toe," says Tre. "Well, do you wanna meet her or not?"

"You said 'her' right? Fine. Any woman has to have more sense than you."

"Yeah, yeah, yeah."

And we're supposed to have special powers? *Yeah right*. Enough with these two. I join officer idiota in the squad car.

CHAPTER 14 – Gloria

I can't believe I let this practical stranger talk me into leaving with him. The furthest thing from my mind is getting into a vehicle with some guy. But I guess he's not just any guy. In fact, I know exactly who he is. It came to me earlier. All-time leader in rushing yards at the university. But I dare not let him know.

Now in his spare car, a 2017 Mercedes sedan, with his name stitched into the upholstery, I'm reminded of the sheer excess these athletes squander through. I could do so much with only ten percent of what he makes. He doesn't even know how good he's got it. And all that gaudy jewelry. Where are we going, a video shoot? This guy tries way too hard. The cologne he obviously drenched himself in nearly runs me out the vehicle. Or maybe it's this sweater he let me borrow. There's no way I was going to let him take me by my apartment. For a number of reasons. He's probably used to girl's throwing themselves at him. Hmph. Well he won't have to worry about this one.

Now, of all things, I find out he doesn't even know this woman. "I can't believe I let you talk me into this," I say. "I thought you said she was your friend?"

"I said acquaintance. And I've—well, I've seen her a couple of times," he answers.

"You've seen her? What?"

"Look," Tre says while glancing over. "You got a better idea?"

"So, some lady you've never met hands you a card that says 'Prophetess', of all things, and immediately you think she has the cure to cancer? Give me a break!"

"Look, if she's in left field or she can't help us, we can leave. It's that easy. I mean c'mon, we just saw black smoke coming out of a man's head while playing live action Mortal Kombat in the park. What do we have to lose?"

What the heck. He's right. The happenings in my life turned bizarre long before this current adventure. What's one more? Not only did I see black smoke floating around a man's torso, I saw Tre do some pretty remarkable things as well. There has to be a connection. No matter how immature, infantile, and materialistic he may appear.

"Just drive," I sigh.

"Besides," Tre continues. "She seemed to be expecting my call. Asked how many were with me. Not sure what's that about."

"You think Zeek will call?" I ask.

"Who cares," Tre blurts. "That guy's got a serious attitude problem. We helped save his daughter and he barely says thanks."

"Well you never know what people are going through," I say reflecting on my own situation.

"Tell me about it," he counters. "So, what do you think we all have in common?"

I watch as Tre vigorously bobs his head up and down to the hip-hop song playing on the radio.

"I have no idea."

——T H E A S S I G N E D——

ZEEK

"Now this is a change of scenery," I mutter under my breath from the front passenger seat as the police cruiser jets down the street. It's definitely a different look.

"Say something, Mr. Myers?" asks the stern-faced officer.

"Nah," I say, glancing over at the emotionless lawman. He looks to be about fifty, hard chin, that same generic haircut every patrolman has in the movies.

I try to shake the anger brewing inside, taking a few deep breaths. Looking over my shoulder, I see the mild-mannered Mr. Sanderlin, cleaning his glasses. Slowly, I do a double take trying to catch a view of the blackness or any other abnormal signs. Nothing. *What am I doing?* Pencil-neck sits in the back humming some country tune as he looks out the window.

"You alright, Mr. Myers?"

I give up. Slouching in the front seat, I finally say, "Yeah, I'm fine, officer."

With the ride lengthening, I wonder what precinct we're headed to? We passed the closest one, East, nearly three blocks back. I try to remain patient but the incessant humming of this clown in the backseat is driving me insane. The detached officer doesn't seem to mind. Go figure. I check the time as my thoughts drift to Christina and Alicia.

"Hey officer? How long do you think this will take? I really would li—"

The policeman slows the cruiser, finally coming to a stop on the side of the road. He places the car in park, opens his door, and steps out.

Am I missing something? Confused, I stare out the window. There's no precinct in sight. Suddenly, the back door opens. The glass plate separating the front from the back, obstructs my view.

"Get out," commands a voice. The perv, steps from the car. The same voice murmurs a word in an unfamiliar language.

"Koon-cha"

"Koon-cha," repeats another. Must be Sanderlin. Not sure what language they're speaking. I strain my neck to get a better look. I can hear Sanderlin's footsteps as he distances himself from the cruiser. Moments later, the policeman returns to the car.

"Wait a minute," I say. "I know you didn't just let that guy walk scot-free?

Tell me you—"

The car buckles as the officer slams on the gas. "Hey! What are you doing?" Still, he says nothing. His accelerating speed makes me uncomfortable. "Hey man! I asked you a question!" No response. I stare the officer down hoping for any rise in the soundless driver. As my eyes cut through the patrolman's flesh, something catches my attention. A small tattooed symbol seems to almost stand on his wrist.

Smoke-like vapor rises from the Policeman's skin. Its color reflects the navy hue of his uniform. Like steam, it hovers around his torso, slowly swirling about. I watch the life-like substance in amazement.

"Can't be…"

My heartbeat quickens. Adrenaline pumps through my veins once more. I look down at my fingers, flexing them. Power pulsates through my nerves. My body prepares…but for what?

"AAHHSSSP!"

The Policeman lunges for my throat. His strength is superhuman. I gasp trying to free myself of the vicious hold. The car swerves as the shadowy substance recollects itself around the disturbed officer. I reach for the door-it's locked. The Policeman attempts to choke me out, but I finally fight him off with an elbow to the head. Using my shoulder, I ram the car door. It bursts open, and I jump from the speeding car head first, my body tumbling down the street.

Twenty yards up, the squad car comes to a stop. The angered Policeman snarls as his haze-engulfed body emerges from the vehicle. Too late. I make my way through a blocked-off industrialized perimeter. I don't know how, but my body tells me to leap, so I do, with supernatural ability, over a 15-foot wall, never looking back.

———THE ASSIGNED———

TRE

"Looks like your acquaintance is doing alright for herself," mocks Gloria as we enter a five-star hotel located in the heart of the city.

"Haha," I say, sarcastically. She's had jokes the whole ride here. "Looks that way."

This girl's different. She hasn't once mentioned who I am. I mean come on, she's had to at least heard of Tre 'TNT' Turner.

Most chicks go crazy about the Mercedes, but she seemed turned off by it. Again, she's nowhere near my type, but having a girl my age not throw herself at a young millionaire is quite...*different.*

We take the elevator up to the top floor, the twenty-first. Only two doors representing two enormous penthouses cover the entire level.

"You wanna knock?" I whisper.

"What? She's your friend. You knock."

"Like I said, acquaintance. As a matter of fact, I—"

The door opens. "Tre Turner. Welcome. Come in."

"Uhh...Prophetess?"

"Call me Anna."

This woman seems to only resemble the mysterious figure I've encountered over the past couple of weeks. They share similar features, but this particular woman looks...normal. Her usual formal attire is now replaced by a University of Memphis pullover. Her hair has the same grayish tone, although pinned up into a tightly squeezed bun. Same age group, though. Late fifties, early sixties.

"And who's your beautiful friend?" she asks.

"I'm Gloria," she blushes, in the oversized sweater I let her borrow.

"Gloria. What a beautiful name. Well don't you two just stand there. Come on in!"

The now seemingly ordinary woman's suite is the size of most people's houses. With three large bedrooms, two and a half bathrooms, a large den, kitchen, and balcony, it was built with the elite in mind. Reminds me of something I might own.

Looks as if she's been here quite some time, her eclectic effects all over the large living space. Vases, figurines, statues, and relics from all over the world. Not the fake airport ones either, these things look pricey.

Gloria and I take a seat on a mahogany-lined sofa. Our host, now going by the name of Anna, sets a tray of lemonade and sugar cookies in front of us. Gloria and I look at one another before scrutinizing the almost suspicious treats. The woman takes a seat on another sofa across from ours.

"So, what brings you children here?"

I start. "Well, you remember earlier how you said, 'as things continue to manifest'?"

The Prophetess—uhh Anna—or whoever she is, pours lemonade. "But of course. Your brother has just passed, and I know that can be a trying time."

I scoot to the edge of my seat. "Yeah, but HOW did you know about my brother?"

"Why, I read it in the paper. You were pretty well known for college football around here, weren't you?" The newly energetic woman points to her sweater. "Go Tigers! More lemonade?"

Sitting, my mouth open, I'm not sure what to make of all this. Not waiting for a response about her precious lemonade, the woman sets off for the kitchen.

"I thought you said she could help us?" whispers Gloria.

"I don't get it. Earlier, she was finishing my sentences and acting as if she's known me my entire life, almost like she was reading my mind."

"Yeah, and now she's serving milk and cookies." Gloria rolls her eyes. "See I knew—"

"Just hold on a minute, okay?" Standing, I make one more attempt at reaching out to the woman I met earlier. "Hey, uhh excuse me, Prophetess?"

"Oh, where'd ya get that silly name from," says the woman, returning from the kitchen with another tray. "Just call me Anna."

My patience wanes. "Where'd I get that silly name from? I got it from you! From the card I took after you gave me that long Jedi-Knight pep talk! Now tell me what's going on! You follow me around, tell me all this stuff about myself. You've finally got my attention and now you act like you don't know what I'm talking about?! Feeding us cookies and sour lemonade…"

"I'm sorry, Tre. Guess I'm just an old lonely alumnus who loves University football. And when I heard your brother passed, I just wanted to reach out to you. You are the school's all-time leading rusher, after all."

I've heard enough. "You know what—" My phone rings, interrupting my vocal onslaught. Boy, she better be glad. I answer the unknown number. "Yeah, Tre Turner."

"Yo, Tre. What's up bro?" speaks an unrecognizable voice.

"Yeah, who's this?"

"It's Zeek."

"Zeek?"

"Yeah."

"Hey everything alright down at the station?"

"Yeah…about that…did you guys go see that friend of yours?"

"Yeah, but sorry man. Looks like—"

"—tell him it is not a dead end. He is the remaining piece and he must come now. Your efforts are not in vain, William Turner, III."

I shake my head as the woman ends her performance by finishing my sentence in a tone that signifies she means business. Expelling a laugh of relief, I finish answering Zeek's question. "On second thought man, let me give you directions."

The mysterious Anna emerges from a back bedroom just as a knock is heard at the door. Her new outfit seems to be more in line with the extravagant attire earlier witnessed by Tre. "See, I told you," he smirks as she walks by to open the door. An Asian inspired floral pant and smock drapes the woman's petite, yet sturdy frame. Long satin-like, silver colored hair glides down her back. Her change in appearance is truly astounding. There's a regal temperament to her now.

"So, you must be Zeek. Welcome. I am Anna."

A grungy Zeek hesitates in shaking Anna's hand. He wipes his palms on his jeans before lightly cupping the tips of her fingers.

"Come in."

Zeek moves slowly until he catches a glimpse of me and Tre. I wave, hoping to lower his guard.

"And I think you have met the others, Tre and Gloria."

"Yeah, we definitely met," says Zeek.

"Good. Would you like a cookie? Lemonade?"

"Enough with the cookies and lemonade," barks an irritated Tre.

"Yeah, I have to agree," I say. "You were playing dumb, weren't you?"

Anna smiles. "Not exactly, my child. I was merely waiting for the third of three to present themselves."

"The third of three?"

"Yes. There has to be three."

"Hunh? Three what? Tre asks.

"My children, let me ask you a question. Do you believe in God?"

Tre and I nod.

"And you Zeek?"

Zeek lowers his head. "Not sure what I believe. I've seen a lot lately."

"What about demons?" Anna continues.

Zeek perks up. "Now there's definitely some of them floating around."

Anna moves in closer. "Well, if you believe in demons, you must believe in God."

My mouth drops. "Wow." Guess I'd never thought of it like that.

"What if I told you a war has raged since Creation?" she asks. "Although the outcome has been decided, the war continues. This is the way. What if I told you, you three have been chosen to wage battle in this warfare?"

"War?" Tre asks. "Hey, I'm not looking to enlist. Besides, I don't see no guns or ammunition hiding under this couch."

"This is a different kind of war, Tre," says Anna. "For we wrestle not against flesh and blood, but against principalities and powers not of this world."

"Okay," I say. "So, what do we use?"

"Your Gifts."

"Gifts?"

"Yes, my child." Anna walks towards me, taking my hand. "Etes-vous sur que vous voulez savoir?"

Before my thoughts can even gather, my mouth answers back in French. "Oui. S'il vous plait dites-moi."

"And have you ever been to France, my child?"

"Why...no. All this just started last week."

"Not only can you speak and interpret any language known to man, your ears can pick out a single voice in a crowd of thousands or hear a single whisper a mile away.

"Cool," I smile. Although briefly. "I think..."

Of course, Tre has to butt in. "No doubt? Okay, so what about me?"

"Tre, you have the gift of healing. Your body can immediately repair itself from nearly any infirmity. Broken bones, flesh wounds, sickness..."

"Now that's what I'm talking about!" he gloats. "I'm like the Black Wolverine!"

"I'm sorry?" Anna frowns.

"Nothing," I say, shaking my head. "Go on, please."

"Tre, not only can you heal yourself. You can heal others as well, with just one touch to their infirmity. You have the potential to save a lot of people, Tre Turner."

Tre's smile fades as if a thought envelopes him.

"So, what about the other things we've experienced?" I ask. "All of this strength, quickness, agility? I mean, I've done some things I've only seen on television."

"You are familiar with the Bible, correct?" Anna asks.

"Yeah?"

"The Bible speaks of a few chosen, possessing abnormal strength for periods of time, small armies being able to defeat enemies ten —twenty times their size. People speaking languages foreign to them, many being healed of various diseases, some being able to see glimpses of the future."

"So pretty much…miracles?"

"But of course, my child. A miracle is no more than an interruption, a suspension in the laws that govern this world, physically, mentally, logically. Everything that has been written about can still happen today, even raising the dead."

"What a minute," says Tre. "Did you say raising the dead?"

"Yes, my child. But these gifts are not for show or personal gain. They are for war."

Zeek finally speaks up. "And just who does this war concern?"

Anna walks towards a large window, peering through open curtains.

"There are those among us who are not as they appear. Demons walk this earth as mortal men. They are persuading many to join their uprising. Any man or woman you see could be one of the Persuaded: your mailman, your doctor, the woman in the car next to you, even members of your family. They normally wear the Shadow and they bear the Mark as a brand or tattoo on their arm or wrist."

"You mean, like the Mark of the Beast that's talked about in Revelation?" Tre asks.

"That is correct, Tre. I'm sure your father has preached about it before."

What? I have to jump in on this one. "Wait. Your father is a minister? Unbelievable…" I've heard it all now. Tre opens his mouth, but obviously can't think of a good enough rebuttal.

"And what's this Shadow business?" Zeek asks.

"The demonic-influenced people I speak of—our kind likes to refer to them as the Persuaded—they manifest a portion of their inner darkness outwardly. It rises like—"

"—like a black, smoke-like, haze," Zeek finishes.

"You have seen it?"

Each of us nods. Anna shakes her head as she paces around the suite. "Time draws nearer than expected. It should not be happening in this manner. We are not ready."

"Wait a minute," I say. "Slow down."

Anna continues. "Every few generations, God chooses Three to assist him in this ever-present battle. Some say Jesus' most inner circle, Peter, James, and John, were the first Three of Three. God assigns them individual and collective powers that exceed any myth or fable."

"Okay!" shouts Tre, bobbing up and down like an excited child. "So, we're like modern day superheroes, right?! Now that's what I'm talking about! How many superheroes do you know, hunh Gloria?"

It doesn't take much effort to ignore his comment. "So, these Persuaded, I think that's what we saw today. That was a demon?"

"Not a demon, per se," Anna answers. "Rather, demonically influenced. The Persuaded are mortal, and can possess supernatural abilities, just as you, but they are still human and can be helped if not fully persuaded. Although it does seem as if they are increasing in number. There has to be a Familiar in close proximity."

"*Oooookay*," Tre says, not trying to hide his sarcasm. "And that is…?"

"A Familiar is a spirit, a true demon. A demon enclosed in flesh. It is not uncommon for disputes to arise in Hell and for demons to be banished or attempt to leave on their own."

"Maybe that's what we saw in the park," I say.

"I suspect not, my child. Familiars are much more powerful than the Persuaded. Your countenance does not wear the fatigue of battling a Familiar. They cannot be saved, thus they must be fought with unbridled force and cast back to the pits of Hell. The power to rebuke is in you but it must be correctly harnessed. Besides, the last Familiar to enclose himself in flesh was the demon Beelzebub. But he was cast out a little over forty years ago. This new Familiar could be masquerading as anyone."

"Okay, this still doesn't make sense," says Zeek. I'm sure by now, Anna's descriptions of supernatural occurrences has his logic turned upside down. "I mean why me?" Zeek goes on. "This guy's dad's a preacher. She's probably some goody-two-shoes," he says pointing to me, although that is definitely not the case. "And me? I've never even really believed in a god, much less stepped foot inside a church."

"This is not about any church, Zeek," Anna says firmly. "This is about a Kingdom. One the enemy wants to control…or destroy. What if I told you there is a God?" she continues. "The same God your wife believed in, and he is just as real as anything you've encountered the last few days."

Zeek's defenses swell up. "Whoa. Wait a minute lady. What do you know about my wife? Who are you?"

"I am Anna, the Prophetess. I see and I know. I know you loved your young wife very much and I see you still live in the past."

"What'd you say lady? Look, I'm out of here."

"Hold up Zeek!" Tre pleads. "Let her finish, then it's your call."

Breathing heavily, Zeek stands by the door.

"God has shown me your paths," says Anna. "He has sent me here to help you. To guide you."

"So, you're an angel or something?" asks Tre.

"Oh no, Tre. As you, I am flesh and blood. I am simply here to—as you say— fill in the blanks."

"So, you knew we would meet in the park?" I say.

"Not exactly, my child. I was led to this city. Once I found Tre, it was only a matter of time before your paths intertwined. I knew once your Gifts began to manifest, it would probably— what do you young people say now—freak you out? Of course, it would be apparent I was an individual completely peculiar to Tre's surroundings. So peculiar, I may be the only person willing to believe the abnormalities happening in his life, thus yours as well."

Makes sense to me. Tre too, as we both nod in agreement. Zeek, however, is not so easily sold. "So, you're saying God, or whoever, set up this whole day—my daughter being abducted, me nearly being choked to death by some demon police officer, just so I could meet you and become some assassin of his?"

"No, of course not, Zeek. It's much more complicated than that. You have to—"

"Save it," Zeek cuts in. "This is ridiculous. I'm outta here."

Anna raises her voice just as Zeek is about to walk out. "I know that like me, you have the gift of Seeing. You see visions. And when the time is right, I won't have to find you...YOU will find me."

Her last statement does little to bring Zeek back in. Tre and I follow.

"Hey, Zeek wait up!"

"For what?!" he yells back. "To hear more ghost stories? I've heard enough."

Now at the elevator, Zeek punches the down button.

"Zeek, I know it doesn't all make sense," I try to reason. "But you've gotta admit, something is definitely going on with us and she seemed to know a lot."

Tre joins in. "Yeah man. You saw that thing at the park just like we did. I'm not trying to be a guinea pig for God or anyone else for that matter. But if there's gonna be something coming for me, I wanna be ready."

The elevator doors finally open as Zeek steps inside. "Look. It was great meeting you guys, but I was doing just fine before today and I'll be just fine after this day is over."

The doors begin to close. "Tell your fairy godmother thanks, but no thanks. *Sayonara.*"

"What is with that guy?" Tre frowns. "Every time I see him, I get a headache."

"Maybe people say the same about you," I say making my way back to the suite.

"Say what?"

"Nothing..."

Back in the suite, I watch as Anna casually puts up the yet-to-be-touched lemonade and cookies. "So, what do we do now, Anna?" I ask.

"Give him time," she responds. "This is much to digest for anyone. The day has grown into night. You two should go home and rest. Today, the enemy tried to distract us. But tomorrow, we will rise."

"I like that," smiles Tre. "Cool. We'll be back tomorrow."

"Nice to meet you, Anna," I smile, as we head for the door.

"Mannn, what have we gotten ourselves into?" Tre asks as we wait for the elevator.

"I...I don't know," I laugh.

"Wait. What's that?"

"What?"

"You smiled," he says. For a brief moment, he almost seems... charming. Key
word—brief.

"And?"

"Why do you act as if you don't like me?" he smiles. I quickly erase the grin from my face, can't give him any fuel. "Maybe it's because I don't," I say blankly.

Tre looks at his reflection in the buffed, polished steel doors of the elevator. Flexing his shoulders, he says, "Nah...can't be that ..."

I thought so. Nothing's changed in the last couple of hours. He's still stuck on himself. Casually, I look him head to toe. "You're not all that."

"But I'm close enough," he snaps back.

"Ugggghhhh," I grunt as the elevator doors open. "Why do I put up with you?"

"Because I'm your personal superhero," he bows. "I'm here to protect you, my lady."

"Oh please. How 'bout I protect you?"

"If I recall, it was I who saved you at the park."

We continue our debate all the way down the elevator.

——T H E A S S I G N E D——

ZEEK

"What's with these people?!" I shout through the drab parking lot. No one is there to answer back as I head for my bike. First, all this talk of soldiers and demons. Now, some lady I've never met is rambling off about Angel? That's where I draw the line. I'll just have to figure this thing out for myself. Or better yet, just leave it alone. It's sure to die down on its own. One thing's for sure, powers or not, I don't owe God, or anyone for that matter.

Three stalls later and my bike still won't crank. This is definitely not the time. It's enough I'm parked at this ritzy hotel. The valet boys are already starting to mumble. Don't worry guys, I'll be gone before you build up the nerve to approach.

Okay, let's try this again. I attempt to jumpstart the aging and stubborn chopper, but she won't budge. Frustration sets in as familiar voices shout at me from across the street.

"Hey Zeek! You okay?!"

I nod, at the same time speeding up my process. Key, clutch, kick. Again. "Come on!" I shout. Tre and Gloria are headed this way and that's the last thing I need.

"Are you okay, Zeek?" asks Gloria.

"Everything's fine," I say, wildly jumping up and down on the start.

"Looks like you're the one who needs a fairy godmother," laughs Tre.

"Haha. Funny guy—ehh."

"Sorry man," he says. "But you've been out here, what? Thirty minutes now?"

"Yeah Zeek. Why don't you let Tre take you home?"

"Yeah man. It'll be no problem. C'mon."

"I...SAID...SHE...WILL...CRANK...ANY...SECOND," ramming the start with each word spoken. Tre looks at Gloria. "Do you think that old piece of metal is really gonna start?"

"Doesn't look that way."

"She's not an old piece of metal," I grumble. "She's a classic."

"Yeah, I bet. Just like that old television in my grandma's living room. It just sits there. Kind of like your bike, hunh Zeek."

"And what are you driving anyway, lover boy?"

"Well, keep in mind I'm in my spare but…" A chirping sound is heard over the parking lot as Tre clicks his car alarm. "2017 Mercedes CLS."

"Figures," I say, frowning at the flashy ride. "No style. No story behind it. Just show."

"Well, the only show you'll be watching is the homeless guy fighting the pigeons if you don't take this ride."

"What about my bike?"

"Trust me. That bike ain't going nowhere."

* * *

Wow. And he says this is his spare car. Some guys have all the luck. Tre *TNT* Turner. Seeing his name stitched in the peanut butter colored armrests makes it easy to remember. And now I sit in the backseat as he goes on and on about us forming his version of the Justice League.

"Zeek, don't you get it?" he shrugs. "The three of us could possess something no one else in the world has. We could be like Morpheus, Trinity, and Neo."

Gloria rolls her eyes. "You watch *waaaayyyy* too many movies. You know that right?"

"I'm serious," he continues. "With these special powers or gifts or whatever you wanna call 'em, we could kick some serious a—" Tre pauses, looking towards the roof of the car. "Okay, sorry God. Starting now, I'ma stop cursing…promise."

Wow. Funny thing is, I believe him. Wish it was that easy for me. "You two can do whatever you want," I say. "I didn't ask for this. I just want my life back the way it was."

"What would your daughter say, huh Zeek?" Tre asks. "What would she say if she knew her dad was a quitter?"

My voice grows firm. "Leave my daughter out of this, okay bro? I just got her back and I don't intend on losing her again. Not for anyone. Not you, not *God*, not anybody."

"Yeah that had to be scary for you at the park," says Gloria.

"Yeah, that too," I answer.

"That *too?* Whadya mean?"

Pausing for a moment, I lean back on the leather head rest. "Me and Chrissy's mom, we got married when we were 18. Chrissy was barely a year old. Her mom, Angel, she—she died that same year."

"Zeek, I'm sorry," says Gloria.

"Yeah, sorry man," joins Tre. "I didn't know."

"Then last year Chrissy got all sick. At first, the doctors thought it was pneumonia. Then they began to change their diagnosis. Some said it was Gehrig's Disease. Others said a rare form of leukemia. They even put her on radiation but none of 'em really knew. All they could tell me was that she was getting worse."

The memories are so vivid. It's not until now that I realize I've never told this to anyone. "A week or two ago, Chrissy's body completely shut down. The docs finally gave up on her and said—said I should make final arrangements. Well, everybody 'cept this one chaplain at the hospital. Anyways, the next day, Chrissy is up playing as if nothing ever happened. They couldn't find anything wrong with her. It was like…"

"Like a miracle…" Gloria smiles.

"Well all I know is I won't—I can't lose her again. She's all I got. And I'm not gonna let you two get me involved in some sort—" Movement outside my window catches my attention. "What's going on?"

The street is flooded with cars and people. Tre slows as traffic comes to a near stand-still. "Looks like Sin City is extra swoll' tonight."

"You mean that old warehouse they turned into a nightclub?" Gloria asks.

"Yep."

She watches as people fill the street. "My goodness. What's so special about it?"

"Sin City?" Tre asks in surprise. "The place is hot, no doubt."

He honks and waves as high skirts and low tops flood the road.

"Typical," Gloria mumbles, folding her arms.

"Should've known lover boy had been here," I say under my breath.

"Wait a minute, what's today?" Tre asks.

"Twenty-fourth. Why?"

"Oh yeah, that's right. Ya boy, Jason Bale is supposed to be in the building tonight."

"The movie star?"

"Yep. And looks like all these hunnies are out just for him."

"He's not all that," frowns Gloria. "Trust me."

"Hater is sooo not your color," blabs Tre.

Jason Bale. Now that's someone I actually wouldn't mind meeting. "He's the one bringing all those jobs to the city, right?"

Tre glances back in my direction. "That's what I heard—well speak of the devil."

People erupt as an all-white stretched Hummer pulls up. A massive man steps from the elongated vehicle. I remember seeing him on the news. He wears a white blazer, white shirt, and blue jeans. His shirt, mostly unbuttoned, hints at his ripped frame. Next, four security personnel exit the limo. Varying in size and shape, the four men all wear similar white suit coats, with the exception of one. The guy with the mohawk and torn sleeves. I remember him too. Dark tinted sunglasses protrude from each of the men's faces.

Jason Bale emerges from the Hummer. The crowd of twenty-somethings goes wild. Along with some who look too old to fit in. I'm not the star-struck type but I must admit, this is quite something to watch. Jason Bale seems to take it all in stride. He mingles with the crowd as his bodyguards watch intently.

"Are you ready to party?!" the actor shouts to onlookers.

The mob erupts. One man definitely seems out of place as he pines for Bale.

"Mr. Bale! Please sir, one moment of your time!" says the older man as he scratches his way through the crowd. The man who looks to be in his sixties is too old to be carrying on like this. Even Jason Bale takes notice, waving to the man.

"Everyone will get a chance to party with Bale!" the actor yells, referring to himself in third person. Guess he really is a star.

"This is ridiculous," says Gloria.

"What?" says Tre. "I kind of like it. I mean he's not Tre TNT Turner but it's kind of hot."

Gloria rolls her eyes. "Give me a break."

I agree.

"Look at that old man," says Tre. "He's persistent. Wonder who he is?"

Sporting bifocals and a dinner jacket with patches on the elbows, the out-of-place chap presses his way towards the idol.

"Bale!" he yells, approaching as close as the guards will allow.

The celeb smiles as he responds, "In the flesh!"

The man's demeanor changes. "You are an abomination! You must be stopped!"

Bale grins as he turns his back. The older man reaches into his speckled blazer.

"He's got a gun!" yells someone from the crowd.

People panic as the obsessed fan pulls out a bottle filled with some sort of liquid and splashes it over Bale's back. Two of the celebrity's beefy guards immediately subdue the man. Bale carefully wipes the foreign substance from his neck. "What the... what is this?"

Pushed to the ground, the man looks up. "Holy water, you demon!"

The actor smirks. "I rather you had a gun. Now get him out of here!"

Two of Bale's security personnel place the lunatic in the stretched Hummer and speed off as the celebrity and his largest bodyguard enter the club. The two remaining guards patrol the outside of the club as they scour the crowd.

"Did you guys see that?" Tre asks.

"Yeah," says Gloria. "I wonder what that was all about?"

"Just another crazy," I say. "This world's full of 'em."

Gloria turns and looks at me. "I'm not so sure about that—wait a minute…I feel…something."

Tre flexes his shoulders. "You're not alone."

Unfortunately, he's right. They're not by themselves. I feel it too. Adrenaline rushes through my body. It's like I've gained a sixth sense. Like Tre, I flex my fingers. *Just like the police car.* I try to shake off the feeling, but nothing seems to work. Gloria sits up in the front passenger seat. She peers out though Tre's window, almost amazed. "Now tell me you guys see that?"

Part of me doesn't even want to look. Tre nods his head, "I'm there with ya, Glo."

Reluctantly, I push my body to turn. A ghastly haze reflects off the profiles of Bale's men. With neutral undertones, its color seems to reflect that of their white coats. In cycles, the smoke-like substance lingers momentarily, evaporates, and starts the process all over. If I didn't know any better, I'd say the men were on fire. The two do a final check before entering the club. The smoke-like matter follows.

"My God."

"Funny thing is, no one seems to notice. Everyone else is carrying on as normal."

"It's amazing."

"I wonder if the great Jason Bale knows he's got Nightmare on Elm Street working for him?"

"He's a prick," says Gloria. "But I think we should go check it out. Someone could be in danger."

"Wow," Tre grins. "I thought you would've been on the conservative side after going toe to toe with that thing in the park."

"Yeah, I agree we should know more about what we're getting into. But just like earlier, someone's life could be on the line."

"I agree, Glo. What about you, Zeek?"

I see it all too well no matter how much I don't want to admit it. "Just drive Tre," I say, looking out the opposite window.

"Huh?" Tre asks, now turning halfway around in his seat. "Are you kidding me? Tell me you didn't see that."

"Look, it's none of our business."

"None of our business?" Tre counters. "What if we said, none of our business when that thing tried to run off with your daughter?!"

What do they expect me to say? This is not my battle. I didn't ask for any of this. Besides, I can't tell who's good or what's evil. Everyone seems a little nuts, if you ask me. "Look, do what you want. I'll walk the rest of the way. Thanks for the ride."

Out of the car, Tre shouts to me from the window. "For real, Zeek? Really? Glad it wasn't my daughter in that park."

Disregarding his last comment, I continue to walk down the congested parkway. I briefly glance back to catch a glimpse of Tre and Gloria running towards the club. They can play superhero all they want. I've got a lot more on my plate to deal with.

A half-mile down the road, Tre's words continue to pound in the folds of my brain. *What if we said none of our business when that thing tried to run off with your daughter?!"*

"He could've kept on driving but noooooo," I say aloud. And they didn't have to go in that club. No matter how hard I try to ignore my thoughts, I can't ignore the senses that begin to flare back up in me. As I look at my hands, I feel a power, a strength beckoning my mind to give the go-ahead to join them. *Just keep walking, Zeek.*

These powers now ignore my rejection as they take over. Images flash in front of me, just like before, but this time more controlled. In what feels like slow motion, I see people fighting. Now, Gloria as she falls from a second story balcony. And just like that, the images are gone. But not the power. My heart accelerates. Adrenaline fills my veins.

It compels me north.

Back to Sin City.

"Hey you can't skip!"

"Sue me," I jab, as Tre and I wrangle through the line.

"Whoa, whoa, whoa," says a large bouncer at the front door.

"Hey Big Pete," says Tre. "It's me!"

"Tre! My man! Give me some love!"

The bouncer lifts Tre straight in the air with a playful bear hug. By the look of Tre's face, it's only playful for the bouncer.

"Okay man. That's...enough...love," Tre manages to squeeze out.

"You trying to get in and party with your boy, Bale?" asks the hefty Samoan.

"You know it, Big Pete." Tre turns my way. "Me and my friend here. We just wanna get in and get out. We'll only be here for like 15 minutes—tops."

Big Pete shakes his head. "I don't know, Tre. Everyone is supposed to pay tonight. Besides, isn't your girlfriend a little underdressed? I mean...sweats?"

What? Girlfriend? Please. And what's wrong with what I have on? Some of these girls could learn a thing or two about modesty. "Excuse me?" rattles off my lips. Tre blocks my view. "Peeeeeeeteeeey," he grins. "Who was the best offensive lineman in the conference?"

"Come on," smiles the wide-body oaf. "Everyone knows the answer to that. I was!"

"Right! And because of that great protection, who led the conference in rushing yards?"

"You."

"Right again my friend!"

My patience wanes as the two continue their rhetoric. *Girl-friend?* Please.

"See, without you there would be no me. Without me there would be no you. We're practically joined at the hip. Now I tell you what, how 'bout I come to your nephew's pop warner practice and run some drills?"

"They would love that, Tre. My nephew wears your college number. Alright go 'head. You and your girlfriend have a good time."

"I am not his girlfriend!"

Tre cuts me off as he drags me in. "Thanks, Big Pete!"

Inside, my irritation is suspended by the flaring of my senses, although not those of the supernatural kind. From the outside, Sin City doesn't look like much; a long dark building with large cast-iron doors. But just behind those same doors reveal a million-dollar production of multi-colored lights and extreme decibels of sound. The main floor reveals an oasis of people gyrating, almost trance-like, to eardrum splitting…*music*. At least I suppose that's what they call it. Why people would want to pay money to stand shoulder to shoulder and get drinks spilled on them I will never understand.

"So, this is what you call—"

Sound jolts through my head. It's like someone turned up the already deafening noise. But not just the music. The talking! Covering my ears, it takes everything in me not to pass out.

"What's wrong?" Tre shouts.

"It's like— I can hear hundreds of conversations all at once!"

Tre takes me by the arm. "Focus!"

My head is flooded with voices. I can hear people as they place orders at the bar, tacky pick-up lines, even a Vietnamese couple as they argue about what time to leave…in Vietnamese!

"I'm trying!" I shout.

Tre's right. It's like I've developed a new muscle. The more I focus, the more the voices subside. I test it out on a nearby couple. Focusing on just them, I can hear their conversation over the shrill of Electronica.

"Glo! Upstairs! Bale's guys."

"Yeah. And isn't that Jason Bale with—Tre!"

"What's wrong?"

Cupping my ears, I answer. "I think—I think I can hear them."

"Up there?" Tre replies. "Wow."

Bale and entourage sit in a roped-off section overhead. Guards position themselves along a glass balcony as they watch down below. Young women line an extended sofa with the movie star seated perfectly in the middle. Two of Bale's men in white fill the remainder of the couch. The largest one—for some reason I remember his name from the interview—*Amnon*, stands next to the sofa.

Most people see farther than they hear, but fortunately that's not the case for me. At least not anymore. And what I hear next isn't as startling once it resonates in my mind.

"I—I think Jason Bale is one of them."

"What? Jason Bale? Are you sure?"

I nod, still trying to pick up the conversation.

"Tell me. What are they saying?"

I repeat the star's words line for line. *"The world. The best thing ever created by the Other. His creation. My conquest. But soon, every son and daughter of Adam will bear the Mark of Bale."*

Bale raises his left arm. His Angels join by raising their fists. From our viewpoint, it looks as if the giant rips open his once buttoned shirt. A tattoo of some sort is sprawled across his chest. It's too far to make out the details of it.

"The tattoo..." Tre mumbles as Bale stands.

"Should I keep going?" I ask.

"Yes!" he answers. "Focus!"

I continue mouthing Jason Bale's words. *"My ministers will spread the gospel of Bale! The young will be generals in our army and the old...cadets. They will happily bear my Mark and we shall rule freely! We will show them another way. A way of—"*

Bale stops and looks around. His countenance grows serious. "One of his henchmen is asking what's wrong," I report to Tre. "They call him, *Lord.*"

"We'll see about that."

"I sense the presence of the Other," Bale continues. *"Perfect."*

"Wait a minute. He just said, 'I sense the presence of the Other.' Think he could be talking about us?"

"Only one way to find out," Tre says, walking towards the elevator. "Let's go say hi."

Upstairs, Tre steps out first. A moderately sized bouncer stands guard in front of the VIP entrance. "Hey!" he yells. "Where's your wrist—"

Tre lightly shoves the bouncer in the chest with one hand. The force effortlessly drives the man into a nearby wall just as two of Bale's men approach.

"Sir, we're gonna have to ask you to leave."

"Not until I holla at cha boy, Jason," mugs Tre, cracking his knuckles.

"Bale is not signing autographs at—"

Bale, as everyone seems to enjoy calling him, motions to his guards. "Let them come," he waves. His men give way. The celebrity grins as we approach. "Sit, my friends. You're pretty strong, my man. I could use a guy like you on my team."

"I don't think so," Tre murmurs under his breath.

"So, what can I do for you two? Autograph? Who should I make it out to?"

Close up, I can see why many would find him attractive, although it does nothing for me. Maybe that's because I can see him for what he really is.

Literally.

"Tre…"

"Yeah Glo, I see. I don't believe it."

A grayish black haze slowly exudes from Jason Bale's profile. The same shape-shifting vapor we saw in the park. The same mist seen hovering around Bale's security team now radiates from his being. The Shadow. The substance almost seems to have a persona of its own, as it pulsates in and out of his skin. Bale's Shadow is more sinister in tone than the others I've witnessed. The very look of it causes my senses to flare. The supernatural kind this time.

"Cut the act, Jason Bale, or whatever your name is," Tre says, balling his fists. "I can see what you really look like."

The actor/demon, formerly known as Bale, smiles. "Yeah, the movies will do that to ya. Guess my make-up artist has the Midas touch."

His men appear antsy, pacing back and forth. The tattoo that covers Amnon's massive chest recaptures Tre's attention. "Hey, big guy. Nice tat. Where'd you get it?"

Amnon grunts as Bale and the others laugh.

"My brother had a fresh one just like it," Tre finishes. "Right before someone murdered him. Sure I couldn't *persuade* you to tell me?"

Bale's demeanor changes, as does that of his minions. He gives them a command in another language. It sounds primal at best, but in some weird way I can understand it as if it were English. Guess that's what I do.

"Hey Tre. He told his boys to get rid of us."

"Did he now? Well tell him this." Tre stares straight up at the more-than-seven-feet-tall giant. "I ain't going nowhere 'til I find out about that tat."

Tre's words infuriate the beastly man— or whatever he is. The Shadow swells around his torso as well as the others'.

"So, you have the Gift, little girl," Bale says, stepping in front of his guard dog.

Is this the Other's way of trying to stop me? 'Cause if so, his tactics have become quite pitiful. I haven't seen any like you in what? Forty years?"

"Enough of the chit-chat!" yells Tre. "I wanna know about that tattoo!"

"You mean my Mark?" Bale smirks confidently. "The Mark of Bale? Why, all my Angels bear my Mark!" The men raise their fists, exposing the same symbol tattooed and branded on the underside of their wrists. Amnon beats on his exposed chest like a crazed warrior. "And you can wear it too, young man."

Tre's eyes narrow. "Ain't no way in Hell."

"Don't be so sure. Besides, do you even know who I truly am?"

"A horrible actor?" I say.

The translucent haze engulfs Bale's body.

"Yeah, with a helluva five o'clock shadow," says Tre.

"Amusing," Bale smiles as he circles us. "So, you can understand the language of the Familiar and—how shall I say—see me in all my *glory*. And for what? You don't even know why you're here, do you?"

Personally, I've seen all I need. "I know you're evil. It saturates you."

"Evil? Hmph. Why do you consider me evil? Because I want my birth-given right? That makes me evil? What about those you trust who lie to you and make you believe something all your life only to find out it's not true. Are they evil?"

Immediately my thoughts go to A'ma. But he couldn't possibly know. Could he?

"Shut up! You don't know anything about me."

"I know enough, now don't I?" he says, now standing eye to eye. I hadn't noticed how close his steps had become.

"The gifts you have now are mere…parlor tricks. With your courage and your irrefutable beauty, I could show you things you possibly couldn't imagine."

He stands so close. I know I should push away. But I don't.

"Glo! Snap out of it!" I hear Tre shout. He's right. Maybe Bale is stronger than I give him credit for. I cannot take him casually. This is spiritual warfare in its truest form.

"And what can you show me?" I whisper back.

"Anything," he says, slightly caressing my left hand.

"Anything?"

"I…am…Bale."

"Okay, Bale. What about this?"

Firmly, I grip his hand. Squeezing down with all my might, I feel strength like never before. I watch, admittedly with a sense of delight, as he cringes in pain. Suddenly his face grows demented. Blackish veins rise to his pores. The Shadow swirls around his torso. Finally getting my chance, I shove the possessed actor. The supernatural heave sends him colliding into the couch.

"That's my girl!" shouts Tre.

Before I can comment, Bale spits out the words, "Destroy them!"

The Shadow rises around his five Angels. Each man manifests his own unique vapory aura. My senses prepare for what is sure to take place. Ironically, the techno music blasting through the club is a good fit for the melee that's about to begin…

BOOOOM!

The mohawked Angel rushes Tre with two fists to the chest, sending him soaring through a nearby wall. Dust and debris fly everywhere. The demented bodyguard laughs as he brushes his hands. I want to call for Tre but there's no time as I engage in my own battle.

The shortest of Bale's men is very articulate in some form of martial arts. It takes everything in me to keep up as we exchange blows. But somehow, I find myself performing moves I've never known about, let alone attempted. We go back and forth with flurries of elbows and forearms. His skillful hands move so fast I lose focus on the leg sweep coming my way. Hitting the ground, I move away just in time from an impending chair to the face. It crashes down just inches from my widened eyes, shattering into pieces. Jumping to my feet, I gather myself. Four Angels stand …waiting. I've got to even the odds.

Waiting no more, they attack.

I use another chair to block one of the Angel's kicks, swinging it around and landing it in its upright position. Using the same momentum to land in the chair feet first, I jump to an adjacent table, landing on my hands. How I do it, I don't know.

I just do.

Somersaulting from the table, my legs land directly around the neck of another opponent. I clench my core diverting all of my weight to my upper body. With Bale's Angel still in tow, my body flips, sending him over the balcony to the dance floor below.

"Three to one. Now that's better." I do a little smirking of my own.

"Hey, Mr. T! Over here!"

"Tre?!"

"In the flesh!"

"Now is that all you got?!" Tre yells, emerging from the space behind the wall.

The mohawked Balak turns as the Shadow thickens around him.

"You guys should really see somebody about that!" Tre mocks.

Balak rushes Tre again with both fists out front. This time, Tre dodges the double punch, grabbing Balak around the fore-arms. He swings the Angel around repeatedly. Finally, Tre lets go, sending him twenty feet into a table.

"Got that one from John Cena!" Tre shouts, referring to the popular wrestling star. He really does watch too much TV. Although I must admit, I'm a fan of the wrestler myself.

"Thought you were gonna be in that wall forever," I say over my shoulder as we stand back to back.

"You know me," he says. "Gotta be fashionably late."

"What are you waiting for!" screams Bale. "Hantos! Rapha! Take care of them!"

With one Angel somewhere on the first floor, Balak under a table, and Amnon by Bale's side, the two remaining Angels head straight for us. Tre battles the tall dark-skinned Angel with long dreadlocks. *Rapha.* The Shadow oozes from each of his thickened strands of hair as he sways back and forth like a Caribbean kick-boxer.

Me and the martial artist, *Hantos*, resume our battle. We stand eye level before he emits a loud sound, followed by a vicious wave of punches. I try my best to land a blow in between his assaults, but it hardly matters. Anna was right. These guys are much stronger than the Tax Collector from the park.

The force of his strike throws me into the clutches of Amnon. A frenzied smile forms on the giant's face as he lifts me by the neck with one hand. His fingers coil around my throat, tightening by the second. I fight to free myself from the hold but—but his power is too much. I can feel the last few gasps of air as they leave my lungs. Before I pass out, I can hear Tre say, "Put her down!" And that's when I go over the railing.

Moments later, I come to in the arms of what looks like, "Zeek? Is that you?"

"Yeah. Looks you guys could use a hand. You okay?"

"I'll be alright," I groan. "Tre needs some help. Those things are strong. And Jason Bale is one of them."

"What?" Zeek asks with a look of disbelief.

"Yeah," I wheeze. "Go figure."

"Hey, you're having a hard time breathing—"

"Go. I'll be fine. Help Tre. Just gotta catch my breath."

Patrons of the popular nightspot scatter everywhere as the melee continues. The VIP section is completely demolished. Zeek looks towards the staircase but people overwhelm the small area as they scurry for downstairs. He sets his sights on the second story partition. It's easily a twenty-foot jump. Without hesitation, he steps back, runs, jumps from a chair, and lands on the partition itself.

———T H E A S S I G N E D———

TRE

"GLO!!!"

The giant throws Gloria over the railing like a rag-doll. If she's gone, I'll kill them all.

"Come on!"

Anger fuels me as I take on three of Bale's men at one time. The dreadlocked Angel swings at me but I grab his fist with my left hand while landing a crushing right elbow to his temple. Working my way towards the giant, I use the same elbow to pound another, standing behind me, in the rib cage. The beast-like man-thing smiles, probably hoping I make it through the rest of his bunch. Don't worry, I plan on it.

"Can I join the party?"

"Zeek!"

Before any of them can get the jump, Zeek leaps over Amnon, kicking him in the back of the head before landing directly next to me.

"Boy am I glad to see you!"

"I've been getting that a lot lately."

The giant bellows loudly, but his master, Bale, won't let him leave his side.

"Gloria?!"

"She's okay!"

I nod as I lift the small Asian demonoid-fighter by his collar, flipping him over my head. He gave Gloria hell, but I'll show him something. The bodyguard lands back-first into a table. "And I got that one from Stone Cold Steve Austin!"

"Take care of this, Amnon, and meet me at the site," says Bale as his overgrown henchman nods. Finally! Bale rushes for the back stairwell but I'll get to him later. Zeek and I temporarily subdue two more baddies as Bale makes his escape. Amnon points and smiles as he waits his turn.

Showtime.

"I got this guy, Zeek. You go after Mr. Hollywood."

Zeek looks the massive bodyguard over. "Uhh, you sure?"

"Yeah! I can heal myself, remember?!"

Zeek sizes up the behemoth of a man once more. "Yeah, but you've never healed from *that* before."

"Now!"

"I'm going!" Zeek shouts back, running towards the emergency stairwell.

I set my eyes on the one they call Amnon. He motions 'come on' with his large hands.

"Not much of a talker are ya?" I say, balling my fists. I watch as the Shadow hovers around Amnon's massive frame. "Enough of this…"

I rush straight for the monster. The brute catches me mid-run with one hand and lifts me by the throat. I gasp for air as my legs dangle underneath. Growing dizzy, I begin to lose consciousness as the enraged giant utters one word…

"SLEEEEP!!!"

Not sure how long I was out—just a few seconds—but the giant is already halfway out the stairwell. I can't let Zeek take on Bale plus this guy. "Hey big ugly! Didn't you just hear me say, I…can …HEAL…myself?"

Footsteps can be heard as his oversized body makes its way back up the stairs.

"Come on now. You gon' have to do better than that!"

Like an ignited cannonball, the colossal warrior charges straight for me. But this time I wait. With his strike imminent, I dodge to the left using a football maneuver, and land an awesome blow to his cheek. I watch as his face buckles.

My celebration is premature. Without looking, Amnon serves a fierce backhand to my chest. It sends me flying back, crashing through another wall. Although my body can heal itself, the immediate sting of his hand and the impact of the wall are debilitating.

Thankfully I *can* heal myself, as seconds later I reemerge from the debris, running straight for the giant. I sound a war cry as I close in.

"AAARRHH!!!"

My shoulder viciously collides with the giant's sternum. The momentum carries us through the second-story glass balcony. Our bodies hurl themselves to the ground below climaxing with a violent…

THUD.

As I recover, I watch as the Shadow slowly dissolves. Amnon lays unconscious on what used to be the dance floor. Thankfully I landed on top of him.

"Tre. Tre!" I hear someone call. Guess I haven't knocked all the cobwebs loose yet. "Tre. You okay?"

"Glo? Is that you?"

"Yeah," says a voice behind me. I turn to see her still clinching her ribcage. She slides closer.

"Are you okay?"

"I'll make it," she tries to smile. "Looks like you held your own."

I finally shake it off as I make my way to my feet. "Well, you know me. TNT, baby!"

"Yeah, yeah, whatever."

"But seriously, I was impressed back there," I say. "You kicked some serious a-" Taking a glance towards the ceiling I rephrase my statement. "Okay, I'm trying. Uhh, you did…good."

"Thanks," Gloria grins.

"I almost thought Movie Star got to ya."

"Who me?" she frowns. "Never. Besides, he's not my type."

"I bet…"

Gloria tries to laugh but it seems to only intensify her pain.

"Your ribs?" I say.

"Yeah, took a good one."

"Let me touch you," I say, moving closer.

"What?!" Gloria winces. "You just don't quit, do you?!"

"Huh?" What she means, or rather what she thinks I mean, finally registers. "Oh, nooo!" I shout with my hands. "Look, just trust me. Seriously."

Lightly, I place my hands on Gloria's rib cage. Bones crackle as they mend themselves. After a moment or two, she takes a deep breath.

"Better?" I ask.

"The pain. It's—it's gone. Thank you."

"No problem," I smile. "Anything for you, Glo." I can tell by her look that she's not sure what to make of me quite yet. Heck, I'm not even sure what I meant as I find myself staring through her eyes. I fought for her like she was…mine.

Gloria ends the moment by playfully punching me in the chest. "Wait. Where's Zeek?" she asks. I had nearly forgotten myself.

"He went after Bale. The roof!"

——THE ASSIGNED——

ZEEK

Jason Bale is one of them? Can't be. Yet, I find myself engaged in battle with the famous actor. But one thing's for sure. He does have some sort of power or agility as he evades my punches. His movement appears effortless, as if he isn't even trying.

"Why do you fight me, son of Adam?" he says. "Do you even know?"

"Your crew tried to hurt my friends!" I answer with a swing.

The celebrity barely moves his head, dodging the blow.

"We did not cause that," he says. "Your friends came for us. How long have you even known the others?"

"I know one of those things tried to take my daughter!" I shout. The statement helps take focus off his last question. After all, how long have I known them?

"I assure you, I am not in the business of taking little children," he answers.

"Save it!" I shout. He blocks another one of my accelerated crosses.

"Fight!" I yell, tired of the slap boxing.

"I am not here to fight you, son of Adam. Am I not that different from you?"

For the first time, I hesitate as my fists loosen. The absence of Jason Bale's shadow makes him appear...human.

"I choose my own path. I don't believe in something predetermining my fate. Isn't that what you believe?" His words. The look on his face as he speaks. It all causes me to lower my guard. After all, why am I attacking a man that's not trying to defend himself? That thing in the park went after me. And Bale's men? Well, they are his security. What else are they supposed to do? But this guy doesn't seem like either.

"You don't even know why you pursue me, do you?" he asks. He's right. "What sense does that make. Tell me. What do you desire?"

I step closer, attempting to learn more of the entity that stands before me. "Who are you?"

"A man, just as you. A man who wants everything and I'm not ashamed to admit it." As he approaches, his words grow softer. "Yes, I am different, much like you, but there's so much you don't know. Let me show you another way. Then you can choose your own path."

Before I can contemplate his words, Tre and Gloria burst through the rooftop door. Seeing me and the star standing toe to toe, Tre rushes straight for Bale.

"So, what's it's gonna be?" he asks, Tre sprinting our way.

"I don't—I don't know you," I murmur while looking towards the others. "At least I've seen what they can do."

Just as Tre is about to pounce, Bale stretches out his arm. Black smoke-like vapor shoots from his hand. But this mist is more concentrated than the Shadow. Taking the shape of an elongated arm and hand, it stretches out and wraps itself around Tre's neck, stopping him in his tracks. He struggles with the gas-like limb.

"Let him go!" I shout.

Bale looks to me, his face growing increasingly dark. "Did you not say, 'at least you've seen what they can do'?"

Bale raises his arm, in turn causing the vapor-like appendage to rise. It lifts Tre off his feet. "Well let me formally introduce myself." The Shadow engulfs Bale's profile.

"I...AM...BALE!!!"

Tre gasps for air as the Shadow-hand chokes life from his throat.

"I did not seek you out," says Bale. "You came for me!"

I've seen enough. I can't just stand here and watch as Tre loses consciousness.

"That's enough!" I yell, my fist aiming straight for Bale's head. It misses. Vapor shoots from Bale's remaining hand, piercing straight through my chest like a sword. Feeling like I just got hit by a truck, it takes everything to maintain consciousness.

The last thing I remember hearing is,

"I…AM…BALE! Lord of this world!"

——THE ASSIGNED——

GLORIA

I watch as Bale wields his true power. He laughs as his vapor arms immobilize Tre and Zeek. Their bodies dangle. Struggling is useless. Our powers also seem useless as we finally face true evil. *A Familiar.* Just like Prophetess Anna said, 'our countenance does not wear the fatigue of battling a Familiar.' Well it does now.

My senses finally react, and I run back to the stairwell. Bale's laughter heightens, probably thinking I've retreated. Instead, I start working on the pipe railing attached to the staircase. "Come on!" I grunt, ripping the 6-foot railing from its cement plaster. I run straight for the door and heave the long railing like a javelin, directly at Bale's head. It spirals through the air as it heads straight for his temple.

Direct hit!

Bale falls to the ground. It was almost too easy. His Shadow dispels as the black vapor-like limbs evaporate, dropping Zeek and Tre to the ground. "Guys!" I yell, rushing to their side.

"I'm okay," Tre says, already beginning to heal. "Check on Zeek."

He moans in pain but seems to be coherent. "Ughh, feels like I just got stabbed."

Back on his feet, Tre crouches over Zeek. "Let me help you." Relief comes almost immediately.

"Wow," marvels Zeek. "So that stuff does really work."

"Hey guys," I interrupt. "Bale. He's…" The Familiar has vanished.

"Quick! Glo, Zeek, can you see something? Hear anything?"

Zeek shakes his head. "I've got nothing."

"Glo. Focus." says Tre. "You can hear things like a mile away."

Still shook up from the battle, it's a little hard focusing, but I try, nevertheless.

"Wait! I think I've got something."

I go into a zone, reciting the words that dart past my ears.

"Have the Three returned my Lord?"

"It appears so. Such a feeble attempt at opposition by the Other. I see why He and my father have fought for so long. They're both so… predictable. Contact our Ministers. I must know more about this new Three of Three. They are—"

The voices stop. "That's it," I say to Tre and Zeek. "It's like he blocked it, or maybe they're out of my range."

"Well let's go!" yells Tre. "They can't be that far."

"No," I say. "We need to know more about what we're dealing with. Bale nearly killed you two. This is not just another guy from the park. This is something bigger."

"I agree," says Zeek.

"Yeah, maybe," Tre concedes.

The faint sounds of police sirens wail in the distance.

"We need to get out of here," says Zeek. "Besides, I got a few more questions for your fairy godmother."

"Zeek…" I smirk.

"Sorry. I mean the Ms. Prophetess lady or whatever…"

CHAPTER 17 – ZEEK

"I think we found your Familiar," says Tre. Now back at the suite, he throws a Forbes magazine on the coffee table. Jason Bale's pic is sprawled across the front. The woman they call Prophetess Anna, picks up the publication. "Jason Bale," she reads. "Self-made millionaire, actor, businessman…where will he stop? Politics?"

"Yeah," nods Gloria. "They forgot to mention demon."

Concern sets across Anna's face. "He's…back. Why did I not see this?"

"Wait a minute. What do you mean, back?" asks Tre.

"This…Jason Bale," says Anna. "He is the Familiar I spoke of."

"You mean the one you said was destroyed, what…forty years ago? But this guy can't be more than forty years old, himself."

"Same spirit. Albeit, different body." Anna rubs the front cover intently. "And those eyes. He has the same eyes."

Okay, this is getting to be a bit much. Jason Bale? A demon? The Head demon for that matter. True, I've seen a few things, but I'm having a hard time wrapping my thoughts around this. This guy is handing out jobs for Pete's sake. What is she not telling us? "So, this guy's a freakin' movie star and you're telling me he's some sort of demon? I'm not so sure about all this." Before I know it, I'm pacing the floor.

"Believe me, Zeek," says Anna. "It is true."

"So, what does he want?" asks Gloria.

"Everything."

"Come again?"

"Yes…everything. The world as we know it. Lucifer rebelled in Heaven and was cast into Hell. Bale or rather, *Beelzebub* rebelled in Hell, so he has decided to make Earth his home. Tre gauges our expressions before making his next statement. "Okay, so there's God, the Devil, and this guy?"

"Yes," continues Anna. "His banishment here was meant to be punishment, however, Bale began to see the world as the ultimate conquest. He no longer desired the province of his father, Hell. But rather the creation of his father's Father…God's Earth. And now the culture benefits Bale more than our kind, which has allowed the Persuaded to swell in number. They must be stopped before they become uncontainable."

"My brother had the same tattoo on his arm as Bale and his crew," says Tre. "These Persuaded or whatever they are— they killed my brother. I just know it. And if Jason Bale is behind it …he's gotta go."

Gloria touches Tre's hand. "I'm sorry, Tre. I didn't know."

"I agree, Tre," says Anna, her hand now resting on Tre's shoulder. "But we must not let our emotions influence us. Bale will prey on that. He used it against my circle."

"Your circle?" asks Gloria. "You mean there were Three of you, like us?"

Anna walks towards the window. "Yes, my child."

"So where are the other two?" Tre asks.

"Only I remain."

"What happened?"

"That story in its entirety is not for this time—"

"Hold up, now," I interrupt. "We deserve to know something. And what did you mean by, 'those eyes'? Was it Bale or not?"

Anna finally faces us. "Just know Bale was able to separate the Three of Three. It then became much easier to take us out."

And this is where all my reservations lie. In the fact that a strange woman I've never met before today, can tell me I've been chosen as a warrior in a supernatural battle, but relay no information about my so-called enemy. It just doesn't make sense. Why should we trust her when she openly keeps secrets? Even Jason Bale himself said he did not seek us out. In fact, it was the other way around.

"Wow…" says a cynical Tre. Looks like I'm not the only one with questions. "So, you mean to tell me we've got to try and stop some demon you and your Super Friends couldn't even kill? What else are you not telling us, *Prophetess?*"

"Tre, Gloria, Zeek. I assure you, this is not my desire. It was not supposed to happen like this, all at once. Your Gifts, the battles, Bale, everything. All I can do, my children, is prepare you for what lies ahead." Anna circles us. "Individually, you possess power, however, your powers are at their strongest when you abide together. Free your mind of every weight that besets you. How you got here no longer matters."

As Anna continues to talk, I can't help but wonder, *how did I get here?* I mean, I understand Tre's vendetta for wanting to take out Bale's men but how does that concern me? Other than defend himself in a fight we started, what has the star done to me? Heck, just a week ago, I wanted to work for the man. And I don't even see how the situation with little Chrissy at the park could be a bi-product of Jason Bale. Yeah, he's different, like us, but does that make him our enemy? Thoughts, not visions, flood my head. I'm not like Tre. And I'm sure as heck not like Gloria or the Anna lady. Which produces the question, *why am I here?*

——T H E A S S I G N E D——

TRE

'*How you got here no longer matters…*'

But that's just it. How did we get here? I've never believed in coincidences and if God did truly select us for this battle, that must mean he knew the Persuaded would take my brother. And if he knew that, why didn't he allow me to help him? And if anyone should know, shouldn't his helper, the Prophetess?

"Come on, Prophetess," I say. "You've gotta give me more. That's the one thing I can't stop thinking about."

"I do not understand," she answers.

"Those *THINGS* kill my brother, I hold him in my arms, and I can't do nothing about it. Now, all of a sudden, I've got the power to heal people? I mean why didn't God give me this power two weeks earlier?"

Anna answers back firmly. "God's agenda is not of our own."

"Now that's what I'm talking about!" I shout back. "Since I was a kid it's been, don't question God, God works in mysterious ways. Well, I think it's about time HE did some explaining. Hell, he's asking me to be a pawn in his war. My brother dies in my arms, now I've got the power to…wait a minute?" I lock my eyes on Zeek. Then Gloria. As I approach, she watches me expressly, trying to gauge my intentions. "Glo, what happened to you?"

"What are you talking about?" she frowns.

"Come on Glo! Before you got these powers!" I feel myself growing aggressive, but I don't care. I have to know more. "Something happened to you, didn't it?!"

"Hey man, just let her be," says Zeek.

"Noooo," I reply. "Just let me prove my point. I'll get to you in a minute." Refocusing my attention to Gloria, I try to quiet the increasing anger bubbling inside. "Okay, Glo, look, I'm sorry, but please just tell us if something life changing happened in your life right before you got these…gifts."

Gloria stares straight through me. I've hit a nerve. "I—I found out…" she stutters. "I never knew my father. I mean not a phone call, a description, his name—nothing in nineteen years." She looks towards the window. "Only to find out a man in my church whom I've known for years—respected—looked up to is actually …well, you know…"

"Whoa," I say, taking a step back. Even I wasn't expecting that. "Sorry Glo. How did you find out?" Eyeing me once more she sighs, "I overheard my mother say—"

"You OVERHEARD," I repeat, cutting to the chase. I knew it! "And now, of course, you have the gift of…hearing. Wow."

"You're a jerk."

That may be true but somebody's gotta get to the bottom of this. "Look, I'm sorry, but this has to be said. Now go ahead Zeek and close us out," I say, taking a seat on the couch. "What else has been going, on besides your daughter?" Zeek ignores me, opting to head for the door.

"I don't need this," he mumbles, but my words catch him before he can leave. "It's okay, Zeek. I'm sure by now we can piece it all together. Let's see. You can…see things, right? So, using God's twisted imagination, you probably failed to see something which caused harm to you or a loved one, right?"

Zeek's face grows blank, still incarcerated by my words. They finally loose him as he stares at me in disgust.

"Oh my God," says Gloria. "Your wife."

"That is enough, Tre!" shouts the Prophetess.

"Like Hell! Look, I hate to bring up family skeletons, but it had to be said! My brother gets murdered, she's crushed by some family secret, Zeek loses his wife, and for what? Just to get our attention? Hell, he could've sent a text message! That's not God."

The Prophetess gets in my face. "Who are you to say what is or is not like God?! This war is bigger than any of the combatants that wage in it!"

Ire rises in me as the normally docile woman steps even closer. I turn my back as not to have any sudden impulses. I'm not used to people being this close to me unless they're ready to go toe to toe.

Anna grabs me by the shoulder. "But you're right! God gives free will! Choices were made in each of those situations and choices were made in each of your lives as well! He did not initiate the misfortune of you and your family members' choices, he utilized them! Mankind's ability to choose is what makes him God!"

Like Zeek, I've heard enough as well. "Whatever," I say, fanning off Prophetess Anna's remarks. "I'm out of here." Before I can open the door, Anna blocks the entrance. "Will you let your brother die in vain?" she asks.

"What?!" I shout, my rage increasing by the second. It takes everything in me to remember this is a 60-year-old lady standing in front of me. Otherwise she would've been clocked by now. "Move Anna," I say slow and stern, making sure she hears and fully understands my temperament. "I don't wanna hurt you."

"Gloria's parents, Zeek, your brother, they all had a choice. And now YOU have a choice!"

"I'm only gonna ask you one more time," I say, grinding my teeth. "Move out of MY...WAY..."

"Or what, William Turner, III?!"

That's it! "Look! I said—"

——THE ASSIGNED——

GLORIA

Before Tre can even raise an arm, Anna barely thumps him with the tips of her fingers. The slight touch somehow throws Tre's 200-pound frame to the ground. Zeek and I watch in amazement as he lands on the coffee table, crushing it. My goodness, I didn't know she had such power.

"They've already taken your brother!" she yells. "Will you let them take your mother?! Your father?! We cannot let the enemy win!"

Still on the ground, tears begin to flow from Tre's eyes. "Martin! I'm so sorry!" he sobs. Even with his vile words, I recognize the torment he's under. He really believes he's the cause of his brother's death. I run to his side, because even I can't imagine what that feels like.

"Shh," I whisper. "It's okay, Tre."

"I know this hurts, my child," says Anna. "But this is bigger than any of us."

"So, what do you want me to do?" Tre sniffles before looking upwards. "What does he want me to do?"

Anna scans all of our eyes before answering.

"Believe."

* * *

Hours have passed since Tre's breakdown. I'm sure if it wasn't him first, it could've easily been me or Zeek with all that's gone on in the last couple of weeks. In the time since, Prophetess Anna has tried to bond with us as a group, discussing everything except our powers. Zeek's eyes seem distant but Anna has made sure to keep him in the exchange. Talks have centered around our families, careers—or lack of—even relationships—or lack of. She relinquishes little information concerning her own background, but still I feel more comfortable around her. She has a way with words, which I guess is a big contrast to A'ma, who usually just barks out orders. Even though she doesn't like to bring up her past, she lets us into her current thoughts, especially as the conversation shifts to Bale.

"I agree. Bale is a strategist. He does nothing without reason. We must find out the specifics of his plans before we can move further."

Zeek finally speaks up. "So, what's next for us?"

"We train, my child."

Tre shouts his somewhat annoying catch phrase. "Now that's what I'm talking about! So, what we got Prophetess? Oozis? 9-millimeters? Wait! Oooh, some sort of laser prototype gun, what?" Sounds like he's back to his old self.

"Not exactly, my child. Do not burden your mind with details at the moment. Take tonight and tomorrow to rest. We will begin training Monday at sundown."

"Cool," says Tre. "Well tomorrow is Sunday. Guess I could go to church."

"That is a great idea, Tre," agrees Prophetess Anna. "I'm sure your father would be proud."

"Not so sure about that."

"Trust me. His heart is ready to receive you. You are his child." Tre almost blushes at the comment. I guess in many ways we are alike. Stubborn, strong-willed, desiring our parent's approval.

"Would you mind if I visited as well?" asks the Prophetess.

"Sure, why not."

"Great. My children enjoy the next 36 hours. Monday morning, we will prepare our minds, bodies, and spirits for battle. Our enemy is formidable and we cannot take him lightly."

"I'll do some research on the web for Bale," I say. "Maybe I can find some info on what he's up to. So much of what he does is meant to get a public reaction."

"That is a novel idea, Gloria," says the prophetess. "Any information can be pivotal. Now be careful, my children. 'Til Monday. And Tre, I shall see *you* tomorrow."

Zeek and Tre make their way to the door. "Hey Glo, need a ride?" Tre asks.

"I'm good. I'll see you Monday," I smile. My grin comes across wider than I mean to convey.

"You bet you will," Tre smiles back as he leaves.

"Is there something you need, my child?"

"Huh?" I turn to see Anna grinning at me. There seems to be a lot of smiling going on.

"Well?" she waits. I tiptoe around the subject like a nervous kid.

"I...I was wondering if—could I stay here tonight, Anna?"

"And what about your mother?" she asks. "Is she not ailing?"

"A'ma? She'll be fine. Besides, I can leave when you head out for church tomorrow." Prophetess Anna seems to be thinking it over. "Please?" I ask, looking over her shoulder.

"I do not mind my child. As long as your affairs are in order."

I thank her by nodding and smiling.

"Besides," she adds. "Girls-night-in is always in order."

My eyes widen at Prophetess Anna's moment of levity.

I call A'ma to let her know I won't be coming home. Initially she snarls at my newfound attitude but a few quick reminders of her own recent conduct quiets her down. A knock at the apartment door cuts our conversation short. Although we hardly ever get visitors, I'm too afraid to stay on the phone and find out. The last time there was a knock on our front door it changed my life, and not necessarily for the better.

Hours later, Anna and I enjoy tea as we sit, legs crossed, on a soft, Italian leather couch. I've changed into a pair of her pajamas. They actually seem quite normal for the unconventional woman. She states she's never worn them, which almost leads me to believe, somehow, they were meant for me. Anna even sports a pair of footies. It's an understatement to say they contrast with her highly decorative golden colored pantsuit.

"So, you can just read people's minds?" I ask. Anna laughs, but the look on my face tells her I desire a serious answer.

"No," she smiles. "At least not in that manner. I see things—visions. But I am capable of reading individuals and that can tell me a lot." A subtle change happens in Anna's voice as a quick grin sets in the corner of her mouth. "And I mean a whhooole lot."

"What's that supposed to mean?" I ask.

"You know what I speak of. I was not always the woman you see today. I too was once young." She's right. Who am I fooling? "I mean, I don't know. One minute I can't stand him, the next, he's saving my life or doing something sweet."

Anna's smile widens. "I understand my child. Just keep your focus. You must serve as the balance between the Three. There will be times when your counterparts are distracted by pride or ego. After all, they can't help the fact they're *men*."

"Anna!" I laugh. I didn't see that coming. Prophetess Anna continues to grin as she pours us another cup of tea. "Focus, my child," she says. "So, about your father. Have you talked to him since that night?"

Her abrupt shift in conversation completely changes my demeanor. "For what?" I counter. "I have nothing to say to that man." Making my way to the other side of the room, Anna doesn't let up.

"My child, you must hear his side of the story."

"I don't wanna see him. I couldn't face him even if I wanted to. Deacon Nichols? My…dad? I still don't know what to believe."

"You must talk to him, my child. You do not want to spend the rest of your life wondering. You have forgiven your mother, have you not?"

"Yeah," I say. "But she's all I got. Her ways are flawed but we all—" I stop. Anna catches it too. "Proceed."

"Still, it's no excuse," I sigh. "How could he just sit there all those years and pretend?"

"Pretend?" says Anna, casually clearing the coffee table. "My child, what if he never knew?" Although she never looks up to gauge my response, her words entice me to think. "You have the Gift of Hearing," she continues. "Listen to your heart."

She leaves the room with a tray full of expensive-looking china. I take the moment to do some conversation shifting of my own.

"So, Anna. That little move you worked on Tre. Think you could teach it to me?"

"Rebuke?" she asks. "Well, it was to be part of your training, but I see no harm in getting a head start on the boys." Did Prophetess Anna just wink? There is much more to this woman than we've seen so far.

CHAPTER 18 —TRE

"MAARRRTINNN!!!"

I jump from my slumber, soaking wet. The nightmares haven't stopped since my brother's death. More vivid than the ones that frequented me before his passing, these lucid images cause me to experience the happening over and over.

I'm really thinking about not attending services this morning. I look over to the night stand but remember my morning ritual has changed. No more whiskey. Guess I'll have to summon strength on my own. It's been months since my last visit to church and I'm sure my appearance is likely to cause a spectacle. The prodigal son, home after such a painful episode in the Turner household.

Maybe me being there will help a little, I think to myself. I haven't really talked to my father much since…

Okay, enough of that. *This is a fresh start. A new beginning,* I tell myself in the mirror before breaking out into song and dance in my ever-so-fresh puppy-dog boxers.

"I got power, oh yeah!"

"I got power, oh yeah!"

"I got P- *I got* O- *I got double* UUUU- *I got* E- *I got* R"

*"I got pow-pow-pow-pow-*POWER!!!!"

I strut around the bathroom like a member of the Temptations. Distracting myself a bit seems to lighten my mood.

I try to remember the made-up song as I enter the church. A large poster with my parents' picture greets members at the front doors. Never seen this one before. Must be new. At least slightly new…

As I look around, I think about the labor my father has gone through in establishing a modern worship center. An African-American man who spent his childhood in the race struggles of the sixties, my father, Pastor William Turner, Jr. is now proud to lead a multi-racial congregation. Last time I checked, around 2,000 people attend services every Sunday. Sometimes I wonder how it makes him feel to have his only two children rarely in attendance.

Mere steps inside and I am swamped by dozens of people before the start of service. Many offer condolences at the sight of the Pastor's firstborn son. Some of these people I've known since I was a little kid, when the church was nothing more than a storefront and a handful of members. Other faces, I hardly recognize. Many, not at all. Most comment on how they left me messages, did I get their cards, and so on. I try my best to remain cordial during the friendly bombardment.

"You desire a way of escape?" whispers a voice from behind.

"Prophetess!—Uhh, Anna," I smile. "YES!" I begin to ad-lib my way out of the press. "Yes, my friends—God bless you all—I must show our visitor to her seat," I say, holding Anna's hand in the air. "Don't wanna be late—uhh—praise God!"

The Prophetess and I make our way to the sanctuary. "Thank you ma'am. It's been a long time since…"

"I understand, my child. And how was your sleep?"

"Not so good, actually. These dreams won't go away. Like they're trying to tell me something." The worship service starts as highly skilled musicians and singers lead the congregation in a fast-paced melody.

"We shall discuss more," she says. "The key is to remain focused."

"So, what did you and Gloria talk about last night?" I ask.

"Would not you like to know?" she smiles before standing and joining the audience in clapping to the music.

Would not you like to know? Who talks like that? Geez.

Finally, I take a cue from Prophetess Anna and try to immerse myself in the service. Might as well. I'm here. People of various ethnicities sing, clap, and even jump, during the highly energized opener. I had almost forgotten the boost one can get at my Father's church…at *my* church. Maybe it's the encouraging words in the songs or the creative riffs and beats of the musicians. Maybe I'm a bit homesick. Whatever it is, I definitely feel something. Not in the manner of enhanced strength or powers, but something more along the lines of peace…hope…love.

The large crowd roars as my father and mother walk onto the stage, a day after burying their youngest child. The couple makes their way to the podium, holding each other around the waist. My father doesn't speak, merely shaking his head. He doesn't have to, as his eyes fill with emotion. His face tells it all. It prompts the packed auditorium into an even louder ovation. Prophetess Anna squeezes a tissue through my clenched hand. I hadn't noticed the tears.

"Me and Liz," the grieving leader finally speaks. "We want to thank you for all your various expressions of love during this time. We have not, I repeat, we have not seen our greatest days. The best is yet to come."

Applause, once again, erupts from the seats. My father continues. "It's no secret my son had his troubles. I'm not ashamed to talk about that. See, when a pastor is doing what he should be doing, the enemy can't get him to fall. So instead, he goes after his family, his children." I look around and see people nodding in agreement. Soft spoken 'amens' can be heard. "But the last few months, I saw a change in my son. He was actually…trying. Trying to get away from some of the demons that plagued his young adult life…" *Demons.* I think about Bale and his men. If only my father knew. "…trying to become a better member of society. He was trying. And so I say to you, young people, do all that you can do to better yourself, to be productive. So what if you won't graduate in four years. Are you trying? So what you had a baby out of wedlock. Are you trying?"

My father's voice grows in fervor and volume. People stand once more as the passion the charismatic pastor is so known for begins to emerge. "Me and Liz," Dad holds mom tight. "See, we work on this every day. And we gon' keep trying until the day one of us leaves this world." Musicians accompany my father's words, mimicking his rhythm and pitch. I've never noticed it until now, but that's where I get some of my swagger from.

"That's my dad," I smile with pride.

"And thank God we still have one child. He's not here today but I—" Rumblings vocalize throughout the audience. "I'm sorry, what? He's where?"

"He's here!" the crowd shouts in unison. A cameraman finds my location, beaming my image to the projector screen. I smile softly, lowering my head. The two parents turn around to see the screen. "Is that you Tre?" my father asks over the microphone. "Go on Tre," murmur folks seated near me.

"You feel like giving your old man a hug?" my father asks in a comforting voice I haven't heard in quite some time. The Prophetess firmly grabs my hand before softly letting go.

I gather my thoughts and my body as I stand. Emotions swell as I make my way down the long aisle. I do everything not to cry but it becomes near impossible as I make my way to the stage. Climbing the steps, I see my mourning parents open their arms. The sight almost brings me to my knees. I want to tell my dad so badly how sorry I am, but as I try to mouth the words, he quiets me.

"Shhh. You don't have to say anything. You're my son, Tre. You're my SON. YOU'RE...MY...SON." Holding nothing back, I break down in the arms of my father as his words speak to my wounded spirit.

Some time later, glancing at my watch, I notice the moment has lasted for nearly twenty minutes. I'm not quite sure how long I held on to my father. I only remember an endless supply of tissue, every so often, being pushed into my hand by one of the assistants. Now, I'm seated on stage next to my mother. She looks over every now and then to smile and pat my knee. My father talks about how I never stopped moving and how he nicknamed me *Squirmy* while still in my mother's womb because of my non-stop activity, even way back then. He then goes on to say the man upstairs shared with him in a dream, that I hadn't seen my last end zone, referring to me scoring touchdowns again in the NFL someday. This leads to an impromptu chant of, *"T-N-T! T-N-T!"* I smile while gesturing 'calm down' to the crowd.

"I've also been told we have some special guests in the house this morning," my father continues. "I'm sure you young people know all about him and I—yes, yours truly has even seen a couple of his action movies. And we're so glad that while visiting our city he chose to worship with us this morning. Now let's give it up for Mr. Jason Bale!"

"What-in-hell..."

I scan the audience though I can see nothing through the now standing mass. No need. The cameraman finds Bale and entourage seated near the back of the church. Cheers erupt as the celebrity's face is plastered on the screen. I can't believe it. My eyes quickly find the Prophetess seated in the middle of the sanctuary. She holds up an open hand as if to say...wait. I turn my attention back to Bale. Sporting a red tie in his otherwise usual white attire, Bale stands as he waves to the crowd, even blowing a kiss. His ovation rivals that of the one given to my father. People whisper as others snap away on their phones. How can they be so naïve? My thoughts quickly remind me of where I was just weeks ago. To the new me, Bale is a manipulative demon. Literally. To the people, Jason Bale is a handsome, talented, rich businessman and movie star. "But how can he even set foot inside a church?" I murmur under my breath.

"Would you like to come up and have a word, Mr. Bale?" asks my father. "What?!" I nearly jump from my seat. Those seated close to me mistake my reaction for excitement. Bale smiles and shakes his head, no. My father persists. "Oh, come on. There's no telling when we'll be graced by your presence again."

"Dad!" I shout, wishing my father was now privy to all the knowledge I've acquired over the last few days. He hardly hears me, the crowd now egging Bale on.

"Okay, okay!" Bale playfully shouts from the back of the auditorium. "But I'll stand right here. An usher quickly brings the star a microphone. "Thanks. Don't wanna get too close to the pulpit," he jokes. *I bet.* My eyes reach for the Prophetess. We seem to be the only ones not amused. "But seriously, I have definitely enjoyed myself in your city. Everyone has made me feel right at home..."

"Feels like Hell huh," I blurt.

"...and I wish you, Pastor Turner, your wife, your son Tre, whom I'm a huge fan of..." My father turns, proudly nodding towards me. "... nothing but the best. I have great plans for this city, and I hope you all can be a part."

For the remainder of the service, my eyes are affixed upon Bale and his crew. My father may have just delivered the sermon of his life, but I wouldn't know. I can think of nothing more than jumping off this stage, leaping a few pews, and putting an end to the 'Jason Bale Show'. Although a distance off, it almost looks as if Bale winks at me a couple of times. *That arrogant...*

I wait for the Shadow to rise around the demonoid superstar or any one of his accompanying Angels. I wait for my Gifts to flare but nothing surfaces, other than a natural disdain for what I see.

After service, young and old alike, rush to shake Bale's hand. Some beg for pictures.

"Do you believe this?" I say, getting to the Prophetess.

"Quiet yourself, my child," she says nonchalantly. "Bale did not come here to fight."

"Well I'm about ready to..."

"He wanted to gather information on what he is up against. We must now practice extreme caution. He knows of your family. It is only a matter of time before he learns of the others, if he has not already done so. I am also sure by now he knows you are receiving my guidance."

"Maybe not," I say. "There's a lot of people here. Just stay back."

Bale makes his way through the crowd, snapping shots and signing autographs. He makes sure his presence is felt. I've seen enough as I make my way through the press.

"What are you doing here, you snake?"

"Tre! What are you doing?" asks a member clamoring for a photo. The big one—Amnon—grunts as his eyes try to intimidate me. It doesn't work. "You want some more, big boy?"

"Trrrrrreeeee," smiles Bale as he autographs a teen's necktie. "Tre Turner. Or do you like to be called William? Your father has a lovely church."

"I thought your kind couldn't even stand near a church."

"Now where'd you hear a thing like that?" he laughs. "I'm not a vampire."

"Close enough," I grit through my teeth, fists balled.

"On the contrary. I love church. Some of my closest friends attend regularly. As a matter of fact, I think I see a few of them here today." Bale's angels chuckle under their tight white suits.

"Why you—"

"So, this is who's been helping you...little Anna."

"Prophetess!" I shout. "I said stay back."

"No matter my child," she says, now standing boldly to my right. Her eyes cut through Bale's flesh without the slightest hesitation as she proclaims, "I fear no evil."

"Oh, so it's Prophetess now," Bale smirks, turning to his Angels. "Well I guess congratulations are in order, little Anna. Oh, pardon me..." Bale takes a mimicking tone as he bows. "...Prophetess."

The Prophetess nods. "The years have been kind to you, Bale. Almost too kind."

"Why thank you little Anna. Guess I can't call you little anymore. What are you now, like ninety?"

"Alive and well."

Bale's irritating grin firms up. "So you are. So you are."

"And to what do we owe this honor, Beelzebub. My apologies. It is *Jason Bale* now, correct?"

"That's okay, little Anna. I've moved on from that identity. Why waste time fighting with the Other? I'm rich, successful, the biggest star in the world. What else could I want?"

"What you have always wanted," answers the Prophetess. "To rule this world."

Bale moves closer but he'll have to step over my dead body to lay a finger on the Prophetess. "It is fine Tre," she says. "He will not attempt to harm me here. It is bad for his image."

"Why Anna," says Bale, too close for comfort. The Shadow slowly rises around his torso. A grayish haze appears to ooze from his pores, although not as strong as I've seen in the past. It's almost like he's controlling it. But no matter. As I look around, I'm reminded no one can see what I'm getting firsthand account of right now.

"Little Anna. Age has made you bitter. Look at you. Your hair is gray, your face wrinkled—"

"And my heart is pure."

"That may be true," Bale whispers, his face just inches from Prophetess Anna's ear. "But one thing I am certain of is that you and your wannabe superheroes are way out of your league."

I've had enough. "How 'bout a wannabe a—uhh, a wannabe butt—kicking."

"Cute. Well it's been great catching up on old times Anna, but I have other pressing matters to attend. I've had enough church for one century."

Bale and his men make their way to the front door. "When it starts, we shall be ready!" affirms the Prophetess.

"So be it," says Bale as he and his Angels exit the church. Smoke-like vapor dissipates in the air as star-struck teens follow the men out.

"I can't believe it!" I shout. "Can you?"

"We must begin training immediately," says the Prophetess with little emotion. "Bale knows who you are. Contact the others and tell them to meet me at my suite in thirty minutes. Even I am not sure as to all Bale has in mind."

"No doubt. Got it. We'll be there." Prophetess Anna heads for a side entrance. "Prophetess! Anna! Where are you going? You need to stick with me."

"I shall be fine, my child."

"Well how are you getting home?"

"I have friends," she says, never turning back.

Friends? There's little time to process her statement as I walk out front to make sure Bale has left the premises. I watch as the white stretched Hummer slowly takes off from across the street. Loosening the knot in my tie, my mind readies itself for battle.

CHAPTER 19 – ZEEK

The obnoxious ringtone of my phone serves as a noon wake-up call. It's Tre. I let it go to voicemail. Another encounter with angels and demons or demons that call themselves angels, can wait. It feels good just being home with my family. No hospitals, no strangers walking in and out at all times of the night, just... family.

Me and Alicia stayed up most of the night and watched as Christina played with her new toys, a surprise from some of the staff at the hospital. To see my daughter do something as simple as play with a new doll has made the last year all worth it.

"Why didn't you wake me?" I yawn from the couch towards Alicia.

"You were sleeping so well, and besides, Chrissy and I were having some girl time."

"Look Daddy!" smiles Christina, while pointing to her freshly plaited locks. "Aunt 'Licia did my hair!" A great improvement over my beautician skills.

"It's beautiful baby. Good job, sis."

"Thanks, Zeek."

Having acquired my first attention of the day, Christina happily skips to her room.

"You never said anything about my hair," beams Alicia, her hand gently sweeping across her recently acquired short-styled cut. "And stop calling me *sis* all the time."

"Huh," I murmur, sticking my head in the fridge.

"Nothing, Zeek."

I hear Alicia just fine, but I dare not entertain that conversation. Alicia has been my rock since Angelina's passing. She's been a mother figure to Christina. I couldn't have made it without her. But Alicia is my wife's sister. Her best friend. True, it's been four years, but I don't think there will ever be a large enough span of time to make me see her any different. Although, I must say I am secretly happy she decided to chop off her hair. She looks a lot less like Angelina now.

"I may have to go meet some friends later. Not sure when I'll be back. Think you could—"

"Of course. Don't I always," she says. I think I sense a slight attitude in her tone.

"Thanks sis—Alicia."

"You're welcome," she smiles back. "So, what's been going on anyway?"

"Whada you mean?"

"I mean…I don't know. You're…different."

The thought causes me to smile. "Yeah, guess I am huh? I'm just happy, that's all. Christina's good, you're good, I'm good!"

"Angel would be happy to see the man you've become."

The statement makes me love the younger sister even more. Maybe not in the way she'd prefer, but in a manner that cherishes her, nonetheless.

Christina drags an expertly crafted wooden rocking horse from her room into the hallway. She bucks the swaying toy, while mimicking the horse's neighs. Funny. I hadn't noticed the expensive-looking present until now.

"I don't remember that one from yesterday," I say.

"It's not," answers Alicia. "It came this morning. Priority shipping."

"On a Sunday?"

"Yep. Came with a note. I decided I'd let you open it."

"Hmph." I tear the envelope as Chrissy shouts, "Giddy up!" to the imaginary animal. A small handwritten note rests at the bottom of the packaging.

It would have been my pleasure in presenting the real thing, but I decided against, as to not appear too forward. So please accept this hand-carved 1948 Rowling classic as an alternative. Hopefully you and your daughter, Christina, can visit my stables one day and ride my collection of thoroughbreds. Let me assure you Mr. Myers, or Zeek if I may, I am all for family and would never harm a child or employ someone that did. Hopefully one day we can sit down and talk. I could use a man of strong conviction like you.

Eternally,

Bale

Panic rips through my body. "Chrissy, get off that thing!" I shout, wrestling my child from the ever-creaking animal. Its entire appearance seems to change as the horse's flared nostrils look ready to spew out venomous mist.

"What's wrong Zeek?!"

"Quick! Get down Alicia!"

Christina screams as I heave her and myself to the floor. We wait. For what, I'm not sure, but I won't be caught off guard.

"It was just a—"

My finger signals silence.

"It was just a gift," Alicia whispers. "What's the matter with you?"

We wait. Moments go by and nothing happens. The more I think about it, the more I know nothing is going to happen. At least not now.

The ridiculous ringtone Christina selected for my phone eases the tension of the moment. Not recognizing the number shown, something, nevertheless, propels me to answer.

"Zeek, my friend. Did your daughter enjoy the gift?"

"Just who the hell do you think you are?! You come after my family?! I will kill you!"

"Enough, Mr. Myers. I mean your family no harm. Think about it. I could have done that already if that was my intention."

I hate to admit it but he's right. "So, what do you want?!"

"You didn't answer my question, Mr. Myers."

"What?!"

Bale speaks in a slow, calculated tone. "Did your daughter... enjoy the gift?"

"What do you think? Of course. She's a kid."

His demeanor picks up. "Well great! I wanted to make sure I got something that would make an impression."

I say nothing, not knowing what to make of all of this. "Are you there?" he asks. "Zeek?"

"Yeah. Is that all?"

"Actually, I was hoping you'd take a ride with me."

"What? Are you crazy? And leave my family here to—"

"Zeek…Zeek. We've been through this already," Bale says calmly. "If it was my intent to harm your family, it would have already occurred. I merely want to show you something. I'm sure a lot has been said about me. I just want to share my side of the story." I look over to Chrissy and Alicia. They watch as I ponder my next statement.

"When?"

"A car is outside waiting for you."

"Five minutes."

"Of course. See you soon."

The quicker I get this guy and his goons away from my apartment, the better. With no immediate threat in sight, I let Alicia know it's okay to get off the ground. "What's going on, Zeek?" she asks.

"I'll tell you about it all later. Just know everything's okay."

"I wanna go Daddy," says Christina while playfully hopping on one foot.

"Not this time baby," I respond, gently kissing her forehead.

"Daddy, can I ride my horsey again?"

I look around the room at all the things Christina didn't have before yesterday as I finally concede, "Sure baby, you can ride the horsey."

Minutes later, my hands ball into fists as a driver approaches. "Mr. Myers," he nods, merely wanting to open the rear door of the white limousine. I look around before hesitantly easing into the crisp-smelling vehicle.

We drive for what seems like an eternity. The clock on my phone confirms about twenty-five minutes. Part of me is tense, not knowing what to expect. The other half is still anxious, but more in the vein of how Christina acts on Christmas Day just before we open presents. Although I wasn't a believer, I never denied Chrissy the wonder of opening gifts. And now, part of me feels like that—ready to see what's about to be opened. And that's the part that scares me.

After a few deliberate wrong turns and repeated circles around the same part of town, we make our way to an old warehouse located on President's Island. Most of Memphis is located on a bluff and the island is a major spot for factories. Not technically an island, but more of an inlet, the island is usually not frequented by anyone unless they work in the area. A good a spot as any, I guess, for a hideout. Or to hide someone.

The silent driver opens my door before nodding to the entrance. One of Bale's security detail is positioned out front. Dark-skinned with dreads, I recognize him from the club. We had a good go at it. I wait for my powers, or whatever they are, to flare, but nothing happens. Looks like I'm going in on my own. A sarcastic grin widens across the guard's face as he mumbles, "Follow me."

Inside, the dimly-lit storage facility has been emptied out. Doesn't seem to have been used in years. Bale's man leads me up a steel staircase. His hand motions me to stop, before leaving me perched on a walkway high above ground level. Must have been used by managers to keep an eye on the workers. Not sure why they would leave me up here. Not a good spot for an ambush, with the view as open as it is. While I wait, several men and a couple of women are escorted in by some of Bale's men—Angels, I believe he calls them, noticeable by their trademark white suits. The people they accompany separate into two lines. The formation looks almost militarian in nature. Some of them look to be pulled straight from work, still wearing various uniforms. A bus driver, doctor, some guy who looks like he works in a cubicle. Maybe they were 'softly kidnapped' like me. Next, a policeman and a thin man with glasses enter.

What the—

Peering down, I now see the policeman is *The Policeman!* Although a ways off, I'm sure of it. And the thin man with glasses is the same bastard that tried to take my daughter. Part of me wants to jump down right now and beat the crap out of them both, but I'm not sure I'd survive the drop. Even for what I've been able to do so far, that's a bit much. And it doesn't feel as if I'm getting much help in the form of superhuman powers right now. Looking more closely, the short man in the white lab coat looks familiar as well. I'd bet money he's a doctor at Christina's hospital. Who are these people?

Bale's Angels take their spots behind the group as the man himself makes his entrance. Jason Bale quickly glances up to my exact location and winks. No one else seems to detect my presence as I hide in the shadows of the rafters. Guess he would obviously know my whereabouts, it's his show. And it hits me just like that. He wants me to watch.

The separated groups of people act as aisles as Bale begins to pace back and forth between them.

"Ministers, I thank you for your time," he opens. "I know you are busy spreading the gospel of Bale and your diligence is duly noted. I would also like to thank you for your quick response to …" Bale looks my direction while picking his words carefully. " …to our little situation. Rest assured it is being handled."

"So, is it true the Three of Three are back?" asks a man in a suit and tie.

"Hardly," replies Bale. "Just a cheap replica. Do not concern yourself with them. Our ministry shall go on as planned."

"I saw one of them," says the doctor. "He could…heal." His voice ignites my memory. The doctor I bumped into in the hospital bathroom. And come to think about it, he had the Mark tattooed on his wrist. But why does Bale want me to see this? It makes no sense. He can't possibly think that letting me sit in one of his meetings would make me want to join his exaggerated book club.

"Yes, Dr. Echols," continues Bale. "They have some powers. But you have my power. Nothing compares to that. And so that brings me to why we are gathered here. You all have been decreed with great responsibility. To spread the gospel of Bale. And for that purpose and that purpose alone, I endow you with powers beyond your wildest dreams. Am I not gracious?" The men and women loudly cheer before he quiets them. "It has come to my attention that one of our brothers has used his power in a manner unbefitting of a minister." Bale slows his pace, stopping in front of the same bifocal-wearing savage that tried to abduct Christina. "What is your single purpose?" Bale asks the unassuming man.

"To uhh…" I can hear him gulp as he tries to finish. "To spread the gospel of Bale."

"I can't hear you!"

"To spread the gospel of Bale, my Lord!"

Bale clinches his teeth. "To spread the gospel of Bale…exactly." His face loosens as he resumes his pacing. "Thank you minister. You all are my ministers and your single purpose is to spread the gospel of Bale. To venture into every aspect of society and recruit for my ministry. To show them another way. And for carrying out this duty, do I not give you the desires of your heart? Do I not afford you abilities you never thought possible? And how do you use these gifts?" Bale once again stops in front of the balding, thin man. "To aid in pleasing your sick, twisted flesh?" The others distance themselves from their nervous colleague. "You endanger our global ministry, and for what?!" To satisfy your cravings! Give me your wrist."

The shaking subordinate snivels out words. "My Lord, I'm sorry. I couldn't control myself."

"That won't be a problem after today. Now give me your wrist!"

The man reluctantly holds out his arm, the Mark tattooed on his right wrist.

Jason Bale extends his hand. Black, smoke-like vapor emits from his index finger, swirling around the man's wrist. Like a lasso, the blackness tightens its grip around his wrist as it appears squeezed. He grunts as his circulation is severed. Another vein of mist seeps from Bale's middle finger, seeming to pierce through the man's skin. The Shadow takes the form of a scalpel as it begins to physically remove the tattooed Mark, skin and all, from the screaming man's arm. The others as well as myself, grimace as a sizzling sound is heard while the Shadow continues to tear through the man's arm. "You do not deserve to wear the Mark of Bale!" yells the angry leader as the Shadow swirls around the enraged actor. Actually, that term doesn't describe Bale anymore …whoever he is. A grotesque scowl covers his face. The piece of tattoo-covered skin falls to the ground as Bale grabs his weakened follower by the neck. Black veins surface in the man's paled face. "Now return what I have given you!" The man gasps for air as the Shadow emits from his profile. As if sucked through a vacuum, the haze is consumed by the even larger Shadow of Bale. The dying man ages before our eyes as he struggles for one last breath. Lifeless, his head bows over as Bale releases his hold. "Do you not understand what I am trying to give you?" An emotional Bale asks patting his tussled hair. "What I want to give the world? I want to show them another way!"

As his guards remove the man's body, I'm not sure what to feel. This is what I wanted, right? For the wicked man who wanted to do god-knows-what-to my child—to suffer the most horrible death possible. Even if he suffered this at the hands of my enemy? Isn't the enemy of my enemy my friend? And why do I refer to

Bale as my enemy? I don't trust him, but he could've made a move on me already. There's so much I don't understand.

Bale addresses his remaining ministers. "My father and my father's father have waged war against one another for Millennia. And for what? Their conflict is pointless. Neither wants to completely destroy the other. But I ask…why does there only have to be TWO choices?"

A look of confidence swells over Bale's face. "But I, Bale, come to the people as an independent candidate. My father's way was wrong. No longer will we creep and hide. I will openly show this world the power that is rightfully theirs."

One of Bale's men approaches. "My Lord, we should be leaving if we're going to catch our flight."

"Ministers, you have your instructions," continues Bale. "Now leave me." Not wanting to be the next example, the various men and women quickly exit. Bale looks up and turns his attentions to me.

"So, tell me, Mr. Myers. What did you think?"

"Think? I think you just killed a man."

"Yes," Bale chuckles. "But is that not what you wanted?"

"I didn't ask you to do me any favors."

"True. But I wanted you to see, with your own eyes. Everything you've heard about me is not true."

"Well I haven't heard much. You give yourself way too much credit."

He laughs. "I like you, Zeek. A man such as yourself would be very useful to my ministry."

"Thanks," I say. "But if it's all the same to you, I think I'll pass."

"Why? Because of what the old woman has told you? Because of the little taste of power you've experienced? Come. Let me show you true power. A power you could only dream about. Let me show you another way."

"Like I said, I'm good. But thanks for—"

"—for destroying your enemy..."

"...for the offer. Now am I free to go?"

"But of course, Zeek. And you don't have to admit it now, but I know there's something in you that wants to know more. How long will you allow the Other to string you alone? There is a revolution happening. Now whether you're a part of it or not is up to you, but trust me, the people have spoken. I will reveal to them the true power."

Bale's Shadow swirls around him like flames.

"They will freely wear my Mark. In fact, they will beg for it..."

The unexpected aroma of bacon causes me to reexamine the apartment number on the front door. Spicy bacon, to be more exact. It smells like my mother's special recipe. She made it often during my childhood, but I haven't smelled the strong, peppery odor in years.

Setting my keys down on the table, it looks as if it's been polished.

"A'ma, where are you?" I ask cautiously.

"In the kitchen, my love," hums a cheerful voice.

Neither the words nor tone belong to the woman I left home a couple of days ago. It's her voice alright, but that's not A'ma. Can't be. Slowly I creep to the kitchen, not sure what or who I'll find.

"A'ma?"

"Hi sweetie, I'm making your favorite…"

I nearly stumble at the sight my eyes uncover. Standing before me is a fully dressed woman that resembles my mother. Her hair is curled, make-up applied, posture erect. "A'ma, you look so… pretty," are the first words that come to mind. Well, because she does. "…and young." I'd almost forgotten what my mother looks like, so many years hidden behind tattered nightgowns, pills, and vodka bottles.

"Thank you, Mija," says the now attractive forty-something-woman.

The stove is filled with breakfast delicatessens. "I feel great," smiles A'ma as she pours pancake batter. The cooking, the clothes, the warm words, it's almost too much. But I dare not let go of this moment. Who knows when or if I'll ever get it back?

"Well are you ready to eat, sweetie?"

"I'm starving, A'ma," I say, sounding like a little child. Kind of feel like one too. "A'ma, I know I haven't been around much lately, but all that's going to change."

"It's okay, Mija," she says. A name she's used ever since my childhood. "We've been through a lot. I want to tell you how sorry I am for holding things from you. I just didn't want you to hurt the way I hurt...the way he hurt me."

"So, the Deacon, he knew right?" I casually ask while biting into a piece of steaming sausage. "I mean he knew he was my dad?"

"Of course, darling. He left us, Gloria, don't you see?"

I don't want to argue. Things are too good now. "Yes A'ma."

"Besides, it's a new day," A'ma says as she stacks more pancakes onto my plate. "New opportunities."

"You're right A'ma. I'm glad you're better. I've been praying for you."

"Hmph," she grins. "Well all that matters is that I'm here and I'm ready to be your mother again. No more taking care of me." A'ma kisses me on the cheek, and my face can't help but beam as I bite down into the endless stack of pancakes. What I would give to stay at this table forever.

"So, it's just you and me now, right sweetie?" she asks.

"Um hmmm," I nod, my mouth filled with homemade biscuits covered in honey butter.

"Good," says A'ma finally biting into the meal she's prepared. "You don't need those new friends of yours anyway."

"Whada you talking about, A'ma?"

"Those nice young men told me about those crazies you were hanging out with. You don't need them anymore. You have your A'ma back."

My fork drops as I force down the remaining food in my mouth with one swallow. "What young men, A'ma?"

"Oh, the nicest young men came by," she says unaffected. Finally, A'ma looks up, chewing as she speaks. "They showed me another way Gloria…and I can show you."

Hearing the familiar words, my body nearly goes limp. I jump from the table, distancing myself from my…mother. Emotion rings from my voice. "What are you talking about A'ma?"

"Everything is okay now, my little Mija. Trust your mother."

And then it starts. Smoke-colored mist ascends from A'ma's body. "No," I cry. The price paid for the previous moment is unbearable. My mother stands before me as one of *them*.

"Don't cry Gloria," she says, now standing. "I can make it better. I promise."

"A'ma! Why! You don't know what you've done!"

"Shhh, it's okay. Now come, Mija."

As A'ma moves closer, the Shadow radiates around her body. "Stay back!" I shout, but the life-like substance glides through her skin, continuing its seduction. My senses flare as my heart accelerates. Adrenaline fills my veins. I too can feel power surging through my body. Power I don't want to use on my demon-influenced mother. But I have to do something...

Rebuke.

My earlier lesson with the Prophetess comes to mind. *Subduing one without causing severe bodily harm.* But where is the line drawn? I haven't had time to master the move. Besides, my emotions flood any logical thoughts.

"Let me show you another way," A'ma repeats, her voice changing by the second. I haven't much time to think either, as the Shadow tightens its grip around my deceived mother. Impatiently, my body waits. Allow my mother to make the first move, physically bring it to her like she's one of Bale's men or try the Rebuke. I have no choice.

"ARRRHHH!"

A war cry roars from my belly as I run straight for A'ma. A demented vapory scowl leaps from her as I advance but it's not enough to hinder me. I stop just short of full-on contact with A'ma, my fingertips barely grazing her abdomen. The light touch throws her body violently to the floor.

My God, what have I done! I can barely look her way as tears pour down the same cheek kissed by that other woman just moments ago. My eyes closed, I cry to myself, not wanting to see the damage inflicted to A'ma. A familiar voice forces them open.

"Why am I on this floor, Gloria? And why am I wearing this dreadful skirt and is this—is this makeup? Is this your doing,

Gloria? You know I despise anything touching my face! Is this how you treat your flesh and blood?"

Although wearing the same new clothes, A'ma's countenance has definitely changed. She looks like the old A'ma. And her rant is increasingly recognizable.

"Esto es ridiculo!"

"Oh, A'ma!" I sob, running to my mother. No, I wouldn't trade this moment for the world.

——THE ASSIGNED——

TRE

A silky fog rises from the street, a result of the brief afternoon rain. Surrounding my SUV, it reminds me of the Shadow. But this haze isn't evil in nature. At least, I hope. "Come on Glo, pick up!" I shout through the phone. She and Zeek have been out of pocket for the last hour. My mind can only wonder as I sit at this prolonged red light.

Sensing someone watching, I slowly turn my head towards the passenger window. Three guys in an old Chevy pick-up stare back. My age or younger, they look like…

Those are Martin's boys! I vaguely remember them from one of Martin's brief loan-request visits, although I can't be too sure. The prior rain fogs the glass. Holding up the peace sign, I yell, "What's up?!" through the slightly cracked window. The fellas stare back emotionless before finally taking off. *Ooookay,* I think out loud, pulling off from the light. My path is cut short by a miniature, pink ribbon-wearing terrier standing in the middle of the street.

Why do the smallest dogs bark the loudest? Guess he's got 'little man's' complex. I blow the horn, but the obnoxious dog is determined to hold his ground in the center of the rain-drenched lane.

"Give me a break—move Benji!"

Easing the SUV up a bit does little to move the diminutive canine.

"Finally!" I shout as the dog's owner runs out into the rain to retrieve the stubborn pooch. The hooded owner smiles and waves as she scoops up the animal.

"Yeah, yeah, just get out the way," I smile back. As I wait, the owner's eyes grow dark. Weird. Fog from the street rises up around her. Wait, that's not fog, that's—

BAMMM!!!

"AAAHHH!" I scream as something crashes atop my hood. "What the...?!" It punches through the windshield, shattering the glass. A Persuaded! He growls as black vapor swirls about. Gathering my wits, I slam on the gas and take off down the four-lane boulevard.

"Wait a minute, I know you!" I yell as the possessed man lunges for my face. He's one of Martin's friends from the truck.

"Shut up, follower!" he shouts back. I try to shake him but the Persuaded doesn't budge. Fog, swirling black mist, and the two-hundred-pound man stuck in the windshield make the roadways nearly invisible. So much so, I barely see a second Persuaded standing in the middle of the lane. Tires squeal as I swerve, trying to avoid the slender man. The two-ton vehicle jolts to one side. Looking out the rear view, I can see the Persuaded sprinting down the street, passing cars with ease. Motorists watch in amazement. His power is definitely amped up. Where'd he go?

The sound above indicates the roof. My eyes confirm as I look back to see a hand punching through the top of the vehicle. "Come on, man! I just got this truck!"

My speed approaches 65 in the 45-mph zone. Wrestling the first Persuaded with one hand, I drive with the other. The second Persuaded continues ripping a hole in the top of my Cadillac.

"Okay, that's it!" I shout, eye to eye with the first demented man. "You want some of me?! Come on!" I grab the Persuaded, pulling his torso through the windshield. Delivering blow after blow to the guy's face, he somehow finds a way to keep his grip. We swerve through traffic as rain pellets shoot through the shattered glass. I can feel the air pour in from behind as the slender Persuaded makes his way inside the truck. Now fully in the cabin, the second Persuaded makes an attempt for my head. Sensing him just in time, I land a forearm to his chest. The brutal blow throws the slender man back to the third-row seat. I turn the forearm into an elbow, bestowing vicious force to the temple of the nearer Persuaded. The foot soldier flies back out onto the hood of the truck. His body contorts as we take a sharp turn into the adjoining street.

"Will you fall off, alrea—" The slender Persuaded chokes the living daylights out of me! I can't see or breathe. For most people, panic would set in, but in this case, my adrenaline only pumps harder. I reach for his hands as his accomplice makes his way back into the front of the cabin. His Shadow glistens as it sways in the dense atmosphere.

"My turn," grins a set of sharp teeth. I'm having a hard time focusing, my head taking a bevy of blows, while constricting pressure is applied to my neck from behind. The assault is coming faster than my body can heal. "So that's how you wanna play it, huh?" I moan under a barrage of punches. "Okay, fine!"

I slam the pedal all the way to the floor. The V8 engine cranks out massive pounds of torque as the speeding bomb accelerates to near 90 mph. I unlatch my seatbelt as the Persuaded continue their strike. Their hands seem to be glued to my face and neck.

"Here we go again," I say, slamming on the brakes.

SCREEEECH!

The car buckles as it comes to a pounding halt. The Persuaded and I fly out the shattered front windshield, head first. We soar through the air before crashing through the window of a Luigi's Pizza Parlor.

"Bad idea," I moan. Not sure how long I was out but a crowd has surrounded me. Quickly, I jump up looking for, "the Persuaded —AOUUWW!" A sharp pain shoots through my shoulder.

"Sir, don't move," says an employee. "I think your shoulder is dislocated." He's right. My left shoulder droops in an awkward position. People squirm as they watch me pop it back in place.

"Wait a second," says a Luigi's customer. "Look at his face." The crowd marvels as lacerations disappear from my body. "Oops," I smile, good as new. The two Persuaded, still knocked-out cold, look like regular men. That is, regular men that just got thrown through a window from a speeding vehicle.

"Well, nothing more to see here folks," I say, saluting the crowd. "Sorry about that. Enjoy the rest of your meals."

"Hey, aren't you TNT Turner?"

"Who me? Oh no. I get that all the time though. Probably a distant rela—"

"Lie still ma'am!" shouts an employee as I make my way to the door. "I'm calling an ambulance!"

A woman, not much older than me, bleeds on the floor. A large shard of glass protrudes from her side. The woman, in obvious pain, grimaces as she tries to stay conscious. "I'm going to help you," I say, kneeling down beside her. "Just relax."

"Are you a doctor?" she asks through clenched teeth.

"Uhh, something like that. Now this may sting for a second, but just trust me."

Distracting her as she nods, I pull the long shard of glass from the woman's side. Shrieks of pain fill the small eatery. Finally dislodged, blood gushes from the large gash left by the errant blade. I place my hands at the top of the wound and close my eyes as I focus. Blood seeps back into the gash as it closes. A few moments later, the young woman feels just fine. She looks down in disbelief.

"Wha—wha—what did you do?"

"I believed."

CHAPTER 21 – ZEEK

Anna's suite was the only place I knew to go. Especially after seven missed calls from Tre. Besides, maybe if I stay away from the house, Bale and his men will have no reason to scope it out. I don't know. I can't even begin to wrap my head around all that's going on.

Anna and Gloria run out to meet me and Tre, who pulls up at just about the same time. His truck is a mess.

"Are you okay, my children?" asks Anna.

"I'm fine," says Tre.

"Yeah, me too," I say.

"This has escalated more rapidly than I anticipated. We must begin. Quickly, inside."

Upstairs, Anna hands us entrance cards used to enter hotel rooms.

"We don't need keys to your suite," says Tre.

"Yeah Anna," Gloria agrees. "We can knock."

"This is not entry to my abode. This is for your suite. Your training complex. Bale knows too much. We are not safe here." Anna steps across the hall and unlocks the door. The three of us follow, making our way inside.

"Wow!"

"Not bad," I say, scanning the room.

"You shall be safe here," says Anna. "This is where we will train. Bale has already gathered information concerning Tre and Gloria."

"He got to you, Glo?" Tre asks. Something about the way he looks at her makes me think about Angel.

"My mom," she answers. "When I got home, she was like... the others."

"A Persuaded?"

Gloria nods. "I was able to subdue her with something the Prophetess taught me."

"This has gone too far. That snake has the nerve to step foot in my father's church. Then he gets my brother's friends, of all people, to try and take me out?! I wonder if that's how they got Martin."

"Today?" I ask.

"Yeah! Just now! I've been calling you all morning."

"I know man. Sorry."

"It's only a matter of time before Bale learns of Zeek's identity," Anna asserts. "You and your family *are* safe, correct my child?" The room's focus shifts to me. My mouth slightly opens before deciding against any vocalization. *What's the point in bringing it up*, I think as my head nods. Besides, we are safe.

"This room is not listed under my name," continues Anna. "So, you all will be safe here. Make plans to tarry for the next several days if at all possible."

With the focus off me, we continue exploring the high-end penthouse. The suite has three spacious bedrooms and a large open space up front. Sleek burgundy couches rest in the opened area. Flat screen televisions drape the walls like framed paintings. Birds chirp carefree melodies against floor-to-ceiling windows.

"How can you pay for all this?" Tre asks.

"God provides," Anna smiles as she picks up a remote and pushes a button. In a flash, the huge draped curtains close shut, followed by some sort of steel reinforcement. She presses another button. The others and I jump as another steel support drops to the ground, covering the front door.

"Now that's what I'm talking about!" Tre snaps.

"Precautionary, my children. Now let's begin."

Anna motions us to take a seat. Wearing a fiery red pantsuit with elongated cuffs and orange heels, we watch the unusual woman. The collar of the suit rises above her neck at least six inches. Shimmering crystals adorn the lifted lapel. Her usually long and flowing grayish mane is today pinned back into a bun. Her tone takes an even more serious register as her highly distinctive accent drives her words.

"You all have been chosen by God. For whatever reason, you three have been assigned this task. No amount of logic will make events prior, or to come, completely comprehensible. No, it is not fair. No, I hath not all the answers. What I do know is that the fate of life as we know it lies in your hands. Bale wants to raise an army of those things you have encountered. If he succeeds… well. Our only chance is if we are a united front. I must know now; do you accept this call? Gloria?"

"Yes, of course, Anna."

"Tre?"

"Football season is just about over. *'Game of Thrones'* got can-celled—sure, count me in."

"Zeek?"

I take a deep breath. Not sure as to what I'm doing…in any of this.

"We cannot do this without you."

"I'm in."

"Good," Anna smiles. "The next few days, we shall grow stronger physically, mentally, and spiritually. We shall learn more of our weapons and how to effectively use them. We will also learn more about our brothers and our sister. We shall grow closer. We shall become a team."

——THE ASSIGNED——

GLORIA

Zeek takes a deep breath before committing to the cause. Hon-estly, he doesn't look like he's all there. I sure hope he's ready when the time comes. Now that Tre, Zeek and I have all given our agreement, Anna continues.

"As I said, I do not have all the answers but those I do hold, I shall do my best to share." My mind wanders to A'ma as I listen to Anna. I've seen firsthand what the Persuaded can do. I don't know about the others, but I'll do whatever it takes to stop them.

"I am sure you are eager to learn more about the Three of Three. Our kind has been mentioned ever since the death of Jesus. No one knows the exact date we came into existence. As I have stated, many believe three of Jesus' closest followers, Peter, James, and

John where the first. After Jesus' death, many miraculous deeds were accomplished by this group, as well as others. The Acts of the Apostles in the Bible records many of these remarkable feats. Since then, stories have been handed down of three being called from select generations. Some in the same life span, others hundreds of years apart. What does not change is the extraordinary individual and collective Gifts they operate in." Anna talks as a storyteller in front of her class. Her well-thought-out words and elegant attire captivate our attention. "So, who taught you, Anna?" I ask.

"The Three of Three that preceded me perished long before my birth but there are some known as the Intercessors who carry the story from generation to generation. They have special skills, although not powers as you. An Intercessor located me and confirmed what had already been shown to me through visions as my gifts began to manifest themselves. Shortly afterwards, I discovered the Second and Third of Three."

"But why weren't you able to save your team?" asks Tre. "I mean didn't one of you have the Gift of healing or whatever?"

"Our Gifts work their best when we are properly positioned, in tune with ourselves, our brethren, and our Creator. Unfortunately, my team was ambushed during a turbulent time."

Tre places his hand on Anna's shoulder. "It's okay, Prophetess. We're strong. We'll get 'em."

"But that's just it!" she shouts back, her face expressive. "It's not just about your physical powers! Your mind must be set free in all areas. Some of you have anger in your hearts. Some of you have not forgiven God, others, yourself!" She's right. "We must release ourselves from any anguish the enemy can use against us. Bale is the master of manipulation. You must not go into warfare with a clouded mind. He will sense it and use it against you."

Zeek raises his hand to speak. "This may sound silly, not sure, but have you ever just tried talking to this guy?"

Now I know Zeek is a little different, but did he just really ask that? He obviously hasn't seen what Bale can do. Tre and I wait for Anna to go completely off, but instead she just smiles and asks, "What would you suggest we say, my child?"

"Uhh, not sure, but I mean, seems like he could've killed us already if he wanted to. You don't think we could reason with him?"

I've heard enough. "Are you serious, Zeek?"

"I mean, he is a movie star, businessman, he can't be completely bad?"

"Zeek, c'mon," Tre says. "That guy tried to kill us on the rooftop, remember?"

"I mean yeah, but we attacked him first. I'm just saying, is it possible, that's all?"

Anna's gaze seems to go straight through Zeek. "Is there something else you need to share with us, my child?" Zeek seems shamed now. Maybe Tre is staring. I sure am.

"No, just posing a question, that's all," he says, finally bowing out.

Anna moves in closer. "Zeek, I understand all of this is new to you, but listen to me carefully. Jason Bale is not a man. He is a demon enclosed in flesh and he will do anything to separate you from your team. Never forget that. Do you understand?"

"Sure, no problem," Zeek responds, cavalier. "He's the bad guy. Got it. So, what now?" Anna leaves the room. Tre runs to help her as she returns with an armful of books. "What now?" she repeats. "You study."

I carefully scan through one of the antique styled paperbacks, some almost falling apart. "What are these?"

"The New Testament, books on demonic possession, readings on Beelzebub and other demons. I know you have witnessed some things, but you must learn more concerning what you are up against." Anna looks directly at Zeek. "And you must believe this evil truly exists."

Tre frowns at the large pile of reading material. Guess studying is not his strong suit. "Thought we were gonna learn some new moves or something?"

"In time, my child," reassures Anna. "But tonight, you study. Please take your assignment seriously. Many souls depend on it. We shall regroup in the morning." Anna retires to her room. "Guess she's serious hunh?" asks Tre.

"Yep," I smile. "And since I've already read the entire Bible, I'll take these here on Possession. Should be great with a warm bed and hot cup of tea. Yummm. See you guys in the morning."

"You're leaving us?" Tre asks as I head for one of the bedrooms. "It's just a little past seven."

"Yep. Goodnight."

Before I close the door, I hear Tre and Zeek discussing who gets what. "Well, guess it's just you and me, brother from another mother," cracks Tre. "I'll leave the Bible books for you. My dad's a Pastor you know."

"And?!" shouts Zeek.

"Hey, you'll love it. Bunch of therefores, wherewithals, and hithertos, kind of like listening to the Prophetess. You'll love it!"

"Wow, thanks," says Zeek.

I shut the door before I can hear anymore. Hilarious.

Morning arrives and I drape one of the hotel's huge bath robes around me as I make my way to the kitchen for some juice. Seated on the couch is Zeek, still reading. Doesn't look like he's moved an inch since last night.

"Good morning, Zeek." Consumed, Zeek doesn't even notice me in the room. "Zeek?"

"Huh—oh hey."

"Man, did you ever go to sleep?" Tre asks as he drags in. Zeek never looks up.

"Uh, yeah, I mean no, not really."

"And didn't your mother ever teach you to read silently?"

"I didn't know my mother," Zeek answers, his head still buried in the book. I give Tre 'the look' for his callous comment.

"Oh, hey man, I'm sorry—"

Zeek fans off the apology as if the remarks didn't faze him. Maybe they don't, considering he's lived with it all his life.

"You know, we really don't know that much about each other," I say. "Prophetess Anna did say we should grow closer as a team, probably help out with our Gifts. Would you mind telling us more about your wife, Zeek? I believed you said Angel was her name?"

Zeek finally looks up as he glances towards my direction. It only lasts for a moment as his eyes drift back down to the Bible he's been reading throughout the night.

"Her real name's Angelina," he starts. "I called her Angel for short." A smile emerges as he remembers his wife. "You know the funny thing?" He raises the Bible. "I'd catch her reading this sometime and ask her what she'd find so interesting and she'd say, *'You should read it sometime.'* And I'd say no thanks. Not me. I mean, what she did was fine. It was how she was raised. But me?" Zeek laughs. "Now look at me. I'm caught up in some sort of war between Heaven and Hell. If only she could see me now."

"So how did she die, Zeek?" I ask, carefully forming my words.

"We were riding down to the coast. I was going too fast. A deer ran out, I—I tried to avoid it. Angel...she didn't make it."

"I'm so sorry," I say, making my way to Zeek.

"Our wedding day..."

"My God! Zeek?" How does one respond to something like that?

"I just wish it would've been me, you know?"

"Maybe she was ready and you weren't," I smile. I don't know where the words come from, but they seem to fit.

"Maybe," Zeek agrees as he wipes his nose.

"Well, she'd be proud of you now," says Tre. "Strong man, good father, superhero..." Tre's usually misplaced humor actually works this time.

"Thanks," says Zeek, holding up the frayed Bible. "And this was the one part of her life I knew so little about. So, I feel like I owe it to her, you know? To at least give it a shot."

"Beautifully said, my child." Anna's stealth-like arrival startles us. "And did you read of your namesake?" she asks. Zeek nods.

"Yeah, I did. Pretty interesting."

"Now wait a minute," Tre motions with his hands. "Okay, you got me. I'm no Bible scholar, I give you that. But I'm pretty sure there's no one in there by the name of Zeek."

"No," answers Anna. "But there is the great Ezekiel."

"EZEKIEL?!?!" Tre and I loudly shout in unison.

"Yeah?!" Zeek mouths defensively. "Gotta problem with that?!"

"Ezekiel's a wonderful name," I say quickly.

"Indeed, my child. In Hebrew it is pronounced *Yeh'khez-kel*. And it means 'God is strong', a name befitting for you. And he possessed the Gift of seeing, just as you."

"Yeah, I read."

"Wow," Tre says. "Impressive, Zeek."

"Yeah, guess you were sleep for that sermon."

"Haha. Funny."

"Indeed," smiles Anna.

We spend the next two hours discussing the various paths that have led us to this point. Tre talks about his reoccurring nightmares and the burden of celebrity at such a young age. Listening to him talk gives me a glimpse into why he's like that. The high-profile life he's carved out for himself would be tempting and difficult for anyone, let alone a 22-year-old. Tre turns off the 'TNT' persona and speaks from his heart. There's so much to him when he just lets go.

Of course, I talk about A'ma and Deacon Nichols. I think I even ranted on about my non-existent social life, but hopefully not for too long. One thing's for sure, we definitely begin to see what it takes to walk in the others' shoes.

"So, as you see my children, it is not just about this!" says Anna, raising a balled fist. "Remember, although strong beyond compare, Samson never reached his full potential. Pride, a haughty attitude, and an insatiable lust for women led to his destruction." Anna walks gracefully towards Tre. "Do not let it become yours." Next, she moves towards me. "Do not let religion rid you of relationship. You do not have all the answers, nor can you do this alone." Her words, although general, sting profusely. On second thought, maybe they're not so general after all.

Concern, almost grief, consumes Anna's face as she makes her way to Zeek, taking his hand. "My child, do not let the uncertainty that troubles you, the fear you have of this new existence, do not allow it to tempt you to see things that are not truly there."

I try not to gauge anyone's reaction, still focused on my own report. Anna faces us as a group now. "If any of you succumb to your personal temptations at the most unfortunate of times, you may suffer a fate similar to that of my circle. And there may be no one left to tell the story."

——THE ASSIGNED——

TRE

"We won't let that happen," I say. "Just tell us what you want us to do."

The Prophetess looks to me, then Glo, and finally Zeek. Her eyes narrow as she speaks. "We train."

Prophetess Anna instructs us to change into workout attire. Finally, we get to the good stuff. Wearing a tank top and shorts, I jog from the bedroom, lathering on a little extra lotion to highlight the guns. Zeek's build, although not quite athletic as mine, is well proportioned. Tattoos slide down his arms. One reads, *ANGEL*. Gloria looks like she feels right at home in a light gray tee and blue shorts.

Wearing her usual over-styled attire, the Prophetess inspects each of us. "Good," she says. "Now, which of you is most robust?"

"Hunh?" we shrug.

"Athletic."

"Ohh." I do my best to contain the laughter. "C'mon. You're kidding, right?"

"We shall see," she says before switching gears. "Now each of you, on the ground! NOW!" Her boisterous voice hurries us more than the actual words. Push-ups, sit-ups, burpees, power squats. Nothing I haven't seen before.

"Is that all you got?" I say to Zeek as we sweat out reps. After a few rounds, we both begin to slow, though neither of us dare give up.

"Getting tired already fellas?" Gloria boasts as she cranks out push-ups, now adding a clap between each one. Whatever.

The drills go on for a couple of hours. Even with our enhanced strength, the Prophetess' workout wears us down. Sweat beads like morning dew on the hardwood floor. "Hey, you think we could get a break?" I ask.

"Surely such a fine physical specimen as Tre *TNT* Turner, does not need a break?" Anna's voice tinges with sarcasm.

"Haha," I murmur. "You have worked us pretty good."

"Indeed, my child. I tell you what. Take this time to refuel. This will be your last meal for the next few days. Our fast starts at sundown."

"Say what?"

"You will abstain from all substantive nourishment. To strengthen the body, you must deny it of the very thing it craves. Only then can one truly see."

"So, no food whatsoever?" Zeek asks.

"Only liquids," replies the Prophetess. "By removing yourself from physical desire, you shall discover your Gifts like never before."

"Well I'm ready," says Gloria. Speak for yourself.

"You all are," smiles the Prophetess. "Go, sup together. Our training and fast resumes at sundown." Anna leaves the room.

"Is she serious?" The words burst from my mouth. "I don't know about ya'll, but I was right there with her till she said no food. I mean, mannnn!"

"Is not that bad, Tre," smirks Gloria.

"Hmph, whatever! I mean, I get the no cursing, no drinking, no fraternizing with scandalous coeds. I get all that. But I need a T-bone, some ribs, a cheeseburger, an apple, orange—something!"

"Looks like you better eat a good lunch."

"Yeah, well let's get outta here. I'm starving."

"Me too. I was starting to lose focus myself. What about you Zeek?"

Zeek makes his way to the door. "You guys go on," he says. "Need to spend some time with Christina. I'll catch up with you later."

"Welp, looks like it's just you and me," I smile.

"Unfortunately."

"Our first date."

"This is NOT a date."

"Blah, blah, blah…"

I take Glo to one of my favorite spots in South Memphis—*Steins*. Gloria seems slightly apprehensive at first. "Don't let the outside fool you," I say of the aged, worn building. Stepping out of the truck, she frowns at the sight. I offer reassurance by taking her hand. "The inside is a hundred times better," I say intently, looking her straight in the eye. "I promise."

As we enter the small weathered eatery, a waitress instructs us to sit wherever we like. I choose a table far away from windows.

"Mmm," Gloria sniffs. "It does smell good in here."

"See, told ya."

"I can't remember the last time I had a home-cooked meal. Well, besides the other day when my mom tried to turn me into a Persuaded…but that doesn't count."

"Yeah, I'm sure that had to be crazy."

The waitress takes our order. I get the same thing every time I'm here. Fried chicken with greens, macaroni, and yams. Gloria opts for the turkey and dressing, another favorite.

"To think my mom is finally getting better only to find out it's just another form of manipulation…"

"Yeah but cut her some slack. The Persuaded got to her. That's not the same as making you feel guilty for not cooking."

"No?" Gloria counters. "Well what about not having a life, not knowing the truth about my father? Not having a boyfriend since the tenth grade!" Gloria stops. Slightly embarrassed, she peaks at me to gage my reaction.

"You sure that's all your mom's fault? I mean, why don't you try letting your hair down or wearing a dress every now and then?" I say, slurping through a straw. "You just may like it."

"Is that so?" Gloria smiles. "For you to take me even less serious? I don't think so."

"You know being feminine is not a crime. You won't lose your powers by wearing clothes that aren't three sizes too big."

"Our lives are at stake and all you can think about is seeing me in some skimpy outfit?! Typical!"

"I didn't say skimpy, I said—"

The waitress interrupts with our food. "Ketchup? Hot sauce? You two enjoy."

Okay, let me try this again. That didn't go so well. "Look Glo. You don't have to prove your worth to me anymore. You stood up to Bale's men. And that giant? I thought he had…well anyways, I believe in you." The sucking-on-a-lemon look on Gloria's face, softens. Maybe now I can finally bite into this chicken. "So, what about your father?" I ask. "Have you talked to him?"

"For what? I have nothing to say to that man."

"Well, if you can forgive your mother, you can at least talk to 'that man'."

Gloria tries to hide the extent of her pain, but it's evident in her words. "I've been lied to my entire life, Tre. And by the people I love the most. So what am I supposed to do? Just forget everything that happened overnight?"

"Of course not," I say. "But we need our minds focused if we're going to defeat Bale. And you still got love for your mom, right? And didn't you say this guy was like a father to you?"

"Yes!" shouts Gloria. "And that's why it hurts so much. I mean my mom? She's all I got. She's been the same ever since I can remember, whatever that is. But the Deacon, the church? They were my escape. They weren't supposed to let me down."

"I hear ya," I say, biting into a crispy edge of chicken. Like you said, your mom is your mom. Besides we all make mistakes, huh?"

"Right!"

"Even your mom. Even the Deacon. Even the church. Even you."

Gloria looks at me with suspicious focus before an impressed grin emerges.

"Did you just use reverse psychology on me?" she smiles.

"Who me? Of course not. But I will say, when you love someone, you don't let one action erase all the good they've done."

"Really?" questions Gloria. "And when did you become Dr. Phil?"

"Funny."

"No, I'm serious. That was actually kind of sweet."

"I guess a friend of mine has been showing me how to care for something other than myself." Our eyes lock for a quick second before the moment ends. My attention turns to the neglected plate in front of me. The chicken practically screams my name.

"Hey Tre?"

"Yep," I barely get out, biting down on the savory drumstick.

"If we get out of this alive, I'll wear something special just for you."

The savory drumstick nearly chokes the life out of me. Food sails from my mouth. "Say what?!"

Gloria laughs as she hands me napkins. "A dress, Tre!" she chuckles. "Something nice I can wear to your father's church! Geeez, what did you think I was talking about?!"

"Yeah, I know," I say, laughing at myself. "Just caught me off guard, that's all."

All of a sudden, I'm not hungry anymore. Go figure.

At nightfall, we reconvene to our plush hideout. "Did everyone enjoy their last meal?" asks Prophetess Anna. Our eyes meeting, Gloria and I smile. Zeek nods.

"Wonderful, my children."

"Oh Anna," says Gloria. "One thing before we get started. A friend of mine gave me an interesting tidbit on Bale."

"Go on my child."

"Turns out he was supposed to have some big press conference in L.A. but at the last minute, he changed it to Memphis. Whatever it is, it must be big. Everyone has to get security passes and right now we're on a waiting list. News outlets from all over are flying in. CNN, MSNBC, FOX."

"My child, have you a specific date?"

"Yeah, umm, Friday. Not sure of the time."

The Prophetess scans the room as her mind goes into thought. "Prophetess, what is it?"

"This gives us just over three days. We must do all we can to be ready."

"Ready for what?" asks Zeek.

"Everything. It is no coincidence Bale hath tarried here for so long. He wants us close. This announcement must be very important."

"I'll try to find out more tomorrow morning," says Gloria.

"Good. Now let's begin. You all have specialized Gifts. The Gifts of Seeing, Hearing, and Healing. But you also share more personal Gifts as well. Discernment for one. This is what enables you to detect the Shadow. You should also be able to locate your brother or sister at all times.

"I thought Zeek was the only one that has the Gift of Seeing?"

"Correct, but you should be able to feel the presence of your brethren. You should also be able to detect the presence of Bale and his minions. Failure to do so means you've allowed something to cloud your Gift. It could be anger, sorrow, frustration, even love. Bale will use this against you."

Me and the others do our best to take in the seemingly limitless knowledge of the Prophetess. The lessons focus on life and warfare tactics. Some things sound like they come straight from an army manual. Others, from the latest Sunday School lesson. After a couple of hours, Prophetess Anna gives us a quick break. She returns from the kitchen carrying a tray holding three glasses filled with a watery substance.

"Alright, my children. Our fast commences now. This vial is filled with water and minerals needed to sustain you for the next three days. You may drink as much as you desire but consume no other liquid or food. Understood?"

Hesitantly, I nod as we taste the sour drink. "What is this?" I frown.

"Your victuals. Now drink up."

"Our what?"

"It means food," answers Zeek.

Gloria quickly knocks out the 20-ounce container. Zeek and I take our time but eventually finish the bitter lemony-tasting beverage. "Some food this is."

"Now remember, you are warriors," the Prophetess starts. You fight for a kingdom. A kingdom Bale wants to control. You must battle beyond any distraction, and emotion, any mindset that can be used against you. Weariness from battle, hunger, grief. Nothing must hold you back. Now close your eyes. All of you."

Out of reflex, we look at each other before obeying the order. "Keep them closed until I instruct you further," commands our secretive instructor. I hear movement as abstract colors reflect against the darkness of my eyelids. After a few moments, Prophetess Anna speaks. Her voice is loud, though not close. She's not in the living room space anymore.

"I have placed you all in different areas. It is important to know the welfare and location of your brethren at all times, even when your concentration has been influenced by outside factors. Allow yourself to remain blind to your surroundings and use your discernment to locate your counterparts."

Suddenly, the warmth of breath bounces against my neck. "Where is Ezekiel?" whispers Prophetess Anna, standing as what I feel to be directly behind me.

"Uhhh, not sure."

"Focus!"

Okay, you can do this, Tre. Eyes still closed, I divert all my attention to the thought of Zeek. Using all of my energy, I zone in. And that's when the change comes. It's as if my body goes to another plateau. Although I can't actually see him, I can feel where he's at. I just know. "He's in the bathroom!" I shout.

"Be specific!"

"The one—the one in Gloria's room. He's leaning on the wall!"

"That's it!"

Wow. My senses go to another level. It's not as robust as the adrenaline or power that rushes through my body when the Persuaded are close. It takes more discipline to invoke this Gift. It's like being at a high level of meditation. Prophetess Anna continues the exercise with the others. After a few attempts, she ups the stakes by moving people in the middle of rounds. Fatigue and hunger begin to consume us as we exhaust our mental and physical energy supplies.

"Well done, my children. It is my prayer that circumstance is not nearly as dire when you face your adversary." As Anna makes her way to the kitchen, I take a seat on the stiff floor. Hadn't even noticed my clothes were dripping wet. The Prophetess returns with another tray. "This will replenish you."

There's no hesitation on my part this time. I gulp down the liquid victuals as if I've been in the Sahara. Kind of tastes like Gatorade now.

"Can I have some more?" asks Zeek.

"Yeah, me too."

"Of course, my children. Drink up. We have several more rounds to complete."

She can't be serious. But of course, she is. After a few more mind-numbing exercises, Prophetess Anna finally dismisses the day's training a little after 11pm. By 11:30, the entire suite is silent.

——THE ASSIGNED——

ZEEK

Anna starts the morning exercises promptly at 7am. We begin with our liquid diet followed by two hours of physical training. Next, the focus exercises. Anna increases the degree of difficulty, moving some of us to the suite across the hall, stairwells, even the elevator. By 11am, pangs of hunger cry out.

"I don't know if I can do this," says Tre. I agree. It's worse than yesterday and now it's almost been 24 hours without any real food.

"Focus!" yells Anna.

"Anyone got some peanuts, M&M's, piece of lint?!" cracks Tre.

"Tre you must—" Anna's eyes gloss over to white. The unusual woman goes into a trance-like state. So that's what I look like.

"What's wrong with her?" Gloria asks.

"She's having a vision," I answer.

"Is that what it's like, Zeek?"

"Something like that."

Anna gasps as she comes to. "AIM!" she yells, now out of her trance.

"What is it Anna?"

"Gloria, I see an army. Hordes of people in line as they willingly give themselves to Bale's rule. And the word, *AIM*."

"What does it mean?"

"I am not certain, my child. See if you can find any information on Bale's latest acquisitions, his mergers, anything."

"No problem, but I may need to get on the computer, make some calls for a couple of hours."

"That is fine my child. Besides, I must rest. Perhaps more shall be revealed to me if I gather my strength. We shall resume at sundown." Anna retires to her room.

"Man, she didn't look so good," says Tre.

"Yeah, looks like those visions are starting to take a toll on her," I say. "Not sure if I wanna go through that."

Gloria throws in her two cents. "Just do what you're supposed to, and you'll be fine."

"Yeah, yeah. And why don't you get on your task, computer girl."

"Don't worry. I always do."

Gloria and Tre spend the next couple of hours stationed in front of the laptop. The two act like high-school freshmen, giggling and playfully hitting one another. Can't say I saw that one coming. Didn't think Mr. Celebrity would go for someone like Gloria, but what do I know? Maybe he's actually changing. Just hope it doesn't jeopardize our work. But who am I to talk? I don't even know how I fit in all this. One day, I don't even believe in God. The next, I'm his super soldier.

I pass the time mostly daydreaming about food or checking on Chrissy and Alicia. The latter asks a lot of questions to which I don't know how to answer. She ends the conversation by saying "I miss you," to which I definitely don't know how to answer. Of course, I miss them, but her voice says more than I'm willing to convey. She's my wife's sister for heaven's sake. I don't care if it's been four years or forty. I read in the Bible somewhere about men marrying their deceased brother's wives to keep the lineage going. Not sure that applies in this instance.

Gloria ushers everyone to the computer desk as Anna is awakened from her nap.

"So, what you got for us, computer girl?"

"Okay, check this out." Gloria pulls images up on the screen. "Bale was being way too secretive about his huge announcement. So of course, every media outlet was trying to get the scoop on the big deal. I made some calls down to the station, which says I'm fired if I don't come in this weekend."

"Join the club," I smirk.

"Yeah…right. Anyways, after a little investigation, one of my co-worker's friends, who works for CNN, found a patent submission and FCC request for a new imploration of technology submitted by one of Bale's subsidiaries, Lab Tech."

"Whoa, you're losing me."

"I'm getting there," Gloria says, pulling up more images. "Bale had to get his big announcement approved seeing it deals with implementing a new way to use experimental technology. How he got it approved so fast, I'm not sure. But I wouldn't be surprised if he had a Persuaded or two camped out in the FCC office."

"But of course," says Anna.

"Right. And this is what he plans to unveil."

A futuristic inscription of the acronym, A.I.M. flashes across the computer.

"Aim?"

"It stands for Analysis Identification Marker. Now check this out."

Gloria clicks the mouse.

"That's the Mark!"

A computer drawn version of the Mark is brought up. "That's also their logo," nods Gloria. "It says the Analysis Identification Marker will forever change the way we exchange information. Soon driver licenses, credit cards, passports, all tangible pieces of identification will be obsolete."

"Bale is going to hide his Mark in broad daylight," Anna exhales.

"I'm still not there."

Anna separates herself from us as she paces around the room. "I'm sure you've all heard of 666, the Mark of the Beast. The book of Revelation says, 'and he forced everyone, both small and great, rich and poor, free and slave, to receive a mark on his right hand, so no one could buy or sell unless he had the mark.'"

"So that tattoo we've seen on the Persuaded. That's the 666, the Mark of the Beast?"

"Not quite, my child. Bale's mark is different from that of which the Scriptures speak. That mark is the mark of his father, Lucifer. Bale will not force anyone to bear his. People will naturally be drawn to his status."

"Got it," says Tre.

"Yes, my child! His influence and gift of persuasion far exceed any physical display of power. The people will flock to him. And what he desires most is to be God. To have the people serve him of their own free will."

Finally, I get it as well. "Wow. So that's what this whole hiring spree's about. Give the people jobs, put the Mark on 'em, build an army."

"And there's no telling how many people they'll come in contact with and influence," says Gloria.

"Yeah, and in this economy, people will do just about anything to get a job," says Tre. "Even sell their souls."

The look on my face conveys reluctant agreement. Tre continues. "You're talking about a couple of years and thousands of Persuaded running around."

"Hundreds of thousands," Anna interjects. "Maybe more."

"Dang. So how do we stop it?"

"We must get the people to see Bale for what he really is," says Anna.

"And how do you suppose we get people to see black, ghost-like shadows floating around?" I question. "I barely believe it myself."

"Not so much the supernatural, my child. The enemy's main power is persuasion. He preys on the weak and confused. We must get them to see that Bale wants to use them even if it's just a physical revelation."

"We need some dirt on the great Jason Bale," says Tre. "I mean other than the fact he's a demon and all…"

"Hey guys, check this out!" Gloria, still seated at the computer, pulls up a local newspaper article. We reassemble around the 12-inch screen. "Zeek, Tre. Remember this guy?"

"Hey, that's the guy from the club that got rowdy with Bale."

I faintly remember his face. "Yeah, didn't he splash holy water on Bale or something?"

Anna steps closer to the screen. "Harold?" she asks.

"You know this guy?"

A picture of the now deceased man is placed next to a link to an article. The link reads: *Local theology professor, Dr. Harold Ambrose, found dead. Foul play suspected.*

"Yes," says Anna. "He was an old acquaintance. Once, a member of the Intercessors."

"Keepers of our story, right?" Gloria asks.

"Yes, but Harold's quest for knowledge consumed him. The more he discovered, the further he withdrew from society. He grew tired of waiting for the Three of Three to return. He began to try and confront the enemy on his own. If only he waited a while longer."

Tre shakes his head. "We were right there when Bale's men got to him."

"Maybe we can use this against Bale," says Gloria.

"I am beginning to understand your strategy," nods Anna.

We spend the next few hours discussing tactics for confronting the untouchable, Jason Bale. Anna hammers across the point about sticking together as a team. She seems determined not to let us meet the same fate as her generation. But if they didn't succeed, how can she be so certain we can?

"Now children, it is my desire that you approach Gloria's plan from a non-confrontational stance, using Bale's propaganda against him. But as you have already witnessed, physical engagement is sometimes necessary. If the enemy confronts you, fight as one. Think not that you can do it alone because of your incredible Gifts. The Three are not better than one. The Three are one."

The eccentric woman the others call Prophetess, continues her battle prelude as she marches around us. "Now, as you have experienced, each of you possess abnormal levels of strength, stamina, and agility. Warfare methodology has even been imputed into each of your DNA for such a time as this. Now you must learn how to harness this power into one simple maneuver that temporarily disables the enemy." Her eyes find Gloria. "Especially those whom can be won back. The Rebuke." Anna stands beside Tre. "I think you may remember, my child."

"Oh, you mean when you threw me across the room?" Tre smiles. "So that's what it's called. The Rebuke?" Anna nods. "That's kind of cool though," Tre continues. "Sounds like an old-school wrestling move. The *Rebuke*."

"I'm glad you approve. I was hoping you would once more help me demonstrate."

"Sure—wait!" Tre steps back. Now this is actually funny.

"You mean, you wanna throw me back across the room?"

"C'mon Tre," I say, egging him on. "You won't feel a thing."

"You do have the Gift of Healing, my child."

"Yeah, you guys need to learn this, Tre," grins Gloria.

"Fine," Tre sighs. "Just hurry up and—"

Without warning, Anna gently thumps Tre with her fingertips. He flies twelve feet before crashing to the ground. Gloria and I do our best not to laugh. Laugh loud, that is.

The training exercises continue past midnight. Hunger and fatigue set in as we exhaust our physical, mental, and as Anna says, our spiritual reserves. But the more I try to dive in this thing head-first without over-thinking it, the more power I feel. Some of the stuff she's teaching us really does work.

Ahhhh, the last morning for lemon-in-a-cup. But at this juncture, I'd drink anything. Surprisingly, everyone is kind of hyper today. Guess our bodies are finally getting used to the lack of food. The day before was consumed with several intense hours of training and some new meditation drills. Not sure if I've lost any weight but my pores feel opened up, eyes are whiter. Come to think of it, I haven't had a cigarette since...*the day*. I'm still not sure of everything, this life-changing experience, this new revelation of God, of demons. But I'd be lying if I said meeting Anna and the others hadn't changed my life...for the better.

"So, what you got for us today, Prophetess?" asks a bouncing Tre.

"There are no training exercises this morning," says Anna. "My children, you have done well."

"Now that's what I'm talking about!" says Tre as he high-fives me and Gloria.

"Although there is one more task you must complete."

"But I thought you said—"

"This task is not a training exercise, nor can I instruct it."

"What is it Anna?" asks Gloria.

"Each of you has faced turmoil and tragedy," starts the Prophetess. "Although you have survived your personal storms, debris still lingers. As I have stated before, some of you have not forgiven others. Some of you have not forgiven yourselves, maybe even God. You must make peace with whatever unresolved issues are in your life. Just like a physical impairment, the enemy will use this against you. Take this day to free yourself of any bondage that currently encases your heart."

No words are needed. We each know all too well the rubble that remains in our lives.

I haven't been to church in weeks. Prophetess Anna's words run through my mind as I pull up to the gothic building. *Make peace.* And that's what I've come to do, though part of me is afraid of what I may find out. If I can jump off buildings and fight superhuman tax collectors, surely I can handle a talk with my... *father.*

Adrenaline courses through me, although not the feeling I get when a fight is imminent. This feels more like the sensation I got as a child when I knew I was about to get in trouble, although this time I can't have possibly done anything wrong. *Okay, take a deep breath. You can do this.*

The smell of the hundred-year-old building brings back memories. Looks like nothing's changed. What am I thinking? I haven't been gone that long. But considering I've spent half of my life here, the time away does seem like an eternity. I walk past a couple of the classrooms. They'll be full in a few hours. After-school care, tutoring, the art class I used to teach. I wonder who's been filling in?

"I didn't fully grasp how much you did around here until you were gone," says a familiar voice. "How did you keep all of this together?"

I turn to see Deacon Nichols' tall, slender frame. He's cut his hair since the last time I've seen him. "Not sure. Guess I never had the time to actually think about it. I just did."

"Well, you did great."

"Thanks. How has everything been? I know I haven't—"

"It's okay. We've managed. I told everybody you were taking a leave to help with your mother."

"Isn't that kind of bordering the truth?"

"Well..." smiles the Deacon. "...I figured there were some things you guys needed to work on."

"Yeah, but she's not the only one, Deacon."

"Call me David." I've never heard anyone call the Deacon by his first name, let alone spoke it myself. "And you're right," he says. "But she is your mother, first and foremost."

"You almost say that like—like the rest doesn't matter." For some reason, these words in particular strike a chord with the Deacon—David. His eyes water, but surely he's not about to cry? Fumbling with his hands, he looks around, now drawing closer. Words burst from his mouth. "I called you—I came by, your mother wouldn't open the door–"

"Did you know?" are the only words I can get out. Deacon Nichols takes his time speaking. At first, it reminds me of that night. But something's different.

"No, of course not. Me and your mother, we were intimate only once. Everything was going well, but then about a month later, she started acting weird. The the calls just stopped, she wouldn't see me. I guess that was around the time she found out she was ...pregnant. I thought she found someone else. I had no idea you were mine. You have to believe me."

I discern honesty in his words. Not sure if it's due to my training or just something in my heart, but the words are true. He awaits my response. "I believe you."

"Oh Gloria, if I knew I had a child, I would have never walked away from my responsibility."

"It's okay, Deacon. I believe you."

"David."

"*David*, I believe you. A'ma used me to get back at you."

"I never intended to hurt your mother. She was a beautiful woman, much like the one that stands before me now. But I was conflicted with whether I should become a priest. Your mother couldn't understand what I was going through, so I guess she decided she didn't want me to be a part of your life."

"I never knew why she would drop me off at this church, religiously, every Sunday. But I guess in her own, twisted way, she did want me to know my father." Tears run down as I look up at the tall, slender man. "And I did just that. I got to know a wonderful man." Fiddling with his fingers, his height is shortened as he hunches over. This time I step closer. "I don't blame you or A'ma. We can't agonize over the past. We have to move forward. There's so much work to be done. To have you in my life in any capacity is a blessing."

Deacon Nichols raises his head. "You are something else. What have you been doing the last few weeks?"

"Learning how to fight for the ones I love."

————T H E A S S I G N E D————

ZEEK

Today's grayish outcast is a perfect replica of the 807's exterior as it finally arrives to its stop. No chopper today. I opt for public transportation, seeing that I'm carrying precious cargo. Christina. "Hold Daddy's hand," I smile as the sliding doors of the bus swing open.

"Daddy, am I sick again?" Chrissy asks as she watches the familiar sight pull up. Her words nearly sadden me. Not sure if she or I will ever look at a hospital any differently.

"No baby. Of course not. We're just going to see an old friend."

Everyone's face at St. Jude lights up as they watch a healthy, smiling Christina skip by. Nurses and crew approach as they marvel at the sight of my precious daughter. Like most children, Christina loves the attention. Alicia took extra time fixing her hair. My baby girl wears a blue dress and white patent leather shoes. Thankfully, Alicia dressed her too. I probably wouldn't have picked such an elaborate outfit. Mine, of course, is the usual. Jeans and t-shirt, albeit clean, accompanied by my favorite black leather jacket.

I too approach several nurses and thank them for their assistance with Christina. Some seem hesitant at first to shake my hand. Guess I wasn't the easiest person to work with. Vivid memories come to mind as we walk by several of the rooms in the children's ward. Christina and I observe children affected by cancer and other diseases. Some of their heads are shaved. Others sleep as tubes protrude from their small fragile bodies. As we pass room 413, emotions spring up. I can't help but to peek into the deathly cold room, a major part of our lives just a few short weeks ago. Now another child rests in the bed recently occupied by Christina. And another parent sleeps in the chair seated next to the bed. As I turn, a well-known voice adds to the surreal moment. "And what do we have here?"

"Chappy Brynint!" yells Christina as only she can. She runs into the arms of the waiting Chaplain Bryant. "My goodness, look how big you've gotten! How old are you now, ten?"

"No Chappy," laughs my tickled child. "I'm five!"

"Wow! Well go say hi to your old friends. They've missed you."

Christina runs off to play with the other kids. Although fully dressed and healthy, she doesn't seem to notice the state of the sick children. They don't see condition or illness. Only friendship.

Chaplain Bryant makes his way over. "Mr. Myers," he cautiously nods.

"My friends call me Zeek."

It takes a moment for the Chaplain to process my statement. "Okay, *Zeek*. And how are you, sir?"

"Everything's great Chaplain. Pretty great."

His eyes watch me until they finally believe what they see. "Well that's good. You look like a new man."

"You have no idea," I chuckle. The Chaplain joins in on the laugh.

"Well, you don't know what it does to me and the children to see Christina so full of life."

"We owe a lot of it to you." An awkward look spreads across the Chaplain's face. "You do? Why do you say that?"

"You gave my baby hope. Even when her stubborn young father couldn't do it, an even more stubborn Chaplain did." Chaplain

Bryant's smile stretches from ear to ear. "You taught her not to give up. And I'll never forget that." As I extend my hand, a tear rolls down the preacher man's face. Instead of a hand, a tight squeeze greets me as the Chaplain hugs me with all his might.

The visit lasts for another fifteen minutes or so before Christina and I make our way downstairs. Chaplain Bryant walks us out. "Sometimes you think what you do doesn't make a difference but then you see a miracle like Christina, and it makes everything worthwhile."

I can't help but pick the faithful man's brain. "Chaplain, I know you've seen Christina come a long way and all, but there's so much evil in the world, so many people dying. How do you know any of it's real?"

"You mean my faith?"

I nod.

"Well that's just it, son. It's *faith*. It's believing in something you can't see. And I choose to believe. That's all I can do. That's all any of us can do."

He's right. It's my choice. It's always been my choice. "Of course, every now and then," he continues, "we're blessed with things we can see that encourage our faith."

"Yeah, you're right," I say, smiling down at Christina as we head for the exit.

"And looks like you kept that new stride, Mr. Myers, or shall I say, Zeek," the Chaplain comments, referring to my limp, or rather lack thereof.

"Like I said, Chaplain, you have no idea…"

——T H E A S S I G N E D——

TRE

I pull up to the cemetery right before the heavy rain. Memories of Martin's funeral are just as fresh as the smell of raindrops falling to the ground. No liquid poison needed for this trip. Nope. I'm done with that life. Just me, my God, and my brother.

I remember the exact location of the tombstone with little effort. As I kneel, my fingers run across script chiseled into a massive granite block. They read,

Martin Luther Turner
Son, Brother, Friend
2000–2019

"Man, I never thought it would end like this. I know we weren't the closest, let's face it. We were so different. You wanted to be a gangster. I wanted to be a ladies' man. I wanted to fit in, you wanted to be rebel. I liked Jay-Z, you liked Tupac." A soft smile holds my face as the words continue to flow. "But I figured, later in life, I'd be successful, you'd finally sow your oats, and we could kick it. Take our families on trips, do cook-outs— you know, the things brothers are supposed to do." Thunderous beads of rain now fall, masking the tears of a wounded sibling. "But I guess it didn't work out that—Martin, I'm sorry! I didn't know. I DIDN'T KNOW!!!" My clothes drenched, I look to the sky. "Oh God! Forgive me!"

I sit silent for a moment. Just the melodic patterns of rain. No one answers. Not in the heavens, on the earth, nor in the ground. Or do they?

"I found out who did it, Martin," I say, more composed. "And I'm gonna make it right. You always said I'd be a preacher. Well, I don't know about that, but God's definitely got something for me to do." I look down at my pulsating hands. "He's given me these Gifts. This power. And I guarantee you one thing."

Once more my fingers rub across my brother's name. "THIS …won't be in vain."

I receive a text message from Prophetess Anna reminding us to be back at the suite by sundown. Funny. I never pictured her as the texting type.

Everyone has already arrived by the time I show up. The room is filled with so much laughter, they hardly notice my presence. Even Mr. Sternface—Zeek, is smiling ear to ear.

"Knock, knock."

"Oh, there you are Tre," smiles the Prophetess. "I was getting worried about you. Is everything okay?"

"Everything's great. I see you guys are having a good time."

"Oh yes. Ezekiel was sharing of his days as a rodeo clown."

"Zeek? Rodeo clown? C'mon man. Really?" Zeek raises his hands and hunches his shoulders.

"Hey man, I've worked all kinds of jobs. But that one takes the record. Three hours. That's it. When the bull came after me, I jumped over the railing and kept on running. I ran past concessions, past the restrooms, past the front door. That was it!"

This is the first time I can recall Zeek being...*funny*. And that's when it hits me. We're finally a family. Which makes my surprise all the better. "Man, that's crazy! Well since everyone is in such a good mood, I guess this is the perfect time to give you these." I pull three boxes from my gym bag, handing two of them to my partners. "One for you, one for you, and one for me."

"What do we have here, Tre?" asks Zeek.

"Well, you guys are always kidding me about watching too many movies and all that, but growing up I always wanted to be the characters I read about. You know just some kind of super-hero. And now, crazily enough, God has given me that chance. And what does every superhero have in common..."

"Super...powers?" shrugs Gloria.

"Well yeah, you're right. But what else?"

Zeek and Gloria shrug again.

"A costume."

"Hey man, I'm not wearing any tights," puffs Zeek. "Forget about it."

"And I'm definitely not wearing some skimpy bikini," says Gloria, rolling her eyes. "Or some tight latex bodysuit. Hmph. Please."

"Will you two just open the boxes?"

After a few stubborn moments, Gloria goes first. Enclosed in tissue paper is a black, ribbed, sweater-like garment. A small black emblem is sewn on the right sleeve. "See, not so bad, is it?" I ask. Gloria's eyes are still affixed to the trendy pullover. "Definitely not what I had in mind," she grins. "Thank God."

"Your turn Zeek."

He mumbles as he opens the sealed white cardboard box. "You see what they're trying to do to me, Anna?" he says, pressing his way through tissue paper. "They want me to look like Justin Beiber. Now if that's how you get down, fine. But as for me, I'm not— Hey!" Zeek finds a black leather vest resting in his box. A bit sleeker than any I've seen him wear, but his reaction denotes approval. A raised triangular symbol is embroidered on the back. Three grooves perforate the side with a circle resting inside the top of the triangle.

"Now THIS is what I'm talking about!" shouts Zeek. Everyone laughs at the familiar words. "Thanks man."

"Yeah, thanks Tre," says Gloria. "I like it."

"No problem guys."

"So what's in your box?"

"Just a v-neck T-shirt."

"Tight, I'm sure," says Gloria.

"Tight? Never. It's called fitted. I can't help if the guns jump out!"

"Black as well?" asks Prophetess Anna.

"Yep. I figured since Bale and his boys love to wear white, we'd let the good guys wear black."

"And what's with the symbol?" Zeek asks.

"Well seeing how Bale has his mark, I figured we could have a logo. You mind?" I reach for Zeek's vest. "See the triangle represents the Creator and the three grooves represent us, the Three of Three. And the circle at the top is for you, Prophetess Anna."

"Wonderful, Tre," smiles the Prophetess. "Very creative. Such symbolism. And here I perceived it to simply be a fancy 'A'."

"Funny you should say that. It is. The symbol has duel meanings. It also stands for the Assigned."

"The who?" asks Gloria.

"The A-ssign-ed," I enunciate. "I know we're technically the Three of Three but that sounds so Chronicles of Narnia-ish." I switch my voice to a crude but effective British-like accent. *"We're the Thray of Thray, keepas of da story."* Gloria shakes her head at my antics but my point has been made. "I remember what Prophetess Anna said when we first met her, about God assigning these special Gifts to three people every few generations, and it just stuck with me. *The Assigned.* You think it's okay, Prophetess? At least for our generation?"

The others and I wait for Prophetess Anna to speak. She seems to be in great thought.

"You okay, Anna?" asks Zeek.

"I am blessed to have you children in my life," she finally whispers. It looks as if she's trying to hold back tears. "And the Assigned is highly appropriate, my child. Highly."

"Awww," I smile. "You guys know what time it is. Group hug! C'mon, bring it in." Gloria, and Prophetess Anna move in closer. "C'mon on Zeek. Don't make me come get you."

"So, we're really doing this, huh?"

"Yep," I say, while squeezing my new family. "Now that's what I'm talking about…"

Prophetess Anna is never quite the same after the moment. We spend the next three hours reviewing the same plan, over and over. A worried countenance has consumed her ever since I gave out the garments. Didn't know a sweater and vest could have such an effect. Or maybe it reminds the Prophetess of something. Not sure what, but the monotony of today's lesson is a bit draining to say the least.

"Now remember my children," she continues. "You must do your best to not physically confront Bale on tomorrow. You are to be as a fly in porridge. Not enough to change the flavor but enough to make it undesirable. There's still so much we have to learn."

"Uhh okay. We got it Prophetess," I reassure her. "Look, it'll be a piece of cake. Big Pete hooked me up with some surveillance footage. We'll show it and have Bale and his boys running for cover. After that, they will not want any of this. Shoot, we might not even get to use our Gifts. And I owe a couple of 'em a lil something extra!"

"Yeah," Gloria agrees. "I told a producer down at the station about the video Tre got from Sin City. He says if it's as good as I say, he'll run it."

"Please focus, my children. I know you feel this power radiating inside and you have had modest success in battle so far but believe me when I say…you have not seen Bale's true power."

"Don't worry Anna, says Gloria. "Bale won't know what hit 'em."

Morning comes sooner than expected. It feels as if I laid my head down just minutes ago. I awaken to a black sweater staring me in the face as it drapes itself on the back of a reading chair. My outfit. Actually, it was a pretty sweet gesture by Tre. My mind does wonder where this could go after...after all of this hero stuff. Who knows? We're so different, but I've seen him change so much in these couple of weeks. Again, who knows? My main focus is reminded to me by the ever-gawking black sweater. *The Fight.* No, we're not supposed to engage Bale and his Angels in any manner, but I'm ready for some action...if it so chooses to find us.

Anna is already up, fully dressed, and pacing the floor by the time I make my way to the common area. She makes a brief smile towards me before the distressed look returns.

"Hey Glo," says Tre, his mouth half full. "Prophetess Anna said we could have some orange juice. Tastes like heaven after that other stuff." I nod in acknowledgement as I reach for Anna's hand.

"Is everything okay, Anna?"

She looks at me with an uneasy gaze before speaking. "I didn't rest well my child." A youthful glow hides behind her aged eyes. Long gray hair rides her shoulders. I don't know how she manages to keep it so pressed. She wears black pants with a shimmery effect and a black custom-fit button-down top. Even in one of the simplest outfits I've seen her wear, she still looks regal.

"Everything will be fine," I say. "We're just going to level the playing field. You can show us more when we get back." I look over to Tre and Zeek in the kitchen. "I'll keep them in line," I smile.

Anna squeezes my hand back. Slowly, the wrinkle lines retreat as she grins, "Well, we all have our assignments, now don't we?" I smile back, now holding both of her hands. I see so much of what I would like to see in my mother. Not sure why, but the moment almost brings me to tears. Seeing through her fiery-like eyes, I can see the adoration she has for each member of the group. She truly thinks of us as her children.

"It's okay, Anna. You've taught us well."

"But not enough."

"But well. Very well."

Tre and Zeek interrupt our impromptu girl's moment.

"We gotta get going Glo, if we're going to put this plan of yours in effect," says Tre.

"I know. You ready Zeek?"

"To go confront demons dressed as superstars?" Zeek smirks. "Sure. Why not? Besides, this'll make for a great book one day."

"Man, who you telling…" laughs Tre.

The team looks good in black, I observe, as we make our way to Tre's car. Zeek sports his new leather vest, t-shirt, jeans, and a ferocious looking pair of shades. His hair also seems extra spiked today. Not as long and tangled as it was the day we met in the park. I wear the Assigned sweater as requested by Tre. For some reason, I actually put some thought into today's wardrobe before putting it on. I opt for jeans instead of jogging pants and boots instead of tennis. Like Tre said, probably won't get to have any real fun today. Tre wears his v-neck t-shirt—it's actually a nice fit —with beige cargo pants and grey chucks. Looks like the stubble has been shaved from his bald head. I have to admit, he's cute. But he'll never hear it from me.

Zeek walks straight past the sedan. "Where you going, Zeek?" asks Tre. "I thought we would ride together. Don't tell me you're gonna trust one of those rinky-dink bikes today?"

Zeek continues walking, turning only slightly to respond. "Yeah. Well, this right here ain't rinky-dink." Tre and I look at each other a bit confused.

"What is he talking about?"

"You know Zeek," responds Tre. "Ain't no telling—wait a minute! I don't believe it."

I turn back around to see Zeek standing in front of a beautiful custom-made motorcycle.

"Now what were you guys saying?" he mouths as he mounts the burly chopper. Tre and I quickly move closer to get a better look. The bike looks like something out of a magazine. Nothing like the—pardon the term—*junk* that Zeek rode before. Chrome finish shines on an elongated body. The gas tank and fender are a pearl white color. What looks like wings and some writing I can't quite make out yet, are drawn on the side.

"It's beautiful Zeek."

"Man, who you steal this from?"

"Nobody. It's a project I've been working on for the last couple of years."

"Angel," I say, reading the side.

"Yep," smiles Zeek, kissing his hands before transferring them to the bike. "My Angel."

"I knew it was some class somewhere deep down inside of you," says Tre.

"Well thanks."

"I'm just foolin' with ya man. Let's take that chariot out for a spin."

"I'm right behind ya."

——THE ASSIGNED——

TRE

Gloria uses her news station credentials to get us in the packed-out ballroom of the Peabody Hotel. She refers to me and Zeek as her 'undisciplined lackeys' who forgot their ID's. I'm used to the moniker, TNT Turner, being enough to gain entrance to the trendiest of spots, but not today.

The room is filled with reporters, cameramen, staff, and even a few fans. Knowing Bale, he probably had them hand selected. A podium is situated at the front of the room atop of a large platform built for the press conference. An erected wall stands about ten feet behind the podium. 'Bale Media' and a logo run across the backdrop many times over. It's the Mark, but drawn with a more modern, contemporary flare. The first shape takes the form of a cleverly designed, 'B' with 'ALE' running downward. A small circle sits in the middle. The next shape is an inversion of the first shape but made to look like an 'M' on its side. 'EDIA' runs upward. This guy is something else.

"You guys see that?" I ask. "Broad daylight."

"Anna was right," says Gloria.

"You know it."

"So, what now?" asks Zeek.

"I'll go find my contact," says Gloria. "We should wait 'til Bale makes his announcement. Otherwise, it might not have the same effect."

I nod in agreement. "Let's do this."

Gloria makes her way through the press as Zeek and I remain posted in the back of the ballroom. The lights go dim as the pep rally atmosphere heightens. An announcer can be heard over the PA system. "Ladies and gentleman, I present to you...Bale!" Rock music plays as strobe lights flash in every direction. Smoke rises from the ground. My initial reaction is, the Persuaded, however this haze is made by a canister. Images of 'Bale Media' and the Mark flash across two large screens positioned near the front. As the smoke clears, bodies clad in white materialize on stage. First a woman and a man I've never seen before, take their places on either side of the stage. The next faces are a bit more familiar. Bale's Angels.

The men take their time strutting across the stage as theme music guides their footing. Looks like they're appearing shortest to tallest. Lastly, the giant, Amnon, emerges. Fans cheer as the overgrown oaf takes his place. "They're not all that," I say, reaching over to Zeek. He stands, hands folded, sunglasses on, taking in the spectacle. The music changes to a more intense beat as the ring leader comes out to a standing ovation. Mr. Bale himself. Photographers snap away as Bale bustles around like a motivational speaker amped on energy drinks. Waving to the crowd repeatedly, he prances back and forth across the full length of the stage. As the smoke subsides, a new one surfaces. The Shadow now engulfs all on stage. Bale, his Angels, staff included. The men pose like rock-stars as the grayish-black haze hovers around each of them. Hairs on my arm rise as my body instinctively gets ready for battle at the sight of the tell- tale sign. I look over to Zeek. Before I can say anything, he nods. "It's funny. We're really the only ones that can see this," he says. I scan the crowd of screaming fans and news-hungry journalists. "Yep," I agree as no one seems to notice the true headliner on stage; eight people, all wearing the Shadow. What a sight. Briefly I imagine being in a room filled with hundreds of them. Thousands. I decide to not let my mind go there.

The crowd finally quiets under the urging of Bale as he speaks into an oversized microphone waiting on stage. "As many of you know, Bale Media has been a growing company ever since its inception five years ago. Employing about 1,500 people, Bale Media could not be classified as a juggernaut, until now." Bale pauses, building his story. "Teaming with scientists, we have created a technology that will change our company, this country, the world. A technology that will bring us focus, direction. I give you… AIM!"

Reporters appear baffled as they hold out miniature recorders capturing Bale's every word. "The Analysis Identification Marker will change the way we share information. No longer will one have to carry around three, four, five different identifications. From now on, all your information can be stored in one convenient place…YOU."

Murmurs trickle through the crowd as Bale draws our attention to the giant screen.

"Yep," I say. "Here we go."

——T H E A S S I G N E D——

ZEEK

A well-crafted commercial for Bale Media plays on the screen above. Tre and I watch as the video shows lasers etching a futuristic version of the Mark unto a wrist. The camera expands to show a young woman in sweats sitting at a computer. She holds her hand up to the computer screen. It reads, 'uploading 98%, 99%, COMPLETE'. Now in business attire, the young woman extends her wrist towards a digital device. Again, the camera expands to show graphs and charts instantly appearing onto a boardroom projector. A table of her peers applauds in the video. This guy really knows how to get his point across.

Another character waves his wrist over an ATM scanner. Money immediately disperses. People wait in line to board a plane. Rather than tickets, their wrists are scanned. The person's image and information are viewed upon a portable receiver. Next, a young mom's wrist is scanned as she purchases ice cream for her young child. I can't help but think about Chrissy as I watch. Each scene is brightened by the cast's infectious smiles.

Reporters, photographers, and fans alike all watch in awe. Bale has really done his homework. On the surface, this looks like a really good idea. And to think of all the jobs that could come from this.

But I'm not here for a job, I tell myself. No matter how good it looks, I've gotta stay focused. Bale readdresses the crowd. "Soon, there will be no need for driver's licenses, passports, or even credit cards. Zip drives will be a thing of the past. Imagine work files, reports, everything you need at the flick of a wrist."

"Flick of a wrist," I mumble. Instantly, I can see the marketing campaign. It's near genius.

"Say something, Zeek?" asks Tre. I shake my head as we continue to watch. Bale and his entourage raise their arms revealing their Marks. As stated, in broad daylight.

"It's time!" shouts the big-time celebrity. "A new day is upon us. Those who want to be left behind, so be it. But those who want to be ahead of the curve, who want to work for a company on the verge of global domination, I say to you, consider Bale Media! In five years, we'll be bigger than Apple and Google combined!"

The mass of reporters erupt. I get so caught up in the moment, I barely hear Tre.

"It's time, Zeek," he repeats.

"Gotcha."

As Bale is about to field questions from the journalists, the screen goes black. A voice booms over the sound system. "Who is Jason Bale?" Bale and crew look around as images display on screen. "Dr. Harold Ambrose. Found floating in the Mississippi, one week ago. Where was he last seen?" A large question mark flashes across the screen. "Being accosted by Jason Bale's personnel security detail he so often refers to as his Angels." The screen displays a grainy image of the security tape showing the guy pouring water on Bale then flips to Bale's men physically escorting the doctor away. Murmurs around the room grow louder. "I assure you, this is all false," Bale says, stepping into the microphone. "It's propaganda."

"You should know!" shouts a resurfaced Gloria. Looks like her video is producing the reaction we were banking on. Bale waves to the crowd once more before leaving the stage with his Angels. His PR staff remains at the podium as they address the crowd. "As you can see, we are experiencing technical difficulties," says the smiling assistant. "Someone is playing a horrible trick on Bale Media and we will get to the bottom of this immediately…"

"Well looks like your plan worked," I say to Gloria.

"Yeah," she nods. "But I'm not sure it's enough."

"I'm with you Glo," adds Tre.

"What are you guys talking about? Bale was right in the middle of his big unveiling and you came and stole his thunder. Where I'm from, that's usually called a success."

"Yeah, but he needs to feel our presence," says Tre, fists balled.

"Right," agrees Gloria. "These are demons we're talking about. Can you imagine how many Persuaded could be running around if we sit back and wait? Bale and his Angels need to be banished to the pits of hell…for good."

"Now that's what I'm talking about. Can you see where they are?" Tre says, watching me.

"Huh? Who? What—no. Remind me, what are we supposed to be doing here?"

"Come on Zeek. You don't seem like the type to back down from a fight."

"What about what Anna said?"

"And you definitely don't seem like the type to follow instructions verbatim," Gloria says, clenching her teeth.

"Can you hear anything, Glo?" asks Tre. I can't believe these two. But as Gloria focuses, I can't help but focus on Bale's commercial. Scanning your wrist to get ice cream? Could it work?

"Bale asked for his car to meet him near entrance three!" she shouts. "Let's go!" The two take off for the exit. Reluctantly, I follow.

——THE ASSIGNED——

GLORIA

Every sound is magnified in the dense acoustics of the parking garage. In here, my gift of hearing is not needed to pick up on Bale's rhetoric. "They must worship me freely!" he shouts as we approach around the winding corridor.

"Don't bank on it!" Tre shouts back. Bale and his five Angels turn to face the Three of Three. Or as Tre calls us, the Assigned. Cars line the ever-turning structure as we take our stand. Twenty yards is all that separates us.

"You think you have thwarted my ministry?" says Bale. "This is just the beginning."

"We'll see about that," I say.

"But I give credit where credit is due," he grins. "Nice move. So did Little Anna help you with that?"

"Leave her out of this, Bale," says Zeek.

"It's too late for that. You came for me. Her fate will be the same as her friends and the same as you, her little students. I don't have time for this. Tell the Other I said, hello."

Bale and Amnon continue walking up and around the twisting passage. They disappear behind huge concrete columns that hold together the tightly confined space. The four remaining Angels block our path. But not for long. Almost on cue, the Shadow rises around the souped-up bodyguards. And at the same time, a power races through my veins. The power to fight. Dressed in the usual white suits, a couple of the Angels take off their suit-coats. Guess they know what we're capable of.

"Now which one of you killed my brother," Tre mugs. The Angels snicker while some crack their knuckles. "Man, forget this."

"Tre wait!" shouts Zeek.

Tre rushes for Bale's Angels. I immediately follow. The mo-hawked Balak lands two fists to Tre's chest sending him crashing onto the hood of a parked car. He can take care of himself. I find my old acquaintance, Hantos. He presses me with a barrage of swift punches and kicks. His speed is exceptional, but so is mine. Moves and combinations come naturally when the Gift takes over. I glance over to see Zeek engaged with the other two brutes.

I take a mean kick to the sternum. It probably would've set me down a couple weeks ago, but this time I fight past the initial jolt and reverse my momentum, landing a stiff kick to Hantos' temple while performing a back flip. I come out of it just in time to see my enemy land hard on the unforgiving concrete. I love that move.

"I like to see you try that again," says Tre, motioning to Balak. The doomed Angel sprints towards Tre as fragments of the Shadow linger. This time Tre waits, timing his assault. As Balak swings, Tre leans back, dodging the punch, while grabbing Balak around the waist. Like me, he uses his enemy's momentum, heaving Balak over his head, sending him flying into the same car Tre himself, crashed into. Tre runs and with supernatural ability, soars in the air intending to come down with a brutal punch to the Balak's face. With not a second to spare, Balak rolls off the car and Tre's hand smashes through the metal hood as if it were gelatin.

The other Angels regroup and formulate a different strategy. A row of custom-made choppers similar to Zeek's, rests in the parking garage. Two of the Angels lift and hurl the bikes as if they were dumbbells. I can't but help wonder if we're that strong as Zeek and I dodge the flying torpedoes.

"I've had just about enough of this," says Zeek. His eyes glaze over as if his every move is being controlled by another force. Ripping the wheel off one of the flying choppers, Zeek uses it as a shield as he runs straight for the Angels, weaving through the hurling barrage of motorcycles. It's like he can foresee their every move. Guess that's what he does. Zeek gets close, heaving the wheel at one of the Angels. The spinning disc hits the Angel square in the chest. The demon in white soars backwards, black haze and all, crashing into the abundant selection of parked cars.

The other Angel drops his motorcycle to deal with Zeek. But before he has a chance, I sideswipe him with a swift right jab. Not today. Two Angels lie unconscious. Two remain. I set my eyes for bigger fish. "You guys can finish up here. I'm going after Bale."

"Gloria, no!" shouts Tre. "We fight as a team!"

"Don't worry, I'll save you some. Besides, I can handle Bale. Remember the rooftop? Just come and find me when you take care of those two!"

"Glo, wait!"

I take off around the corner, trying to gain some ground on Bale. Tre doesn't see it, but I am fighting as a team. I can hold off Bale until they arrive. Then we can end this once and for all.

After a few turns around the carousel-like garage, I see what appears to be a white stretch limo in the distance. Sprinting closer, I view what looks to be someone in a hat—a driver— opening the rear door as two figures wait, one larger than the other. Bale and his oversized guard, Amnon.

"Hey Bale, it's over!" I shout, just as they are to step inside.

"For whom? You?" he says, now standing within earshot. "Because for me, it's just beginning. Sure, you've created a slight headache, but it's nothing my PR team can't handle. And by no means is it over."

"The people are smart. They'll see you for you really are. No one will freely bow to you."

"You sound like Little Anna. She's really done a job on you three. I should've destroyed her all those years ago. No matter. There's always tomorrow."

"You'll never get the chance!" I yell, running straight for Bale. The massive bodyguard, Amnon, steps directly in front of his lord, but I was expecting that. He swings wildly as I drop into a slide and glide right through his legs. Now behind him, I rise, landing an elbow to his back and a kick to Bale's chest, sending him straight into the steel reinforced limo door. Direct hit!

Time to show these guys who's in charge. With both immobilized I advance, but Bale's eyes open just as the Shadow swirls furiously about. I'm not sure if Bale hits or kicks me, but the superhuman blow throws me back at least twenty feet.

"I am Bale! I...AM...BALE!!!" is what I hear as I come to. As I look up, I can barely make out Amnon shaking off the blow I delivered to him.

"Destroy her. You know where to meet me," says Bale before stepping inside the limo. The driver hurriedly takes off. *Okay Gloria, gotta shake this off,* I think as Amnon creeps forward. I know I'm supposed to get up, but so far, I can't. Maybe Tre was right. Maybe this wasn't a good idea. Maybe I was trying to do too much, to prove myself. Maybe that debilitating punch has got me second guessing myself. None of that matters now as I notice the huge frame that stands above. My focus returns just in time to see his huge foot hover over me. He smiles as the Shadow spreads from his profile. The concrete floor ripples from the exact spot recently occupied by my head. Thankfully I rolled out in time. Cracks spring out in every direction while the ground trembles with the force of an earthquake.

I spring to my feet as the beast swings for my head. He misses, nearly taking out a concrete support beam in the process. Rubble explodes from the weakened column. His punches are powerful but I'm much quicker. I land a flurry of punches to his abdomen but the monster just smiles before lifting me by the neck and slinging me across the corridor. The force is almost overwhelming but I summon the strength to get back up. He runs straight for me, wildly swinging for my head, but I drop into a split as his huge fist crushes another concrete beam. Squinting from all the dust and debris, I hit the rampaging monster squarely in the groin. He wails in pain. Finally.

Standing, I kick Amnon in his left shin. "Finally, we see eye to eye," I say as the giant falls to one knee. I land kicks to his temple, now to his chest. Part of me gloats as screams bellow from the pit of his belly. The Shadow weakens around him as he consumes the punishment.

"And who says boys have all the fun?"

Stepping back I focus my power. This next blow should send this monster back to the pit of Hell. I run full speed towards the chopped down giant, leaping into a high-kick. Suddenly, the aggravated monster jumps out of his stooped position...

BOOOOOMMMMM!!!!

An enormous boot—or something—I'm not sure—sits on my chest. It takes me a minute to understand its purpose. It's here to drain the remaining life from my body. Dust crowds my airway as I wrestle with the odd sensation.

Sharp, excruciating pain is replaced by a dull, numbness. I no longer hurt although I'm not sure if I still have the use of my limbs. The numbness sets in a little while longer before...

...before the change. That feeling you get when you first revive an arm or leg that has been sleep, rushes through my entire body. I'm not sure what I see. Colors of some sort, not sure. They're unlike any I've ever seen. Can't really explain them. But I am certain of the melody that races past my ears. An enchanting tune filled with what sounds like every instrument I've ever heard. A blaring sound of horns, drums, strings, rising in power and volume before smoothing out into tranquil vibrations. *The wind*. That's the only way I can explain it. It sounds like the wind...if the wind were a melody.

A figure comes to meet me. Can I even say it's a figure? It has no body, no shape, no definition. Yet I know it to be a specific entity. Although indescribable, it's beautiful. I've witnessed it before in all its glory, though that was ages ago. Somehow, I just know. As it draws closer, I have the uncontainable urge to scream to the top of my lungs. Not in fear, or anger, but in adoration. It consumes me and I know it to be...everything. And that's when it no longer matters.

I'm free.

What would I do if I came out to find a demon sitting atop my crashed-in hood? I find myself asking this question as me and Zeek make mince pie out of Balak and his friend with the dreads. The two put up a good fight, but it's nothing we can't handle. Finally subdued, I notice how hard it truly is to keep white clean. Oh well.

"I thought those two would never get the hint."

"Yeah, I know right," smiles Zeek. He pops his neck as I rub my hands, our little skirmish over. "I was just starting to have fun," he continues. "Shame about those choppers, though."

"Yeah. Whada ya say we go help Gloria. I don't want her having all the fun."

"Let's go."

We take off running up and around the meandering parking garage. Every floor looks exactly the same. I make a conscious effort to notice what level we're currently on. Zeek and I call out for Glo but get no answer. I suggest we split up as we continue our search. Nothing out of the ordinary. Just cars and the occasional passing glance of onlookers.

"Tre!" shouts Zeek. "Tre!" he shouts again, louder. "Hurry!"

I take off in the direction of Zeek's voice. It only takes a few seconds to find him. He's not alone. "Gloria?" I call. Zeek holds her head in his lap. I rub my face in disbelief, but when my eyes open, it's still the same. Gloria's motionless body. "I told you to wait!" I shout at her, not knowing what else to say. "I told you to wait!"

A coarse line of blood falls from her mouth. Her face is intact but the black sweater—the sweater I got for her—is saturated with dust to the point it looks white.

Emotions override the thought process. Memories of my brother submerge my consciousness. And just like that, everything we've been taught goes down the drain. Teamwork, discernment—I couldn't locate Glo by just thinking of her location. The pain moves back in, taking up its usual residence. Thought it had been evicted but looks like I was wrong. It consumes me to the point I barely notice Zeek trying to get my attention. His face appears mad, but it takes a moment to recognize his words.

"Snap out of it, Tre!" I finally make out.

"It can't end like this!" I say, the tears running uncontrollably.

"C'mon man, do your thing!" he shouts, still holding Gloria's head in his lap.

And then I remember. My Gift! The one thing I didn't learn but was given to me. Quickly, I fall to my knees, placing my hands around Gloria's face. Nothing. I try her chest, but nothing seems to happen.

"Again!" yells Zeek.

I take his spot in the man-made crater of obliterated concrete, close my eyes and focus as best I know how. When I reopen them, nothing's changed. Glo's gone.

"NO!!!"

And so, the collection is complete. The one thing that was given, fails me. Gloria is gone, just like my brother. Once again, guess I was too late. But I won't mourn. I won't doubt. I won't ask why me. At least not now. "I'll stay here with Glo," I whisper to Zeek. "You go after Bale." Zeek's slowness to answer denotes his contemplation. "Now!" I scream. There's no time for that. "Do YOUR thing!"

"I'm going!" he yells back.

My eyes drop to Gloria, but a swaying large object in my peripheral commands my attention.

"What about him?" Zeek asks.

The *him* in question is probably the vicious fiend who did this to Gloria. Amnon. The giant walks back and forth some forty yards away and now spots us as well. Just as good. "I got him," I assure Zeek. "You know what to do."

"Send him to Hell," Zeek says, running off.

I make sure Gloria's body is situated and comfortable before standing and rubbing the white dust from my shirt. I look for the giant once more. Once relocated, my eyes never leave Amnon's face as I walk straight for my narrow-eyed enemy.

"I missed ride," says the gruff-voiced giant.

"Did you do this to her?" I ask boldly.

"I destroy friend," he grins.

The way he talks, it's strange. Simplistic, like a child. But something oddly familiar. We now stand six feet apart, his natural shadow eating my light. A huge man indeed, but I wouldn't care with or without my powers. Far as I know, they could already be gone. But the man—the demon that killed my friend stands before me and I will do all within my power to make him pay.

"You want same?" he asks.

I want to answer but find myself gasping for air as I recall the origin of this disturbed voice. The voice that speaks in disjointed syllables.

"You killed my friend," I sob. "And you killed my brother!"

The giant looks confused. "My brother!" I remind him. "Martin Turner! T-Mart!" The latter name rings a bell. His face lightens, reminiscing on his conquest.

"I kill brother," he cackles.

My body is overcome with grief and hatred at the same time. To know I've fought the man that took my brother's life only to retreat and leave him alive starts to weaken me, but I quickly turn the guilt into fuel. Everything in me wants to rush in head-first. It would take several blows from the huge beast-like man before I even felt anything. My body is charged with loathsomeness. But before I can rush the animal, a calmness surfaces. At the same time, a cool breeze tickles past my face. For some reason, thoughts of my childhood come to mind. Words once thought forgotten reemerge. I turn my back on the giant as I recite passages long disregarded.

——THE ASSIGNED——

ZEEK

I didn't want to leave Tre, nor Gloria for that matter, but I know nothing I could've said would change his mind. And I can't blame him. Bale's men went too far, and someone has to pay. Running through the garage, it takes a moment to remember where I parked my bike, but the image finally visualizes in my head. If I can't remember where I left my chopper, how can I possibly see where Bale has gone? On the other hand, what's the alternative?

But as I focus on a point on the wall before me, something does happen. I feel *my* Gift manifest. An image of Jason Bale flashes before my eyes. Now a car—no wait—a limousine. I jump on my bike, barreling out of the parking garage. The structure itself has suffered extensive damage at the hands of the dueling factions. As since millennia ago, one good, one evil. Although the outcome has already been decided, the war continues. *This is the way.*

At least this is what I've been told. So much has happened, I'm not sure what I believe. I fly down the highway like a bat out of Hell, or rather…Heaven. My Gift of Seeing leads me to the interstate bridge. As I ride, my mind traces back to before any of this started…

And that's what keeps me riding. Angel. Christina. Angelina for the courage of her convictions no matter what I or anyone else thought, and little Christina for fighting through death and coming back to me. I owe them my best. So, I ride.

Memories accelerate my new chopper through the thickening traffic. After a few short minutes, I pull close to a white limo. Is this the one? My question is answered in a flash as black vapor shoots from the limo's rear-window. The Shadow separates into streams of mist as it attempts to attach itself to the plethora of vehicles traveling on the highway. I can tell which attempts are successful as some of the drivers' countenances immediately change. The Persuaded motorists attempt to run me off the highway as I weave between lanes at 80mph. Somehow, I maneuver through the increasingly dangerous freeway. Must be the Gift. Trying their best to flatten me, Persuaded drivers crash with one another. Cars barrel through the air like missiles before plummeting to the ground like fallen satellites. The slightest sway of my body saves me from dire consequences. I never lose sight of the limo as I swiftly approach. Out of nowhere, the lengthened vehicle fishtails in the middle of the highway, burning rubber as it comes to a rolling stop. I hit the brakes just as my chopper collides with the limousine. The collision sends me head first, soaring through the air. As I fly, images of the accident, flash by. I can see Angel. Man, she's beautiful. That smile. It's the reason I fell in love with her. What I wouldn't give to see her again. Maybe that time is now. Nearing the end of my descent, Angelina draws close. Her mouth opens to speak. I stop breathing not to miss any of what she has to say. My wife utters one word.

"Live…"

I smile at the simple declaration. And after what seems like an eternity with an Angel, I fall to the ground, landing on my feet. Rising, cars swerve to avoid me. Leaving six-inch deep impressions in the asphalt, I step forward. Bale waits for me in the middle of the highway.

"You are beginning to cost me too much!" he shouts.

"Glad to be of service!"

"So, what if you have prolonged my plan? Your attempts are brief at most. I'll be back on track in no time. But you? You will die." Bale looks around as people step out of their cars, watching the unfolding melee. "A man such as myself has the right to defend himself when being attacked by a crazed fan."

"You know what…Enough of the rhetoric."

——T H E A S S I G N E D——

TRE

"Yea, though I walk through the valley of the shadow of death, I shall fear no evil. For thou art with me. Thou rod and thy staff, they comfort me. Thou preparest a table before me in the presence of mine enemies." The words come so easily. Scriptures my father taught us when we were children. Today, they prepare me for battle. "Thou anointest my head with oil. My cup runneth over."

My back still turned, I can hear the man-beast's intense breathing. But nothing worries me now. Nothing else can be done to me. If it is my destiny to die, then so be it. If I am to live, then God will be with me.

"I kill friend! I kill brother!" yells my adversary. Though incendiary, the words only bring more passages to mind.

"Now unto him that is able to do exceeding abundantly above all that we ask or think according to the power that worketh in us." Reenergized, I face my opponent. Huge hands clenched into fists sway at his sides. The Shadow flares around his torso adding to his massive dimensions. But no matter. I'm ready. "I can do all things though Christ which strengthens me."

"And I KILL YOU!"

Amnon charges. I take off as well, spearing the giant to the ground as we meet. The concrete floor rumbles underneath. On top, I head-butt the massive man, but with ease he throws me ten feet with one arm. I land squarely on my toes, running straight back for more. The giant lunges for my head, however I duck and land a crippling hook to his rib cage. Firmly aggravated, he returns the favor, catching me with an uppercut that sends me straight into the air. Pain crowds my senses as I feel the gash in my face open. But by the time I hit the ground, it's closed. Jumping to my feet, I meet the charging brute with a roundhouse kick to the chest. It sends him through two concrete beams before his body rams into a nearby car. Smoke and debris billows around me, impeding my vision.

——THE ASSIGNED——

ZEEK

With Bale in plain view, I rush straight for him. The arrogant idol stands motionless until the very last second. Out of nowhere, he catches me by the throat with one hand, lifting me in the air. His Shadow hovers and shifts in the ever-changing wind. I attempt to loosen his grip, but this guy is strong.

"You think you and your friends can stop me?!" he shouts, still holding me with one hand. "Do you know how many of your kind I've destroyed?!" Not waiting for an answer, Bale throws me thirty feet, at least. I land on the hard asphalt pavement.

Resting on all fours, I hear footsteps approaching. "See that's it," he says. "You've already got the hang of it. Now call me lord, and I'll consider giving you a position at my side." Still on my knees, I spit blood from my mouth.

"I'm still new to the whole *lord* thing, so I think I'll pass."

Bale circles me. "The Other does nothing but take. He took your wife. He nearly took your daughter. But I gave her back to you."

"What?" I look up to gauge his expression.

"You heard me," Bale says without pause. "Those were my doctors, Zeek! Think about it!"

And I do. I think about Dr. Amali and the black haze I now know to be the Shadow. Could it be true?

"Through my power they resurrected your daughter! Now join me and help me show the world another way!" Making my way to my feet, I try to make sense out of all of this. I'm not sure what to believe. He couldn't have possibly saved Christina. Could he? "No. You lie. You're a liar, Bale!" He stretches out his hand. "I gave life back to your daughter. And I can give life back to your wife. Your Angel."

The torment starts all over again. "Stop it!" I yell. How could he possibly bring back Angel? Much as I don't want to admit it, my wife is dead. But at the same time, I've seen things in the last few weeks that have challenged everything I ever believed. Though this guy is a manipulator, a murderer. He does possess power, but could it be used for that purpose? Was it used for Christina?

An exhilarating fragrance flutters past my nose as I internally debate these questions. It makes me want to find out more. Almost persuading me to take the next step.

------T H E A S S I G N E D------

TRE

When the smoke clears, my Persuaded foe is nowhere to be found. Damage to vehicles and the garage itself is easily traceable, though no sign of the not-easily-hid, Amnon. Surely, he hasn't retreated. He must be here somewhere.

SHHRRIEEEEK!!!

Sparks fly everywhere as a car on its side speeds straight towards me. Immediately I run, not taking time to ask questions. Glancing back, I see a large bald head peering from behind the speeding wreckage. Amnon is pushing the car like a football sled. His Shadow widens itself to the length of the car. The calculated haze almost looks as if it's helping push the vehicle! I've never seen anything like it, but now's not the time to marvel as I evade being mowed down like grass. War-cries bellow from the supernaturally charged giant as he moves the car almost effortlessly.

Running straight for a steel enforced wall, I have to make a choice. Even if I allow myself to be pulverized by the car-projectile, it would take a few moments to completely heal. And there's no telling what Amnon could do to me in that time. Not sure what my limits are, but the Prophetess' team didn't make it, so obviously we have some. No, that won't work. It's time to end this.

Just as the wall and car are ready to make a TNT sandwich, I run up the wall and flip outwards. Amnon heaves the car straight into the concrete barrier. He musters up every bit of muscle to make sure I don't survive the deafening crash. The monster is so busy with the final thrust, he never sees me flip over his head.

"I kill you," laughs the illiterate ogre. He takes a few seconds catching his breath before turning.

"And the violent take it by force!"

WHHHAAACKKK!!!

I too use every active muscle in connecting a kick to the giant's chest. Amnon soars backwards into his own creation, the car-sled. His mammoth body collides fiercely with the upright vehicle, further denting the ill-fated chassis. Before he's able to shake it off, I calmly approach. No sign of the Shadow now. Or his renowned power. Although I can feel a supernatural strength overtake me as I lift the enormous demon enclosed in flesh over my head. With all my faculties fully intact, I make a declaration.

"This is for Glo!"

My body leaps straight in the air, still dead-lifting the colossal giant. Falling to one knee, the weary Amnon crashes down to the other. Backbreaker.

Cries once more emanate from the wounded fallen Angel. But these are cries of pain. With power still surging through my body, I stand, again lifting Amnon in the air. With his body dangling above, I make one more declaration.

"And this is for my brother. For what profit a man to gain the whole world and lose his soul!"

CRRRAAAAACCKKK!!!

Another backbreaker. The beast is now still. Tears silently fall from my eyes as I continue crushing my enemy's spine. The weight I carry is lightened as the Goliath's body dissolves into black, smoke-like haze. "It is finished."

————T H E A S S I G N E D————

ZEEK

The sweetness of the fragrance intensifies as thoughts of Angel consume me. I want her so bad. Worse than life itself. The thought of just seeing her again nearly persuades me—I'm being Persuaded!

Bale's greatest talent is on display. The sweetness I smell is the stench of the Shadow as it wraps its lucid tentacles around me. No matter what my heart feels, something about this can't be right.

"Join me," smiles the convincing mogul.

"Not today!" I yell, lunging for Bale. We crash into an approaching sedan. I stun the surprised icon with an elbow to the face before returning the previous favor, throwing him nearly thirty feet onto the hood of a 1995 Taurus. Bale's torso smashes through the window.

Police and news trucks arrive on the crammed highway. Most can't get through for the spectators and parked cars. Ignoring the onlookers, I make my way for Bale. Blood flows from his mouth. "Wow, you bleed," I say.

A deceptive grin emerges as he speaks. "Indeed I do, Son of Adam."

"Looks like you've had enough for one day."

"You think I would show my true power in front of all these people? My time has not come. They must worship me freely, my friend. Don't worry. This is not over."

"I'm ready whenever you are."

Bale frowns as he spits more blood from his mouth. The taste seems foreign to him. Meanwhile, policeman and news crews make their way through the crowd towards Bale. "I'll leave you to your fans," I say. "Looks like they got a few questions for ya. And I'm gonna make sure you get penned for Gloria's death. If I can't send you back to Hell, me and Tre'll make sure you experience hell on Earth."

Bale says nothing, only smiles.

"Mr. Bale, we'd like to talk to you!" shouts an approaching policeman.

"Bale, is it true you and your men had involvement with the murder of Dr. Harold Ambrose?" asks an insistent news team.

Guess that's all he can do. Guess I've done all I can do as well. At least for now. The crowd hardly notices as I make my way through the press.

I still don't know how I got here. What did I do wrong? What could I have possibly done differently? I ask myself these questions as EMT zip a leathery black bag containing Gloria's body. The quick glimpse of Gloria's pale, lifeless face as the bag is zipped to the top, sickens me. I pleaded with Prophetess Anna, now on the scene, to do something, but she said there was nothing she could do. I asked her if I was doing something wrong, if there was another way to use my power, but all she could say was, "I am sorry, my child. I should not have allowed you to engage Bale."

And now to know that Bale is still alive, even if he does get arrested, gives me no solace. Neither does destroying his chief Angel, Amnon. At least not to the point where it makes up for Gloria.

"I'm sorry folks, we've done all we could do," says one of the paramedics.

"She gave her life for her beliefs," says the Prophetess. "God be with you, my child."

I turn my head as the paramedics place the body bag in an ambulance. I can't believe this is happening again.

"Because of Gloria, the enemy's attack has been thwarted," says Anna, placing her arm around me. "She was a fine warrior."

"Yeah Tre. Her plan worked," says Zeek. "Bale will pretty much have to start all over."

"But that's just it! He's still here! Glo's not! It's not right!"

"I'm sorry, Tre," says a saddened Prophetess. "I should not have sent you to face Bale. Please forgive me." She releases me and takes a few steps towards a waiting car. "We should go, my children. Someone must give word to Gloria's mother."

"You're right," says Zeek. "I'll go with you."

"Join us my child," motions Prophetess Anna.

"No," I shake my head.

"Tre, Gloria would want it to come from us," agrees Zeek.

"No."

"My child, we must—"

"No. It will not end like this! Not this time. NOOOO!!!"

Turning away from the others, I walk back to the ambulance. With one snatch, I rip the solid steel door right off its hinges.

"Hey! What are you doing?!" shouts an EMT.

"Get out!" I yell back. The technicians do just that. I unzip the bag containing Gloria's pale body before looking upwards. "I've already lost one person I cared about, and I know I can't get them back. They reached out for me, but I wasn't there. But this time I'm here. I'm right here! You gave me this Gift for a reason. Let me use it!"

The now whitened color of Gloria's black sweater tries to distract me as it serves as a reminder of her defeat. But I won't let it. I place my hands on her chest and wait. No response. "Come on, Glo! Get up!"

"Tre, what are you doing?!" shouts Zeek from the door.

Just like the sweater, I ignore him too. "I said get up, Glo!" Pressing down again, I garner the same reaction. Nothing. Looking up, I see Zeek shake his head. Even the Prophetess has turned her back. Refocusing my attentions towards the heavens, I have an uncanny urge to laugh. And so, I do. "You see that? Everyone's given up. It's just me and you now. Look, I don't know how, I don't know why, but I believe. You hear me?! I believe! Now let me do my job. Isn't this why you gave it to me? Will you allow Bale to get the victory?! I'm here, I'm in position! Now let me do what I do!"

Again, I place my hands upon Gloria's chest. A glow radiates from my palms. As I lift my fingers, a loud gasp shoots from the body bag. Gloria's chest rapidly moves in and out as blood pumps to her heart. Trembling, her eyes slowly open.

"Tre," she whispers. "Wh—where am I?"

"You're here," I say, holding her hand. "You're right here."

"I—I don't believe it!" Zeek shouts, now standing at the rear of the ambulance. "What did you do?"

"I believed," are the only words that come to mind.

——THE ASSIGNED——

GLORIA

My new family surrounds me as I try to warm myself on Prophetess Anna's couch. Three blankets are still not enough to block out the numbing feeling of frostbite ravaging though my system. Guess that's what happens when you're dead. I've heard the story ten times now, but I still can't believe it. I was dead nearly two hours before Tre finally brought me back? I mean, I know it has to be true although the last thing I remember is seeing our video on the jumbo screen. I vaguely remember wanting to go after Bale, everything after that is a blur. The guys told me I pursued Bale and Amnon alone. What was I thinking? Thankfully I remember none of that. I gather the giant, Amnon, took my life, but Tre doesn't like to talk about that part. Actually, most of the story has been told to me by Zeek and Anna. The normally boastful Tre has been pretty quiet these last few hours. Whatever he witnessed really got to him. He couldn't be that messed up over me, could he? Anna even said she had given up hope. "But not Tre," she keeps repeating. Anyways, knowing he took out Amnon makes me feel pretty good. At least we know Bale and his kind can be sent back to Hell. Maybe it's my upbringing in the church that made me feel as if I could go into warfare on my own. Or maybe humbling myself to A'ma, Arnie, and Sandy all this time has made me too eager to prove myself. Whatever it is, guess I've got a lot more to learn.

"Sit closer," I instruct Zeek and Tre, sitting on either ends of me. I can use every ounce of heat I can get. "So, all that really happened?"

"Every bit," says Zeek.

"Correct, my child," says Anna, taking her usual stance in the middle of the room.

"So, you came back for me, Tre?"

Normally cocky and self-absorbed, he seems at a loss for words. "I mean—well you know…"

"Thank you," I say, giving him a big hug and kiss on the cheek.

"Are you blushing?" asks Zeek in disbelief. "The great TNT Turner?"

"Whatever man," Tre smiles. "Anyways, so what's the next move Prophetess?"

"We train and we wait," she responds. "As you've experienced firsthand, Bale is not be trifled with. But at least now he knows we are here to stay and he will have to calculate that into every decision he makes."

"You think the charges will stick?" I ask.

"I am not sure my child. Bale is a very cunning entity. He has always been."

Anna looks solemnly to the floor. We almost join her in uncertainty until she utters her next words.

"But so are the Assigned."

"Now THAT'S what I'm talking about!" yells Tre.

"The darkness of this world shall not prevail, my children. Thanks to you. God has chosen three warriors worthy of honor."

Her words warm me in a way proven unsuccessful by any amount of blankets. I could stay in this moment forever.

"So did ya'll see how I laid those guys out?" asks an animated Tre. "I'm like the Dark Knight!"

Guess the moment's over.

"Give it a break!" I laugh, throwing pillows at Tre's head. On second thought, I like this moment even better. I wouldn't have it any other way.

———T H E A S S I G N E D———

ZEEK

My apartment is a welcomed sight after this past week's events. Christina meets me at the door with outstretched hands, a joyful reminder of why I do all this.

"There's my Chrissy pooh!" I shout, stooping down to her level.

"Me and Aunt Alicia made frech fries," she smiles. Of course, she means French fries but I'll take whatever she's serving. "You want some?"

"Sure sweetie."

"Are you hungry?" asks Alicia, attempting her best efforts at avoiding eye contact. Instead of encouraging the cold atmosphere, I make the first step.

"Hey Alicia, I just wanna thank you for...for everything. I couldn't do this without you."

"Yeah, well I guess one of us has gotta have a life. Hope you've been having fun. I do have my own apartment I need to tend to as well, you know." Alicia turns her back and proceeds to the kitchen.

"Alicia," I say, making my way around the kitchen table. "I assure you, this is not about having fun." I find myself trying to explain the past week. "I haven't been out with anyone. I've been ...helping people. Remember the people who helped Chrissy in the park that day?" Alicia seems to be taking it all in. "Well those are my new friends and I've been trying to do good by them. Just like I wanna do good by you and Chrissy."

Alicia eyes light up as she finally looks at me. "So, what are you saying, Zeek?" she asks. What *am* I saying? I couldn't possibly date and marry my deceased wife's sister. Could I? Christina bails me out by wrapping herself around my legs. "Let's play Daddy!"

"Sure baby," I smile. "Look Alicia, I don't know what I'm saying. At least not now. Just know that I'm here for you. Is that okay?"

Alicia smiles. "Sure, Zeek. Now play with your daughter while I fix you a plate."

Sunset quickly turns into night as Christina, Alicia, and I play every game imaginable. Whatever Chrissy's little mind can conjure up, we play. I wouldn't dare deny her this moment.

As Alicia gives Chrissy her bath, I take a moment to catch the evening's news. I had almost forgotten my morning's activities, but video of the battleground better known as the Peabody Hotel parking garage promptly reminds me. News reporters discuss the incident in detail.

"During a long-awaited press conference Bale Media had hyped as a new dawn in technology, *present* technology was used to show explicit video of what appears to be Jason Bale and his security detail involved in some sort of altercation with the deceased Dr. Harold Ambrose. Ambrose, known as a somewhat outspoken theology professor at Rhodes College, was found floating face down in the Mississippi River." Images of the grainy surveillance video from the club are shown.

"Movie mogul and CEO, Jason Bale, abruptly walked out on his press conference after the anonymous video was shown. His bodyguards then got into a brawl with an unidentified group in the parking garage causing extensive damage. Later, the movie star himself got into some sort of altercation with an unknown man before being taken into custody for questioning. At the moment, Bale is not a suspect but is merely wanted for questioning.

Only time will tell if this puts a dent into the successful juggernaut known as Bale…"

Turning off the TV, my mind can't help but think about his words. *"I can give life back to your wife. Your Angel."* It probably wouldn't have even crossed my mind if I hadn't seen Tre raise Gloria after being dead for two hours. Could someone with more power raise someone after four years? I try not to entertain the thoughts but they overwhelm me. To give Christina the gift of her mother would be amazing. What am I saying? It's crazy. Even if Bale could do it, what would I have to give up? My life? My soul? So much to ponder. Part of me wants to ask Anna about Christina's resurrection, about Angelina. But she probably wouldn't understand. Besides I've pretty much concluded it wasn't Bale who made Chrissy whole. I'm pretty sure it was God. But what about Angel? I'm certain Bale didn't dish out everything he had. Why wouldn't he want to show his true power? What is he planning now? What if this is just the calm before the true storm? Guess I'll learn more as our training continues.

The thoughts subside as a pajama clad Christina jumps in my lap. "Whoa, little kangaroo. Isn't it about your bedtime?" I smile.

"Daddy, can I play with one more toy before I go to bed? Please?"

The parent in me wants to say no, but how can I possibly deny her? "Okay, one more. Now what's it gonna be?" My baby girl stands at attention as she makes her case.

"Daddy, can I ride my horsey again?"

The *horsey*. The gift from Bale, himself. I've done pretty well keeping her mind off the present, hiding it in the back of the closest underneath a stack of dirty clothes. I made sure to let Alicia know she wasn't to speak of it. But now, almost two weeks later, here we are, yet again.

"Is there anything else you'd rather play with instead?" I ask, already knowing the impending answer.

"Un unnn," Chrissy shakes her head. "Please Daddy. I wanna ride my horsey."

What harm could it be, riding the wood-crafted toy? I look at the daughter I didn't have a month ago before finally conceding,

"Sure baby, you can ride the horsey…"

Part One

of

T H E A S S I G N E D

www.ingramcontent.com/pod-product-compliance
Lightning Source LLC
Chambersburg PA
CBHW060535180626
46817CB00002B/583